THE LONG FALLING

THE
LONG
FALLING

KEITH
RIDGWAY

HOUGHTON MIFFLIN COMPANY
BOSTON • NEW YORK
1998

For information about permission to reproduce
selections from this book, write to Permissions,
Houghton Mifflin Company, 215 Park Avenue
South, New York, New York 10003.

Library of Congress Cataloging-in-Publication Data
Ridgway, Keith.
The long falling / Keith Ridgway.
p. cm.
ISBN 0-395-90530-3
I. Title.
PR6068.I287L66 1998
823'.914 — dc21   96-45669 CIP

Printed in the United States of America

QUM 10 9 8 7 6 5 4 3 2 1

For Oliver

ONE

GRACE

It rains on Cavan, Monaghan; rains on the hills and the lakes and the roads; rains on the houses and the farms and the fences between them; on the ditches and the fields, on the breathing land; rains on the whole strange shape of it. Puts down a pattern.

And then it stops.

And the places of the country look different in the sun. They look new. Places out of place; as if brought by the clouds and dropped like litter. There is a scattering of these named things; a spread of small towns, tiny farms, white houses squatting by the deep blue of the lakes. They may look beautiful from a great height, pinpoints of colour gathered together, narrow ribbons of road linking them like veins on a green leaf. But from the ground they are ugly and wrong and a shock to the eyes. A shock. The towns are stains against the sky, the farms are muddy pools of concrete and metal, the white houses are like plastic bags stuck to the branches of a tree. Only in the rain can they hide. Only in the grey drizzle and the absence of colour are they well placed.

There is a church in Cootehill, just outside the town, on the road to Shercock. A tall and grey and silent place, dark against the dark sky. It is a building with eyes, the kind of building that looms, casting shadows across the graveyard that sits snug at its side, the gravestones looking like they might have fallen from the building itself, sticking into the soil like blunt knives, rupturing the wet ground in irregular

3

rows of names and dates. It looks bigger than it is – the power of suggestion. Murders and stormy nights. Mad priests and fallen statues. Faces in the stained glass, whispers from beneath the stones. It never moves, but the sky moves behind it and changes it, making it solid and making it soft, depending.

Grace Quinn rumbles by the church in her husband's small red car, which is old and ragged, with rust at its edges. She glances at the grey stone bell-tower, but there is nothing in her look, it is just an accidental thing, careless. It has become her habit not to see the place where her son is kept.

She is past the church and out past the mart, turning off the Shercock road at the signpost to Ballybay. The road home from Cootehill. Crossing the Monaghan border somewhere there amongst the hills and the lakes.

It used to be that she would only cycle this road, but then she learned how to drive, and realised for the first time just how bad it was. Riddled with holes, pock-marked like the land it ran through, corrupted with humps and troughs and sudden bends, impossibly sharp. For years she had heard others complain, heard whole radio shows devoted to the potholes of Cavan and Monaghan, and she had never really understood what it was all about. On a bike you pick your way. On foot it does not matter. But now she knew.

She got used to it. At first she was terrified, especially after dark, green eyes picking her out from the hedgerows and the gates, sudden movements in the ditches, the shocking thud of a wheel into a hole, her head lurched, her eyes dancing, her hands slipping.

There was one section of it so narrow that she was forced to stop, sometimes reverse, when she met an oncoming car. But the surface there was strangely smooth and flat, as if they had decided that it was too narrow to leave potholed. At night she could tell by the absence of lights up ahead that there was no car coming in the opposite direction, and she would work up speed, perhaps sixty miles an hour, before slowing down suddenly as the road widened again and there was a sharp turn to the right.

It was here that it had happened, on this long narrow part of the road, after dark, the year before. She had forgotten the date. If she thought about it hard enough she could probably remember.

Grace enjoyed the car now. She enjoyed taking turns she knew nothing about, getting lost in the web of roadways that seemed to spread out in all directions before returning pointlessly to where they had begun. She liked to drive, concentrating, thinking of nothing but what she was doing. She was new to it, and could get lost in it. She would stop sometimes, turn the engine off, allow other things to come back to her, but only distantly, half-considered, partial. The car had become her place. She thought it very strange that that should be so, aware that there was something wrong in it, some blackness at the edge of her thinking.

Everybody knew her husband, and everybody knew her. Neither of them was liked. She, initially, because she had come from England, he because of his manner. Now he was not liked because of what had happened, and she because she was his wife.

She no longer knew why she had married him. She had no memory of the reasons, of what she had been thinking, of the emotions involved. She had no memory of love. They had been married thirty-two years before, in Manchester, her home town. He had been twenty-nine, she nineteen. He was the only man she had ever slept with. He gave her money each week. She did not spend it all.

The previous summer he had been out drinking and he drove home and killed a girl. He put her in the back of the car and drove on. At the house he had stood in the hall and dropped the telephone, and picked it up and dropped it again, and called for his wife and made her dial the number. He wouldn't talk to her. He began to tell the woman on the line that he had hit something in the road and he thought that it might be hurt. He slurred and she made him repeat himself. He could not tell her where he lived. He couldn't get the words out.

Grace went to the car, pulling her dressing-gown close to her, glancing at the clear black sky. She saw a hand pressed up against the window. He was talking still. She could hear his wet voice, curled around the truth like a hand trying to hide it. She ran across to the Boltons' place and they rang for the doctor and the police. When Grace went home finally he had been taken in to the station. They came and asked her questions. She should have seen the crumpled front of the car as soon as she went out into the yard, but she did not. She saw the hand only, lying against the glass, a strange colour. But she knew immediately that it was a girl's hand, and that the girl was dead. It seemed a simple thing to understand.

There was more alcohol in him than was allowed when they got him to the station. They kept him there all night, and all the next day, and the next, asking him questions, while Grace walked around the house, looking at things that she had not looked at in a long time.

When he came back there had been journalists who called, asking questions; and there had been voices on the telephone that cursed them and screamed, and who did not care that it was Grace who answered and not her husband. Eventually he had the phone disconnected. It woke him. He could not sleep with the threat of it.

At the court he was given a six-month sentence and lost his licence for five years. The newspapers were full of it. On the radio they complained. After a few days it was forgotten.

He was away for the full six months. He did not write.

6

She did not visit. She learned how to drive. She had to, living so far from everywhere. One of the Bolton boys taught her, patiently and politely. But he was not friendly, he was cold. She offered to pay him for his time but he refused it. He would walk across the fields in the early morning and wait for her outside, by the car. He would not come in, even when it rained. It took two weeks, a lesson every day, before Grace felt confident enough to take the car out on her own. She wanted to get him something, to thank him. He shrugged and said he didn't want anything. He said he'd nothing better to do.

He offered to help her with the farm, but there was nothing left of that. She could look after the lot herself – four sucklers and an old scrub bull. Everything else was gone. Sold to neighbours, about sixty acres of it, slowly, since Martin had left.

Grace could not afford to fix the front of the car. She drove it as it was, reminding everybody. People did not like her for that.

Her husband came in for his tea and Grace gave him a chop and potatoes and peas and bread and butter and a glass of milk. He did not look at her. He had a habit of swaying slightly back and forth as he ate, his knees bouncing up and down under the table. It looked as if he was praying, Grace thought, wondering if he did pray that way. If he prayed at all. He had not gone to mass since he killed the girl. His hair was mostly grey now, and cut short so that you could see skin beneath it. He would not go bald.

He ate his peas first. Then he ate all of the potato. Then he ate the chop, picking it up in his hands finally to suck the last of it off the bone. Then he lifted the glass of milk and drank it down in one go, leaving a white moustache on his upper lip like a child. As Grace boiled the kettle and filled the pot he buttered a slice of bread and sat back

7

to wait for his tea. She used to have the tea made and sitting on the table as he ate his meal, but he had not liked that. He said that he liked the tea piping hot, and that a scum formed on the top of it while he ate. He showed her, making her look at the tea in his cup, asking her would she drink tea with bits of brown stuff floating on the top of it like that? So now Grace would wait until he was nearly finished with his meat before switching the kettle on to boil.

She put the teapot down on the table and covered it with a cosy.

'Do you think it'll snow?' she asked him.

'Ah I don't think so.'

She stood beside the table and took his plate and cutlery.

'Leave the knife,' he said.

'It's very cold, though. Isn't it?'

'It is. It's always bloody cold. It's January, sure.'

She took his glass away as well and walked to the sink. Through the window she could see the grey sky becoming black, the light disappearing, taking with it the little colour of the land. In the distance there was smoke from a cottage chimney, pale against the sky, lingering in the cold air as still as a painting. Silence. Just the sound of her husband sipping. In the distance the hills. Her face upon them, reflected in the glass.

She saw drops of rain on the image of her skin. Rain. Water before turning. How cold did it need to be?

Their children were gone.

Sean – his hands cold in the water, his face suddenly bigger, older, as if he had grown up while her back was turned. He was only three. His father said that it was Grace's fault, that she should have been watching him. He called her stupid. But she was not to blame. A calf had drowned in the same ditch only days before, and her husband had still not fenced it off. She took Sean out to

8

look at the stars and had turned her back for only a moment. Stupid.

She had not gone to the funeral. Her husband had not wanted it. He told her that people would understand. Understand that she was racked with grief and guilt. No neighbours called. She mentioned this to her husband. He looked hard at her and shook his head and told her that she was lucky that the police had not called, never mind neighbours, and that she was a stupid woman, more stupid than an animal.

Sean was buried somewhere in the graveyard by the big church. She did not know where exactly. She did not want to know. She liked to imagine the grave, a tiny mound of earth, flowers resting by the stone, nice words. Sometimes she imagined the headstone white, sometimes black marble with gold letters. Sometimes it was just a cross, a white cross without writing.

There was Martin. Martin, her boy. Her love. He used to help her around the house and make her laugh, his beautiful deep brown eyes and his black hair like her father's. He would hold her hand when they went walking, even when he was older, and he would smile and tell her of how he had got into trouble in school and she would be unable to scold him.

Martin was afraid of his father. When he was nineteen he sat his parents down and told them his secret, and his father hit him and his nose bled. He went to Dublin. He wrote her long letters and she missed him very much. He was doing well in Dublin and lived in a beautiful house. He wrote that it was a different world, a different century. She had heard the same about Galway from the Bolton boy. She wondered whether every place was better than the place she was.

She longed to visit Martin, to find out about his life, see what he had become. It had been five years since he had gone. When his father had been in prison Martin had

9

wanted to visit her but she had put him off. He had left. She did not want to make him come back.

She kept his letters in a drawer in the kitchen, away from her husband. Sometimes she thought that they had been disturbed. That he had stumbled upon them and seen what they were, and had read the words from his son. But she was not sure. She could not decide what she wanted.

Grace lay down on the bed and gazed out of the window, looking for birds or an aeroplane or for anything distinct in all that grey. There was a light rain falling, drops of it bouncing silently down the glass like scratches, tiny scratches without colour. She listened but could hear no noise. It was as if she was sealed within a silence that grew out from herself, as if she had done something to shape this grey world, to design and construct it. She stared and listened and felt prompted for a sign, as if the colourless sky was hers to alter and change and scatter. Sean was gone. And Martin was cut off from her. And she felt that these things, these partings, had happened because she lived with this grey silence crouched over her, because she held it down at the edges, because she breathed it and had taken it into herself and knew nothing else.

She flapped an arm at the clouds, let it fall slowly back to her side. Nothing. She closed her eyes. There were colours hidden there. Strong reds, the veins of other lives.

She heard the sudden noise of her husband's chair scrape the kitchen floor. And in her mind it started off a babble of sounds that intrigued her, movements which she recognised but could not name. She did not know if she was remembering or dreaming. She did not know which way she faced.

He had come home after six months and seemed hollow like a man who is not interested in his life. Every second night he walked to Matt Clancy's place, and the two of them drove to Cootehill or Rockcorry to drink. They came back after midnight and her husband would walk home from Matt Clancy's and make himself a cup of tea and get into the bed beside Grace. He never let Matt drive him all the way home. Grace did not know why.

The narrow part of the road, the place where he had killed the girl, was between Matt Clancy's house and theirs. There were flowers left there still, Grace could see them every day as she drove past. She didn't know why they left flowers there. The doctor had said that he could not be sure whether the girl had died where she had been hit, or whether she had died later, in the back of the car. But Grace knew that she had died in the car. She had seen her hand against the window. If they put flowers anywhere, thought Grace, they should put them on the back seat of the car, covering the stains that she could not wash out.

It was very cold. She drove carefully, going around the corners as slowly as she could. There had been a frost overnight. They said on the radio that it would not snow, but Grace looked at the sky and was not sure. It felt cold enough. She went into Cootehill and bought coal and groceries and stopped into the White Horse for a drink, something she did not do often. Some people might nod at her, but none would talk. She had always been the outsider, the English woman, mad to have left it for here. When she had first arrived she had tried to make friends, but they had all seemed wary. Then, when Sean had drowned, and her husband had said all that he had to say, people she had never seen before began to avoid her conspicuously. They stared. They made comments. She heard herself called odd names, local words that she did not understand. It made her angry. She removed herself from things. Ceased to try. She had Martin. He was everything she needed.

For long years she had been forgotten about. Ignored. Eventually, some people, the younger ones usually, or newcomers, would say hello, chat with her, appear friendly. She was suspicious at first, but she had been edging closer to some of them, had begun to consider again the notion of friends, when it had happened. Her husband had killed the girl. It was worse this time. She did not know why, but it was as if she had done it. She felt the cold eyes, heard things said as she passed. Perhaps it was because she drove the car now.

She did not look around as she walked into the White Horse bar. The barman nodded and took her order. There were not many there. It was the middle of the afternoon and a quiet time. She sat down at a table by the log fire and waited for her drink to arrive before she began to read.

After a while she was conscious of someone walking over and standing in front of her.

'Excuse me, Mrs Quinn?'

He was ... who? She squinted. Then she remembered. He was a policeman. One of the men who had questioned her the previous summer.

'Oh, hello.'

He was a short man, very ruddy-faced and almost completely bald. His shirt was too tight. His voice was soft but the words were rushed, making him seem out of breath. Grace had liked him, he had been very polite with her and he had asked her whether he could drive her anywhere, to stay with relatives or friends, while her husband was at the station. He had looked a little sad when she had said no. He had been the only one who had asked her about the type of man her husband was. How he treated her. And he had been the only one who had not believed her. He hadn't said anything, but she could tell.

'You may not remember me, I'm Detective Vincent Brady.'

'No, I remember you.'

He lowered himself on to a stool on the other side of the small round table, close to the fire. He smiled at her. Brady.

'I saw you sitting here and just thought I'd say hello, see how you're getting on.'

'That's very nice of you.'

'So, how's the farm?'

'Oh, there's nothing to it now. My husband keeps it ticking over.'

'And how's he?'

'Fine.'

He looked at her for a moment.

'And yourself?'

'Fine.'

He had a patch on his neck where he had not shaved properly. He stood up.

'Well, that's good. If there's ever anything I can do for you, then just give me a shout.'

'How?'

He paused, looking down at her. He seemed about to sit again, then changed his mind.

'I'm stationed at Cavan.'

'Okay, thank you.'

He smiled at her before turning and walking back to the bar. He sat down beside another man who Grace also recognised. He had been at the house as well. He smiled at her and she smiled back, then looked down at the newspaper again.

A small lake near the house froze over. Grace poked at the ice with a stick, making small white rings like knots in wood. Then the ice cracked suddenly and she scrambled backwards as the crack shot out to the centre, the sound a beautiful long crunch that made her hold her breath and whisper an exclamation as it ended. God. She took up her stick again and widened the crack, the water bubbling up like dark ink. The pieces of ice were sore to the touch and she could not hold them for long. She put her wet fingers to her mouth and tasted the water. She stood and stretched her neck and looked upwards at the sky, feeling the air on her skin, chilling it and waking it, each nerve seeming to tingle and be alive, sensitive to changes in nearby things that could not be seen or heard or smelled. It was hard for her to understand. She had created something in her mind, an idea, and it was touching her from the inside, as if she were a glove.

She took the suitcase out from the top part of the wardrobe where it had been for years. She dusted it down and laid it on the bed and opened it. Inside she found an old magazine with pictures in it of naked girls. She leafed through it. There was no writing, just pictures. She smiled at some of them. The girls made such funny faces.

She opened the wardrobe and the drawers and took out all of her clothes and placed them, carefully folded, into the suitcase. Summer clothes at the bottom, winter clothes in the middle, underwear and scarves and handkerchiefs at the top. Then she went into the bathroom and collected all of her toiletries and put them into a plastic bag and put it into the suitcase. She could barely get it closed. She lifted it. It was very heavy. She held it in one hand and then in the other. She walked around the room with it, shifting it from hand to hand as her arms became tired. It wasn't too bad.

Then she realised that she'd forgotten her shoes. She retrieved another plastic bag from the kitchen and filled it with her shoes from the wardrobe in the bedroom. Then she put on her coat, hung her handbag from her shoulder, lifted the suitcase and the plastic bag full of shoes and walked out of the bedroom, into the kitchen and through to the living room. Then she walked back again. Her arm hurt. She put the suitcase down and swopped it to the other hand. She walked again through to the kitchen, trying not to stagger, to walk as if she were not carrying anything, and on into the living room. It would be all right.

She unpacked the suitcase and put everything back where it had been. The magazine back into the empty suitcase, the suitcase back into the top part of the wardrobe. She made it seem as though she had never been there.

The girl's parents lived about a mile away. One night they came to the house and wanted to speak to her husband. He wasn't there. Grace asked them to come in but they said that they'd prefer not to. She tried to say something to them, but they shook their heads and hushed her.

'We aren't bitter, we just want to talk with him,' said the woman.

'Just tell him we called. We'll call again,' said the man.

'Would you not fix the car?' asked the woman.

'It's his concern, not hers,' said the man.

They were an old couple, much older than Grace. Their daughter had been their youngest child, only nineteen, the same age as Martin when he had gone. Martin had been in the same school. Grace thought of what her husband had done. To separate a mother from her child. It was an awful thing to have done; a murderous thing. It made her cry.

First time since he killed the girl.

He came in late, after one o'clock, from drinking in Rockcorry with Matt Clancy. Grace lay in bed, listening to him in the kitchen cursing loudly and clattering. She heard something breaking like a plate or a cup, followed by a silence. Then he started to shout. His voice became high-pitched when he shouted, like a boy's. Grace closed her eyes and tried hard not to clench her muscles. She tried to make her body relax and be completely limp. He made his way slowly towards the bedroom. He seemed to be falling against the walls, rubbing his shoulder along the wall to support himself, his hair brushing lightly against the wall-paper, making a whispering sound which matched his breathing. He did not shout while he made his way to her.

He opened the door and Grace saw him black against the dim light from the hallway, silent for a moment and still, before he said:

'Did you fucking break this?'

'No.'

'Did you fucking break this thing?'

He hurled something at her and it hit her forehead. It was a piece from a broken cup. Grace put her hand to the place, feeling a small cut and a sharp pain where her fingers were. She pulled her legs up and got her knees in front of her chest as he was coming across the room towards the bed.

She was in position now with her legs up and her hands over her head, her fingers interlocking at the top of her head, her forearms protecting the sides of her face. He hit her with the back of his hand but the blow landed on her left arm and did not hurt.

'Bitch,' he shouted.

He pulled at her arms to try and get them away from her face.

'Move your fucking hands. Move your fucking hands.'

She kept her hands where they were but made no attempt to keep herself steady. His pulling at her rocked her back and forth. He hit her with his left hand, trying to get at the front of her face, but she ducked her head further and his blows fell half on her knees and half on the heels of her hands.

He stood back slightly and gave her one big pull. She tumbled from the bed and had to put out her hands to break her fall. She hit her back on the bedside table somehow and cried out. He bent over her and grabbed her wrists and pulled her upwards. She made herself heavy.

'What are you doing?' he asked, quieter, as if puzzled. 'Get up. Get fucking up.'

She made herself heavy like a child would and he could not lift her. He let go of her wrists and she fell to the ground and tried to get back into position, curling up on her side into a ball, trying desperately to relax her muscles. She heard him spit and felt a wetness on her thigh.

He walked away, towards the door, muttering. Grace opened an eye and looked out between her arms at his feet moving unsteadily towards the hallway. He stopped. She saw him turn.

'You're a stupid bitch.'

She saw him move rapidly towards her and closed her eye. He kicked her very hard on the shins and she could not help but scream. The pain of it was very bad. He kicked her again very hard, trying to get her stomach but the kick landed on her elbows and her knees. Grace screamed again.

She began to cry. She clenched her eyes as hard as she could, until she thought she would push them back into her skull, and bit her lips until the pain in her mouth distracted her a little from the pain elsewhere, and tried to be quiet. But she could not help the sobs as they came up from inside her somewhere and forced their way out through her chest and her throat and her mouth. She felt tears run down her face but did not know how they escaped from her eyes, and she felt saliva fall from her mouth but did not know how it escaped through her lips. The sobs shook her until she thought they would burst her open.

She heard the bedroom door slam. She opened her eyes to see that the room was empty, that she was alone, and she let the sobs come through her, exploding out of her in a howl that hurt her throat and caused her to be still, exhausted and throbbing with pain, alone in the dark room, on the floor.

She lay still for a long time, afraid of the new pains that

she knew movement would bring. She fought to win back control of her breathing. She could hear no sound in the house. Everything was quiet.

He had never kicked her before.

Imagine falling from a great height. Without panic. Imagine taking in the view on the way down, as your body tumbles gently in the air, the only sound being the sound of your progress. Your progress. Imagine that it is progress to fall from a great height. A thing worth doing. Though it is not a thing for doing. You do nothing, you simply allow it to happen. Imagine relaxing into the sudden ground. Imagine the stop.

The church is silent as the darkness around it deepens, and the rain falls lightly against its walls and its slanted roof, bathing it like spray from the sea might bathe a ship. There is a half moon, a slice of cold light. In the wet grass nothing moves. Not far from the dark silence there are islands of sound as the pubs empty and the car doors slam. But the church itself is left alone and unheeded. It is easy to imagine that it listens. But it gives no sign. It is seen only from a distance, a strange structure in the corner of the eye.

He is kept there, beneath the wet ground, hidden. She sees the flowers, sees the petals knocked loose by the rain, scattered on the grass. She sees the headstone, smaller than the others, plainer. She sees herself by his grave, as if she has fallen there with the rain. She sees her mouth in the uttering of words, sees her knees pressing petals into the mud, sees her hands scoop the earth from around him, until she holds him in her arms and can see what he looks like and fixes on his face so that she will remember what he looks like.

She wakes in the dawn and the sky is blank.

Her husband came in at half-past six and ate his dinner,

listening to the news on the radio. Grace had a sandwich and a cup of tea, nervous and watching. The way he used his knife, the way he sucked air into his mouth to cool the food, the way he rubbed his hands on his thighs as if he were trying to warm them. He did not look at Grace and she could not tell what he was thinking, if he was thinking anything. There was nothing on his face.

Grace wanted to talk to him and knew that she would not. She had allowed herself to give up. She glared at him but he did not notice. She tried to force a thought from her mind into his, but she did not know how that was done.

'Is the kettle on?' he asked suddenly, surprising her.

She saw that he had finished eating, his plate pushed away from him, his glass empty.

'Yes,' she answered, though it was not, and turned to flick the switch.

He stared at her, his tongue wrapped round his front teeth, causing his lips to bulge as he worked at pieces of lodged food. She stared back at him.

'What?' he snapped.

She shook her head gently and turned to see to the warming of the teapot. She heard him rustle a newspaper, noises coming loudly from his stomach.

When the tea was made he poured himself a large mug and disappeared into the living room with the newspaper. Grace cleared up before pouring herself a cup and sitting down at the kitchen table. She was still nervous.

Later, she heard him get up and go to the bathroom. Then she heard the cupboard door rattle in the hall, and the shake of keys. There was silence for a moment and she pictured him putting on his coat and counting his money.

'I'm off,' he shouted.

She did not reply. She heard the front door open and then slam shut, and she waited for a moment before going into the bedroom and looking out, lifting the curtain a little and pressing her cheek to the white wood of the window

19

frame. She saw the shape of her husband disappear into the dark.

For a long time Grace sat in the kitchen, nervously checking the clock, unable to decide what to do with the time. She turned on the radio and listened to pop music and the voice of a DJ who read out lists of names between the songs. He spoke fast. Through the window she could see a clear half moon and a clutter of stars and she knew it would not rain. The weather forecast on the radio confirmed it. She made more tea, but could not drink it. She thought about music and snow and water. She waited on the clock.

It was after eleven when she turned off the radio. She was afraid that she was about to panic. She could not sit still, could not keep her hands still, could not keep her eyes still. She felt the beginnings of a headache and took two tablets. In the bathroom she looked at herself in the mirror. She was pale. But she felt hot. She filled the sink with cold water, and gently lowered her face into it, holding back her hair. She did not move until her lungs demanded it. As she lifted her head she hit it against the tap. She cursed and pressed a palm to the pain. It came back bloody. She stared at the blood for a long moment, feeling a little dizzy. She sat down gingerly on the toilet seat and patted her face with a towel. The cut was not a bad one. The bleeding stopped almost immediately. She washed her hands and went back to the kitchen.

She waited until midnight, calmer now, distracted by the small bump on her head. Then she put on her coat and took the car keys and went out. It was a still, cold night. There was a frost. The sky was clear, a mess of stars spilt across the darkness, the moon bruised and only half there. Grace shivered. It was colder inside the car than it was outside. She started the engine and turned the heat up full. She sat there for a while, letting the windows clear, telling herself that she could stop this at any moment she wished.

She drove slowly, hunched over the steering-wheel slightly, peering ahead. She met no cars, no pedestrians. The road was deserted. It was only five minutes or less before she reached the long narrow section of smooth tarmac. She pulled in and stopped. The headlights lit the road as far as the next corner. There was no movement. She could not see it, but about halfway down was the place marked by flowers where he had hit the girl. Grace turned off the lights, and then the engine, and let the darkness and the silence settle around her.

Shapes appeared to her gradually, coming out of the black as her eyes adjusted. The road was enclosed by hedges on either side, as high as the car. She could not see over them. Looking ahead was like looking into a tunnel. A tree hovered over the hedge on her left, bare branches pointing at the sky, the stars appearing between them like tiny leaves, or like bright spring buds. Grace did not like this darkness. She had never become used to it. She was scared as a child would be. She rolled down the window, but rolled it up again when she began to hear noises, rustling, which she could not explain; something moving in the undergrowth, watching her and sniffing at the air. She shuddered and became impatient.

She did not want to think.

She thought about Sean and Martin. She tried to picture them. She grasped at the image of Sean that was left to her and filled it out to adulthood and imagined him as he might have been. She knew what Martin looked like now from the couple of photographs he had sent, but she did not know how he moved, what his presence might be like. She imagined the two of them sitting in the car with her. Her boys. She tried to hear their voices. Martin's was quick and light as it had been when he had left. She knew it was different now. She had heard the strangeness of it on the telephone. But she imagined it as it had been. For Sean she could not get away from childhood, so that she thought of him as younger than Martin. He would have grown up in this darkness, as his brother had, cycling home late at night along this very road. She felt them in the car with her. They would be relaxed. They would chat in loud voices, not caring about the silence they disturbed. Then they would stop, suddenly, mid-sentence, utterly quiet.

In the distance their father turned the corner, walking slowly with his head down and his hands in his pockets. It was unmistakably him. His short strides, his cropped hair, the deadness in his step marked him. Grace watched him closely and a calmness filled her.

'There he is,' she whispered, as if Sean and Martin really were in the car.

She did not take her eyes off him, and it was strange, the things she felt. She did not know this man. This sixty-two-year-old, empty, hunched figure, slouching under the stars and ignoring the world. He was something in her path, that was all. Her determination became solid and clear, like a light switched on in her head. Everything seemed very simple.

She lowered her eyes briefly as she fumbled with the keys. When she looked up again he had disappeared. She squinted and leaned forward but she could not see him. A nervousness came to her. She turned on the headlights. There was still no sign. She started the engine and moved forward very slowly, inching the car along, close to the tall hedge at the side of the road. She could not see him. She thought perhaps that he had seen her and was hiding. But that was impossible. She moved the car out into the centre of the road. She was confused. She could not understand what had happened to him. She felt a panic rising. Surely he couldn't have seen her. Then suddenly there he was, perhaps two hundred yards ahead of her, lit by the head-lights. Without thinking she braked.

At the side of the narrow road, where flowers tied in ribbons were propped up against the hedge, her husband

22

was kneeling, his head bowed, his hands clenched together. He looked tiny, like a child. Only the soles of his shoes, sticking out from the back of his coat, gave away the fact that he was a grown man. Kneeling. Praying. At the spot where he had killed a girl.

She could not bear to look at him. She bowed her own head, her hands on the steering-wheel showing white knuckles. Anger rose in her. She thought of the magazine in the suitcase and felt as though she had caught him doing something obscene, something disgusting, something at the side of things. She put her foot on the accelerator and the car moved forward.

As she looked up so did he. He stared first at the head-lights, then above the headlights, straight at her. His face was blank, nothing registered with him, he did not see what was happening. Grace put her foot to the floor and stretched out her arms rigidly in front of her, holding the steering-wheel steady. She kept her eyes on his eyes, waiting to see something, some sign that he knew. There was no sign.

At the last moment she could not look. Everything went blank. There was a noise like something collapsing, and the car seemed to lift up and come down sharply, and then again, as if taking a second go. The steering-wheel slipped from Grace's hands and the car scraped along the hedge until she gained control again, braking gently. She went quite a distance before stopping. She was gasping for air, realising only now that she had been holding her breath. She was shaking and there were tears on her face and a strange sound from the engine.

It was hard to turn round because the road was so narrow and her hands and feet kept on slipping, and there was something wrong with the car. She moved slowly back up the road, looking ahead nervously. She had travelled much further than she thought. It seemed a long time before she saw the dark shape at the side of the road. It looked like nothing. A bundle of old clothes. The legs seemed to have disappeared. Only an arm was visible, stretched out at a strange angle, the hand white against the ground. She did not stop the car. He was dead. A little further on the flowers remained, undisturbed.

At the house Grace examined the car. She could see no difference in the damaged front, but there was something wrong with the exhaust. It was hanging down and touching the wheel. She got some string and tied it up as best she could, lying on her back under the car. She could not see very well. She did not want to. She got a sponge and hot water and washed the front and the sides and the back. Then she took a newspaper and dipped it into the mud and ran it over the twisted front bumper.

She went inside and for a moment she could not think what she should do next. She put on the kettle for a cup of tea but then decided that she should have a bath. She ran the water and undressed, moving very slowly as if she were not feeling well, or as if she had been ill in bed for a long time and was only now able to get up. She expected to feel numb, but she did not. She felt as though every muscle in her body sought her attention, not painfully, but as if to point out to her how her body worked. She was conscious of every movement, every sensation.

She cried a little in the bath. Not emotionally. It was a physical release, an exhaustion, all the adrenaline leaving her veins. When she had stopped crying she felt that she wanted to sing. But she couldn't. She kept on thinking that some day she would have to tell somebody everything that she had done. She could not tell them that she had gone home and had a bath and sang. They would think she was mad.

MARTIN

Martin walked up O'Connell Street in the rain, distracted by the trees. He squinted, his head at an angle, his hands in his pockets, and moved slowly. The trees were in the middle of the street, on the wide island which separated the two flows of traffic. They were withered things, bare and lifeless, with barks shiny as leather. Snaking around the branches, evenly spaced one from the other, were countless dead grey light bulbs, sprouting from a green flex that dripped and cut the wood as if strangling. They looked like growths, the bulbs. Like warts or blisters. Decorations, Martin supposed, left over from Christmas. He had not noticed them before, but wondered now whether they were left there all year round. Maybe they were hidden by leaves in the spring, lost in the summer greenery that was impossible to imagine now. It didn't matter. He didn't like them. They were disgusting. He half expected them to burst open and spill a yellow mess down the trunks.

He was cold in Henry's jacket, and the scarf that Philip had left in the house the night before was stringy and damp. His haircut bothered him. They had taken too much off. He wore Henry's black cap and it was too tight and left a red mark across his forehead whenever he removed it. And when it was on he looked as though he might be bald underneath. Chemotherapy bald. He had no umbrella. He could feel the rain beginning to soak through him, dripping from the peak of the cap and down his face. He could have taken a bus but it had not been raining when he had left the house, and he had decided to walk. Halfway down Grafton Street it had started, light but insistent, a very wet kind of rain. He had hurried because of it and now he was too early and sweating.

He ducked the sharp points of passing umbrellas and wondered where he could shelter for a few minutes. He walked at the edge of the pavement, glancing at the trees, closing his eyes at the roar of buses that rushed past him, their misty wake darkening the suede of his shoes.

He was aware of a beggar up ahead, an old man in a filthy grey duffle coat with a huge, tangled beard, and skin almost black with dirt. His white eyes shone out from his face like lights. He stood with his back to the traffic and watched the scurry of people with a nodding, malicious head, thrusting his arm outwards, open palmed, and appearing to mutter. Martin changed course and headed diagonally towards the shopfronts. But the man saw him and moved to intercept. Martin adjusted direction again, moving back towards the kerb. The man smiled and followed him, limping badly. Martin cursed and came face to face with the hirsute features and the gap-toothed grin.

'Any chance of twenty pence there, sir, for a cup of tea?'

'Excuse me,' said Martin, trying to move around him. The man stepped back and sideways, getting in front of him again.

'Just a few pence please, sir, for a cap for the rain. Nice cap like yours.'

'Fuck off,' hissed Martin. He pushed past, increasing his speed and keeping his head down. He had walked only a few steps when he heard a roar behind him.

'Ya big fucker. Don't you push me. No fucking manners. You're a big man aren't ya, in yer big fucking leather jacket. C'mon. C'mon.'

Martin glanced back to see him standing on his toes, his fists raised like a boxer, swaying slightly.

'C'mon, ya coward, come here an say that again.'

Martin turned and kept going, walking as fast as he could without running. There was silence for a moment and he thought perhaps that he had escaped. Then the voice came again, soiled, cracked, and he knew the man was after him. He saw people stare.

'What's wrong with ya, ya big fucker. Ya walk like a girl. C'mon.'

Martin felt the man's hand poking at his shoulder and shrugged it off fiercely and jogged a few steps, smiling an awful, embarrassed smile at those who stared. The man fell back a little but kept shouting, and Martin wondered what to do. He looked around briefly and saw the man hobbling after him, his fists clenched, spittle on his chin. His shouting had settled into a rasping rant cluttered with snot and coughing.

'I'm after ya, don't worry. I'll get ya. Little fuck. Think ya can push me round like a fucking dog. Like a fucking animal. Fuckers. Yer all fuckers, every single one. C'mon.'

His head was jerking back and forth and his arm was pointing clearly at Martin. His limp was worse. He dragged his left leg and wheezed with the effort. People formed a kind of tableau each time Martin looked over his shoulder, pausing in their stride, swinging around with puzzled looks, considering Martin carefully, summing him up. He quickly thought of what he could do. There was too much traffic for him to attempt to flee across the street. If he simply kept on going the man would surely follow him, and that way they would arrive together at the place where the coach came in. The idea was too terrible.

Martin ducked and trotted and dipped his shoulder. He reached the entrance to the Gresham Hotel and sprinted up the steps. A porter stood behind the glass, peering out into the rain, his cap pulled low over his eyes. He opened the door for Martin and stepped back.

'Rotten day,' he said. Martin nodded.

'Yeah. Rotten.' He took off Henry's cap and rubbed at his forehead and moved away from the door hurriedly, expecting to hear the loud cursing voice following behind him. He walked past reception, conscious of the squelch in his shoes, and caught sight of the bar. He glanced back to the main door. The porter stood with his back to him, his hands clasped together, his thumbs working at each other. Through the glass was the tousled grey hair of the beggar, his fist raised and shaking at the blue uniform and the peaked cap, his voice crying out something Martin could not hear. He found himself thinking of the rain falling into the man's open mouth, of how refreshing that would be, how soothing.

In the almost-empty bar he ordered a pint and sat by the fire and dried himself a little and drank.

Memory. It fought him for days and nights on end, and then disappeared. It left him sometimes for months. And then it rose up suddenly to face him like his own ghost.

His mother rang and the breath left him. He had known immediately. He saw his father's face in the darkness of his closed eyes, heard his voice in the silence of his head, felt his hands take a grip of him. His father. Dead on the road. Gone from them. Like that.

He could not remember now what she had said exactly. 'He's dead', or 'he's gone'. They had not talked then. He could see her standing in Bolton's hall, at the foot of the stairs, the phone beneath the mirror. The memory. She spoke to him from his memory. She had told him to come the next morning, that they would bury him then. He wondered why she did not want him to come down immediately, and he wondered why she had left it till then to ring him. His father dead a day.

He had put the phone down and gone to work.

Memory. Since Henry had left, the memory had become stronger, had fought him almost nightly. His father's voice.

His words. The smell of him – cattle and grass and damp dirty clothes. His laugh in the open air and his laugh indoors. And his mother. Her long hands. Her brittle hair. Her voice. Her words. And with Henry gone the memory grew and took Henry in and showed him to Martin as he knew him to be, and imagined him, and feared him. Martin had marked off the days until Henry's return on the calendar in the kitchen. A big swathe of black ink, obscuring days and weeks of what Martin knew would be vacant time. Difficult time. Memory time.

And then his father dead. Like that.

Cast back. Recall. It was only days ago. But it was constant, as if it had happened before, as if it was always happening. As if it was always happening and he had slipped into it for a while and played a part. As if it was a place.

In the graveyard he had helped his mother though she did not need his help. She rested her wrist in the crook of his elbow and followed his steps across the grass. There was a light rain, and the morning was cold.

There were few enough there. There was a brother of the dead man who had appeared out of the blue with a Cork accent and called himself William. He had seemed confused, as if unsure that he had found the right funeral, that this was the same Michael Quinn that had been his brother. He had asked Martin for details, histories, chronologies; thrown names at him which Martin had never heard.

'I saw it in the paper. Just as well I did. Did he still have the scar?'

'What scar?'

'Big ugly brute of a thing on his thigh, his right thigh. Split it open with a fork gettin' the hay in when we were boys.'

He could not imagine his father as a boy.

'I don't know. You'd have to ask my mother.'

William looked at him with dark eyes that Martin thought he knew.

'Maybe I shouldn't do that just now.'

'No, of course.'

There were people from Cootehill. Martin knew some of them but did not know why they were there. Maybe a funeral was neutral, separate from the life preceding, a thing unto itself. An event. Some were friends of his father's. Matt Clancy, with his wife beside him, holding a huge yellow umbrella. The Boltons. Not Pat though. Not Pat. Then there were two who Martin did not know. Two big men in black suits and grey raincoats. Shabby. The one with the bald head smiled at Martin and Martin smiled back.

As they made their way through the graves, the living, Martin could not take his eyes from the coffin. A stained wooden mystery box. Shining. It held the rain to its sides in tiny drops. It made its way through the headstones on the shoulders of strangers, the grave-diggers maybe. The priest led the way, tall and thin and sullen. The coffin followed, an eight-legged insect with a hard headless body. Its wings plucked. Then came the family, such as it was. The family. Martin and his mother and William Quinn.

Around the grave they gathered, only the priest at ease. He stood at the head of the dark space in the earth and held a prayer book in his hands from which he read. Martin did not listen to the words. He concentrated on the coffin. Stared at the wood. Wondered whether wood rotted quicker or slower than flesh. Father flesh. Did father flesh rot quicker or slower than son flesh? Dust did not come into it. Just dead leaves in the rain. Mulch.

He could not see how the lid was secured. There were no nails visible. He wondered whether it was simply resting there, whether it would slide off if kicked. He felt an awful urge to go over and kick it. Awful. Kick at it like a child would kick at a toy. His foot twitched. He felt the

30

rain on his hands, joined together at his crotch like a foot-ball player waiting for a free, flinching at the run up. His foot twitched again. He stubbed at the ground with his toe.

They did something with ropes. The coffin was lifted and moved through the air and then lowered, hovering every few inches as though hesitating. Martin tried to record things, to be super-conscious, to remember, remember, remember. Be a camera. Do it. Squint. He was aware of his mother, looking sideways at him. He glanced at her. She was not looking at him at all. She was looking past him. He looked back to the coffin as its lid came level with the ground, the flat earth, the body of it beneath the surface now. He should watch it disappear. Film. He could not. He glanced back at his mother. She was still looking past him. He could do nothing other than turn his head to follow her gaze. He did not know what she was looking at. He saw the headstones dotted into the grass and the grey earth which sloped up to the church. He saw the grey walls of the church rise up and seem to stretch, blank and dead towards the sky. He saw the sky, the same colour as the stone, the rain falling from it carelessly, barely a veil. He did not know what there was in that that could hold his mother's eyes so long.

When he looked back to the grave his father's coffin had disappeared into the ground, only the ropes to be seen now, still rigid with the weight of him, then relaxing suddenly as the load came to rest on the wet dark soil below with a barely audible splashing sound, like a sigh. Like the sigh his mother gave beside him. A sigh so full of relief that the entire gathering looked up at her, and then one by one looked away again.

Only the Clancys and the brother came back to the house. They took the tea and sandwiches that Martin made and

31

spoke little and left after an hour. At the door Martin's new uncle shook his hand and gripped his elbow.

'He was a good man. My sympathies.'

Martin stared.

'When did you move to Cork?'

'Ah God, forty years ago now. I married a girl from Kinsale. We didn't stay in touch, me and Michael. Our parents died when we were very young. Our grandparents raised us. Up near Scotstown.'

Martin nodded. He was not sure.

'Well. Thank you for coming.'

He asked his mother whether she had known about him.

'I think he's made a mistake,' she said. 'There was a Michael Quinn in Tullyvin died about ten years ago. He was a cousin of your father's. Your man is the image of him.'

Martin cleaned up and prepared to stay the night. But his mother said no, that he should take the evening bus back to Dublin. That he should not miss work the next day. He told her that he had been given the rest of the week off.

'Why?' she asked, puzzled.

'Well, I didn't ask for it. They just told me not to come back till Monday.'

She nodded.

'I don't like to keep you here.'

He argued with her, but she would not be persuaded that it was a good idea. She sat in the kitchen with a half-smile on her face, her eyes a little wide. He felt that she was trying to convince him that she was all right. She had aged, but sideways, as if her days were longer than his. Her hours. Minutes. Her seconds were stretched out. She was weary. Which was, he supposed, only to be expected. At least now . . . Her hands were pallid pale, a length of moonlight doubled, one on the other, resting. Her thin shoulders. Her thin air.

32

She drove him into Cootehill for the bus. She didn't speak. They sat in the car outside the White Horse waiting for it to arrive. As it pulled in she turned to him and asked whether it would be all right if she came up to Dublin and stayed with him for a while.

'God yes. Of course. I meant to say. There's an open invitation.'

'You wouldn't mind?'

'Of course I wouldn't. I should have said it to you.'

He had meant to. Hadn't he? His eyes flew on the clotted windscreen.

'With Henry away and everything it'd be great. We'd be company for each other. Come up as soon as you like.'

He glanced at the bus.

'I've got to go. I'll ring you later. We'll arrange it.'

He kissed his mother on the cheek and left her. He crossed the cold road and climbed on board the bus and told himself that he would not come back. He paid the driver and found a seat. When he looked out he saw his mother where he had left her, unable to start the car. He watched her for a moment. She grimaced each time she turned the key in the ignition. Nothing happened. Martin stood and stepped into the aisle, not knowing quite how he could help her, but thinking that perhaps the bus driver could do something. Then there was a loud metallic roar and he turned to see a puff of dark exhaust fumes. The car jerked forward. It sounded like it might cut out, but then revved up loudly and moved off, his mother crouched over the steering-wheel. Martin sat down again. He watched it clatter through the dusk to the corner near the church and disappear.

She could not drive to Dublin, he decided. Not in that. She would have to take the bus.

There was no sign of the beggar. Martin peered carefully to each side, looking for the wild grey hair amongst the

33

garish umbrellas and the wet heads running for cover. The rain was heavier, bouncing off the concrete with a soft hissing noise, puddles forming by the kerbs, cars slowing to a crawl, everything a little less useful. He could not see the man anywhere.

He put on Henry's cap and pulled it down over his eyes, and zipped up Henry's jacket with Philip's scarf tucked into the collar. He stepped out into the rain and walked towards Parnell Street in other people's clothes.

As he turned the corner he stopped and looked. There were two large white coaches parked halfway down the street. He was late. Passengers hopped and struggled from the doors uneasily, still on country time. They grabbed their luggage quickly and tried to disappear into the ordinary flow of the street.

Martin saw his mother amongst them. She laboured with a suitcase in one hand and a plastic bag, obviously full of shoes, in the other. There was an umbrella sticking out dangerously from under her arm. She made it as far as the wall of Fibber McGee's pub before settling her load on the ground and looking up and opening the umbrella. Martin smiled at her and she saw him almost immediately. She made an attempt to pick up the suitcase again, to come and meet him halfway, but Martin broke into a jog and reached her before she could move.

'I'll carry that,' he said.

She straightened up and looked at him. She smiled. Her hair was mostly grey and hung in wisps over her forehead. She was a little pale, but her eyes were alive, bright, and he noticed them most. She was different already. A little jumpy. Nervous. She kissed his cheek.

'I'm so glad to see you.'

'Sure you only saw me the other day.'

'It's different here.'

He nodded and picked up the suitcase. He took his mother's arm and led her back towards O'Connell Street.

'How are you?' she asked.

'Oh, I'm fine. A bit wet.'

'Here, get under the umbrella. I like the cap.'

'It's Henry's.'

'Oh.'

He hoped she would not compliment the jacket or the scarf. He asked her about the journey and about the weather in Monaghan. She barely answered, distracted by the noise of the city. She stared around herself like a child. When they came to the top of O'Connell Street she stopped and stood to look down its length to the river. Shop lights and car headlights glimmered in the greyness of the rain, giving the street a look of warmth which surprised Martin.

'It's lovely,' she whispered. 'So different. The buses have changed.'

'Just shows you how long since you've been here. I've never seen any other type.'

'They used to be orange. These ones are much nicer. Where's ours?'

'We'll get a taxi. The bus stop is too far and it'd be too awkward with the suitcase.'

He moved to the kerb and waited, hoping to spot one coming down from Parnell Square. He looked around. Glanced behind him.

A grey mess in the shape of a man bobbed unsteadily through the grey light.

He was swaying, a small bottle in his hand, coming their way. He didn't appear to have seen Martin. Maybe he would have forgotten. He was drunk enough. He was also drunk enough to remember. Martin swung away, positioned himself in front of his mother. She was so insubstantial. A taxi turned the corner from Parnell Street and slowed down. Martin closed his eyes and swallowed.

'Here we are,' he said.

He stuck his head out around the umbrella. He was

just a few feet away, apparently oblivious, but veering nonetheless in their general direction. The taxi stopped in front of them and the boot flew open.

Martin heaved the suitcase inside, closing the boot as quietly as he could, keeping his head down. He walked backwards, bumping into his mother, and opened the door for her. She lowered the umbrella. She seemed to take forever to get herself in through the door, Martin's panic rising again as he felt, he was sure of it, someone close behind him. She was in.

'You! Ya big bollocks. C'mon. C'mon.'

Martin threw himself into the car and slammed the door.

'My God,' said his mother. 'What is it?'

The man was up against the car, his hand on the roof, his face huge in the window. Martin tried to look straight ahead, to ignore him. The voice was loud, even through the glass.

'You fucker! Come out here and push me around, ya bollocks. I'm not an animal. I'm not an animal.'

'It's the bleedin' Elephant Man,' said the taxi driver, putting his foot on the accelerator and pulling away from the kerb sharply, the beggar stumbling as his support sped off. Martin's mother looked out through the back window while Martin looked ahead.

'My God,' she said. 'What was he talking about?'

'I've no idea,' answered Martin, aware of a slight tremble in his voice and the look from his mother which followed it. He turned to stare out of the window and saw the drunk's spittle still on the glass, a smudge of it disappearing slowly in the rain.

GRACE

It clung to her. In the dim light of Dublin, with the rain falling and the cars glinting and the crowds of people gathered by the roads, it clung to her. She could not close her eyes to blind it, or hum to kill its sound, or dig her nails into her palms to distract from it. It clung to her.

In the taxi she could smell herself, her clothes damp, her skin loose on her frame, her lips cold. She was wrapped in it.

It had touched her first in the churchyard and had not left her since. And here in the streets where she had hoped to shrug it off, it came at her renewed, and wrapped itself around her and stuck.

Not guilt. Not that. That she could have carried.

It was confusion. Doubt. The failing of her mind. It held her. Clutched her like an instrument, a device. Clamps and arms and notched levers. Springs and cogs and rust from the ages. Attached to her shoulders and her back, invisible, performing a subversive surgery on her sense of balance, her life.

She looked in front of her and saw her hand, raised. She had not put it there. She considered it, and used it then to scratch her eyebrow.

Martin talked and told her where they were. How did he not notice? How did he not recoil? She watched the faces that were shuffled through her gaze, and nodded when her son said something that she understood. The taxi moved slowly, clogged in the rain.

'It's mostly flats, though our street is mainly whole houses. There's some who claim to have been there for generations. I don't know though. Mostly it's couples like us. Well, not exactly like us.'

Grace nodded. The streets passed her in a spray and were colourless. She sought out something bright. Some sign that she had come to a new place.

'Here we are,' he said.

She looked up at it and breathed out and nodded, pleased that it was as it was. Different. Unfamiliar. It was an old, narrow terrace house with wooden window frames painted yellow, and a yellow door, and a metal drainpipe the colour of mustard.

'Yellow,' she said.

Martin laughed. It sounded odd to her.

'Yes it is, isn't it? Yellow.'

She stood in the rain while Martin paid the driver, and she considered the bricks and the lace blind in the downstairs window. As she looked up, the glass glinted at her and the gutter seemed to hum, and the rain fell in her open eyes and she dropped her head to rub at them. By her feet the drain bubbled furiously, the water splashing on the pavement with the fresh sound of city rain that she had forgotten.

Martin opened the door and dragged her suitcase up the stairs while she walked through the narrow hall to the kitchen and looked out at a small paved yard and whitewashed walls. Even in the dying light and the grey rain they shone at her and her breathing eased. She was suddenly hungry.

She opened presses, rummaged in the fridge. She found a couple of tomatoes and took them out and found the cutlery drawer and a sharp knife and sliced them on the draining board. She licked her fingers and went back to the fridge and found some cheese and butter and half an onion in a plastic bag. The bread was in a wooden bread-bin with a mug tree on top. On the wall behind the mugs there was a small notice-board. There were some forms and a photograph of a man she did not know, Henry maybe, and a postcard of a naked man lying face down on a beach towel. His skin was slick.

When Martin came in she was sitting at the table biting into her sandwich while the kettle came to the boil on the sideboard.

'I'm sorry,' she mumbled. 'I was hungry.'

He looked at her without moving, and she was afraid for a moment that he could see the apparatus that was strapped to her back and which she had briefly forgotten, but which cut into her now like a vice and sent her head spinning. She put down her sandwich.

Martin laughed. Laughed and moved forward and saw to the kettle, to the making of tea.

'I was going to take you out for something,' he said. 'Into Rathmines, I thought.'

Grace closed her eyes and found words.

'There's no need. I'll cook for you later. Have something now. A snack. I'll cook for you later.'

'You don't have to.'

'I want to.'

She had not cooked for him in years.

He made tea and sat in front of her and they drank and looked at each other and talked. He smoked a cigarette. She looked at his deep eyes, and his black hair. He had changed his clothes. He wore a blue shirt beneath a grey wool jumper, and jeans. There was about him the sense of his father as a young man. The darkness, the good skin. But there was a difference. She was in there too.

He took her on a tour of the house. She saw the bathroom, added on at the back, reached through a low passage from the kitchen. And the front room, cluttered and comfortable. And then upstairs.

Her room, the spare room, was bright and warm. It was

39

at the back of the house, and she looked out at the rooftops and the rain and the bright white square of the yard.

'Was there a garden?' she asked.

'It was paved when we got here. I suppose there must have been at some stage. Next door has one.'

She looked and could just make out a patch of grass.

'We did the walls ourselves,' said Martin. 'In the summer. Henry got some in his eyes and we had to go to the doctor. It's kind of turned us against it. I finished it on my own, goggles and all.'

Grace looked at the windows in the back of the house opposite. There were two of them. They seemed smoked to darkness, as if stained. On the roof, slates had slipped and gathered in the guttering like playing cards.

'It's so strange to be so close,' she said, and turned to him and smiled. He nodded.

'I'm still not used to it.'

They went out on to the tiny landing and Martin hesitated at the door to the other room. Grace looked down the stairs, and then back at him.

'Is this your room?'

'Yes,' he said cheerfully, pushing the door open and stepping in. Grace stayed where she was and peered in after him, mainly at the floor.

'It's lovely.'

She stood in silence for a moment before turning suddenly and going down the stairs. She heard her son follow, his steps light and quick. She was embarrassed and felt her cheeks flush.

'Well, that's it,' he said. 'Small but cosy.'

'Yes,' said Grace, going back in to the kitchen and taking cups and plates from the table, keeping her back to him. She stood at the sink and turned on the taps.

'Are you all right?'

'Oh yes. The house is lovely.'

'Leave that stuff. Do you want to unpack?'

'Yes,' said Grace, turning around quickly, looking for something with which to dry her hands. 'I should.'

'You don't have to. I mean, do what you like.'

He stood looking at her. His face was clear of things. She wanted to touch him. She wanted to embrace him and have him rest his head on her shoulder. She took a step forward. Her hand came up. She stopped.

'I'm disordered,' she said.

Martin's head shifted slightly sideways.

'What?'

'I mean, disorientated. That's all. I'm just not quite sure where I am.'

He nodded.

'Do you feel all right? I mean, are you sick?'

'No.'

She sat down. In her mind there was a rush of cold, as if a door had opened somewhere. She heard it swinging on its hinges and put her hand to her head.

'The Boltons will keep an eye on the cattle. There's just the four sucklers now. Three white heads and a Friesian. The Friesian will calve maybe next week. He'll have to watch her. The son, what's his name, he said he'd look after them. Fodder them and water them and see they're all right.'

'Okay,' said Martin, and sat next to her.

'I locked up the house. They're good people. Mrs Bolton is very kind. They came over on Monday after I'd heard. Mrs Bolton told me to forget about everything. They'd see to it. She said I would need all my time.'

'She was right.'

'She wasn't.'

Martin's hand was resting on her arm. She looked at it.

'I mean,' she said, 'I think I would rather have been busy.'

Martin nodded.

'Were they okay about looking after the cattle while you're away?'

'I never told them.'

He looked puzzled, and it was a look that reminded her of how he had been as a child. When she teased him. Confused him. She smiled.

'Why not?' he asked, and smiled back at her.

'I don't know. I just didn't.'

She laughed.

'What's so funny?'

'Nothing. I don't know. Oh I'm sorry. It's just the look on your face. You look like someone's played a great big trick on you.'

MARTIN

She cooked the kind of meal that he had not had in years. Chops and potatoes and carrots and peas. He wondered how the mind remembered tastes, and he thought that it must happen in the same way that the mind remembered voices, for suddenly he could hear his father's, gritty, mouth full.

She had cheered up. She had seemed, at first, a little strange. As if confused. He had been afraid that she would break down, cry on him, or want to talk. But she seemed all right now.

After dinner they sat and watched television, silently for the most part. They watched Albert Reynolds, the newly elected leader of Fianna Fail and the new Taoiseach, as he spoke for the first time about taking the place of Charlie Haughey. His eyes seemed startled by it. He smiled into the lights, nodded.

'All change,' said Martin's mother. Martin eyed her, tried to gauge her mood.

'I know that guy,' he ventured.

'Albert Reynolds?'

'No,' he laughed. 'The guy who asked the question. The journalist. He's a friend.'

'Did we see him?'

'No. Just heard him.'

'What did he ask?'

'Something about a reshuffle.'

43

'Is that a good question?' She smiled. Did not look at him. She seemed fine.

'Excellent question.'

She sat in Henry's place on the sofa. She was different somehow. Not changed, different. He couldn't understand it. It was as if she was magnified or exaggerated. Bigger. Or else it was the air around her. As if she filled the space around her like a sound; like a sound or like a light.

Martin made tea. She dipped her biscuits and tucked her bare feet beneath her.

Just after eleven she announced that she was going to bed. Then waited for a while, then said it again, and stood. She kissed him on the forehead and went upstairs. He listened to her footsteps, the sound of her moving about. It made him think of Henry.

He lingered – watched the screen change in front of him and took nothing in. He recalled Henry's reaction to the news of his father's death. The shock and the silence, then the embarrassed mumbles of sympathy that had made Martin smile – almost laugh. Henry in Paris, trying to remember what Martin thought. Trying to work out whether it was good news or bad.

It was one o'clock when he went to bed, climbing the stairs as quietly as he could, pausing at the door of his mother's room, listening. There was silence. He went into his own room and pulled across the curtains before putting on the light. He undressed quickly, standing naked for a moment in front of the mirror, running his hand over his chest and his shoulders, feeling the smoothness of his skin. Then he slipped on a T-shirt and a pair of boxer shorts, switched off the light and climbed into the big double bed, enjoying the chill of the sheets and the pillows, shuddering into them and wrapping himself in their folds.

His mother in the next room. Memory. He remembered what it had been like to sleep in a room next to his parents', wondering if they could hear him. He remembered lying in bed, the sound outside of his father walking past, the rumbling feeling it gave him, the frightened sense of small spaces and hard surfaces, of the cold wall where he rested his head, crouching back from the light beneath the door. The feeling returned.

He remembered lying in bed trying to masturbate as quietly as possible. There had been a trick to it. A splitting of the concentration. A dividing. Doing and watching. Whispering and listening. Both. He had done it so well that he had needed to forget how it was done. He had needed to work at that. Relax, they had told him, all of them. Relax.

As he set about it now he shuffled through memories with a speed that astounded him, picking out here and there the one that closed his eyes a little tighter or moved his head on the pillow as a dream might. He sorted on, his mind throwing random pictures at him that he could not predict. Too many of his father. His mother. His younger self. He opened his eyes to the darkness and the bed, to the memories of Henry which the bed kept for him, the newer memories, the ones that did not alter him. Skin, Henry's skin. The expanse of the sheets which Henry's absence filled now. Martin, moving his hands, the skin of his arms brushing the skin of his thighs, closing his eyes again, able to, willing to, and seeing an open space filled with pictures, not memories, pictures, tiny pictures, living, breathing, a long line of them, connected by touch, a communication of sight and touch and no words, just breathing, just skin. Martin's breathing changed as if the oxygen in the room was suddenly thinner, as if he lay at a great height, a dizzy height, afraid to look down, afraid to look up, afraid to look. He held his balance and held it still a little longer, and held it still a moment more, and then felt it failing, slipping, stumbling, gone, and him falling, as if through water, as if the very skin of his body was the

45

world entire, and all of it falling, collapsing, dropping through water like a stone in a pool.

He laughed out loud at coming so quickly, then snapped his mouth shut as he remembered his mother. The covers were pushed back from him and his shorts were around his ankles, his T-shirt up around his neck. Laughter still rippled through him for a moment before he became still, and confronted the mess on his stomach and, impressing him greatly, high up on his chest. He realised as he lay there, recovering his breathing in a wonderful state of relaxation, that it was the first time he had come in well over a week. He reached out for tissues. He lay back in the cold silence and enjoyed the lullaby of his own breath.

Something strange came to him then, a thought which opened his eyes to the shadows of the room, the light which leaked through the curtains. It had been the first time he had come since his father had died. It had been the first time in his entire life that he had come, ever, without his father in the world. His father did not exist. He had never been able to say that before. He no longer had a father.

He listened to the quiet of his room and the small noises of the street, imagining perhaps that he could hear his mother breathing, her heart working, her chest gently rising and falling, her head lying easy on the soft pillow. He thought: my mother is breathing and I am breathing and my father, for the first time in either of our lives, is not breathing.

GRACE

Grace woke up with the light on her face and did not know where she was. An unfamiliar brightness billowed out from the closed curtains and fell speckled and dusty on the surfaces of the room, a room which for a moment she did not recognise.

And then an unfolding in her mind, a laying out of things.

She felt the warmth of sunlight all over her, caressing her, teasing her eyes. She tugged back the covers and breathed deeply of an air that was fresh and clean. The usual morning ache of her bones was not sharp, and she was able to rise without pain and step across the carpet and snap the curtains open. She squinted and yawned and got back into bed.

In the snug warmth she lay like a child and stared through the glass, out into the space between the houses. She could see the sky, a perfect blue patch of it stretched from the roofs to the top of the window frame, like the skin of the sea hung up to dry. It stretched and did not tear. There was nothing upon it. Lower down, the grey-black slates of the rooftops and the grainy bricks of the walls reminded her of Manchester and her father.

She thought of the distance she had travelled. Manchester, Monaghan, Dublin. It formed a triangle and she had not been outside its shape. It marked out her life. Three places. Three people.

After a while, with nothing left in the frame of the

window to stare at, Grace got out of bed, and dressed. She could hear no sound from the other bedroom. The house was still and quiet.

There was a bunch of keys hanging from a nail on the kitchen wall. Grace stared at them for a while, and took them down then, and walked to the front door and opened it and looked out. It was cold. She tried various keys in the lock, finding the right one eventually. She wondered what time it was; everything was so quiet.

She got her coat and thought for a moment of leaving a note. But she doubted that Martin would be up before she returned. She closed the front door quietly behind her and stepped on to the pavement, glancing up at the closed curtains of his room. She smiled to herself, thinking that if she could do some shopping she might cook him a breakfast and bring it up to him. She turned to her right and walked slowly away from the house. Perhaps she shouldn't disturb him. He might be embarrassed. She did not know what he wore in bed.

She wandered through an untidy neighbourhood of old houses, walking slowly along Lennox Street and turning into Stamer Street, while cars passed her and pedestrians ignored her. She liked the mild city noise, the bright morning. She argued with herself about place and distance. About whether she was wrong to have come here. About where to stop in the listing of mistakes – how far back to go. She felt herself a long way from Monaghan but told herself that she had not even left. She could not understand that. She went through it again. Something held her up. Some connection she had missed.

She reached traffic lights and stood on the corner and read the street names. Harrington Street. Heytesbury Street. They were English names. South Circular Road. Stamer Street. They were disappointing names. They held no pictures. She felt that she would not be able to remember them.

48

On the corner, across the road from her, there was a church. She had glanced at it only. It was a big church, obscured a little by the tall trees which surrounded it, but stretching above them in a square tower of grey stone darkened by the city smoke. As she stood at the corner her gaze rested there, in the sooty granite of the tower. It loomed up. It rose. Grace was startled to find herself staring. Shocked at what it brought back to her. It clutched at her shoulders and her back as if it reached over and took hold of her, and reminded her suddenly and coldly, like a piece of ice slipped beneath her scalp, of the place where her husband was buried. The picture formed in her mind, as if carved, engraved, of the church outside Cootehill, of the cold air that she breathed hanging there above his grave. The church in front of her, and the church where he was. They were covered by the same sky. The same air. She breathed him in.

Grace turned and fled.

She hurried back down Stamer Street, this time with her head down, looking only at the pavement, the cracks and the dirt. It was not guilt. That was not it. It was panic. Again. But this time it came to her not as something random, but as a thought that was as hard as it was irrational. She had sent her husband to the place where her son was kept. She had sent him after Sean. Thrown one over the other like a cover, like a sheet. Why had she done that?

She had wanted to find her son's grave, the tiny place where he was hidden. She had wanted to read the words that marked it. But she had not known where to look, had not known who to ask.

She had walked slowly away from her husband, searching through the headstones for the name of Sean Quinn. She thought it would be close by, but it was not. Martin had walked behind her, and she had wondered

49

whether he knew where it was. He had said nothing, and Grace had wanted to ask him, to say, casually, 'Will we visit your brother's grave?' But she had been ashamed, and she had stayed silent. At the gate the policemen had waited for her. She thought that was as it should be.

It had not occurred to her to worry about being caught until that moment, ashamed in the grounds of the strange church, a mother ignorant of the whereabouts of her child's grave. A mother like that. The policemen, Detective Brady and another man, stood at the gate and watched her approach. She thought, assumed almost, that they were going to arrest her. They would read her rights to her, handcuff her, lead her gently to a car, drive her away as the other mourners looked on, stunned. But they did not. They bowed their heads respectfully, and shook her hand, and Brady said to her, 'If there's anything I can do,' and told her again to call him.

The way he looked at her. The way he paused as he did it. He knew. She felt that he knew.

They had come to the house on the day after the funeral. Grace had been in the bedroom, sorting through clothes, packing slowly, when she saw the two of them outside, looking at the car. She watched as Brady crouched down and peered beneath the front bumper, then walked around the car, bent over, looking for signs, holding his tie against his chest. When he stood up he was panting, out of breath. He talked to the other man for a moment, the same one who had been in the bar of the White Horse and with him at the funeral. They talked very quietly, with their heads close together, two policemen whispering in front of Grace's house.

They asked her whether she knew of anyone having threatened her husband. She told them of the visit by the girl's parents, when they had come looking for him. 'Oh, is that so,' said Detective Brady, his big red head nodding slowly, the skin stretched tightly over his skull as if it might tear. They had left then, gone to see the Killeens.

Later, Detective Brady had called back on his own and talked to her for a while, drinking tea and sweating, though the kitchen was not hot.

'Were the Killeens any help?'

'No, Mrs Quinn.'

The way he said it, almost sadly, and then stayed silent. She was sure that he knew.

Martin wanted to take her to meet a friend of his who worked in a café in the city centre. Grace would rather have stayed where she was, trying not to break open. She was about to say so, but it occurred to her that she might distract herself with streets and bustle and new people. She nodded. They ate breakfast, Martin showered, and they set off in the late morning to walk through the bright air and the cold and the crowds.

He dragged her. He knew how to walk without bumping, knew how to weave and accelerate and get past. She apologised her way after him, becoming hot and uncomfortable. Martin was like a salesman. He pointed things out and waited for her to say something in approval or to nod her head. He talked and talked. He took her into some shops and seemed to expect her to take over, as if shopping was a thing that would come to her naturally, and when she showed no sign of it, he whisked her outside again and on somewhere else, all the time naming things, telling her things that she did not understand, names and stories and gossip that confused her, jokes that she did not get, references that she knew nothing about. She was bewildered and bored. The swirl and babble of the crowd made her silent and tense. She wanted to be out of it.

Eventually, with Martin slowing slightly and glancing at his watch, they came to Trinity College and the Bank of Ireland. He stopped and encouraged her to be impressed.

The buildings were smudged black by exhaust fumes, though the sides of the bank's pillars and the central section of the college front were bright in the sunshine as though newly cleaned, their old stone the colour of mushrooms. Martin looked at her. She smiled, nodded. Caught her breath.

On the pavement where they stood, a girl crouched over a roll of thick paper held flat by stones. Beside her was a open book. She was copying a painting, using sticks of messy chalk. Grace glimpsed the scene and flinched. Two women held down a half-naked man, pressed him to a table like a work-table, a kitchen table. His head hung over the edge, his upside down bearded face stared out. The woman in the foreground pressed one hand down on his neck, and held a knife in the other. Her face was set in a grimace as she prepared to cut his throat. Again. His eyes were wild and terrified, his face stretched in shock, his hands flailed. Blood fell from him, splattering the ground and the robe bunched at his shoulders.

Grace stared. Her mind clicked slowly over this. It was not for her. It was not deliberate. It was simply a picture on a street corner, pressed to the ground she covered. A bad coincidence. Clumsy.

There was something wonderfully straightforward in the face of the woman with the knife, something quite dignified. It was as if she was killing a hen or a pig, or gutting a fish. It was work. It fed her family. Woman slicing onions. That was all.

'We should go,' said Martin, tapping his watch.

Grace dug into her purse and pulled out a pound coin, taking a step forward and dropping it into the box which lay beside the book. She glanced at the girl, smiling, but the girl did not notice.

The café was on a side street near the river. Flags on silver

52

poles cracked in the wind. The thick green water chopped and ran towards the sea.

The place was tiny, its windows grey with condensation, its air still and hot. Smoke hung in the yellow light. Conversation and laughter and low music sounded in the small space like the echo of a larger one. Grace and Martin squeezed themselves into creaky wooden chairs at a small table pressed into a corner.

Martin immediately lit a cigarette and began to watch the doors leading to the kitchens. Young waiters and waitresses went in and out, carrying plates and cups and saucers. They did not use trays. After two or three had come and gone, and Martin had smiled a reassuring smile at his mother, he suddenly waved his hand at the doors and grinned. A boy, a slim fair-haired boy, had emerged, and, smiling broadly, began to make his way towards them through the clutter of tables.

'Hello,' he said brightly, and leaned towards Martin and stopped and glanced at Grace and stood up straight.

'Hi,' said Martin. 'How are you?'

'I'm great. Great. How are you?' He put his hand on Martin's shoulder. Grace stared at it. As if by magic it was lifted away and fell to the boy's side.

'Fine. This is my Mum. Mum, Philip.'

He smiled down at her, his neat face very handsome and very young. His blue eyes stayed on Grace's eyes, and he paused for a second, smiling.

'I'm very pleased to meet you,' he said.

'Hello.'

They looked at each other for a moment. Grace could think of nothing to say.

'You two are the image of each other,' said Philip. 'Do you know that?'

'Are we?'

'Martin has your mouth. Or maybe your eyes.' He looked

53

from one to the other. 'I don't know what it is. You're just identical.'

They both ordered the same food, Grace following her son's lead, not really understanding the names of things. Philip told them that the busy period was coming to an end and he'd join them for coffee after they'd eaten. He smiled at Grace. He delivered their food and told them to enjoy it and she saw him then, a moment later, watching her from across the room. He smiled again.

'He seems very nice,' she said.

'Yeah. He's fine.'

She stared a little doubtfully at the vegetables and the pasta on her plate. She tried a mouthful. She could recognise some, and guessed and wondered at others. She did not like peppers. She picked them out and piled them up at the side. She did the best she could with the rest, at one stage picking something hard and bitter from between her teeth. Martin wolfed his down.

When he had finished he lit another cigarette and looked at her.

'All right?'

'Yes. I'm fine.'

He played with his box of matches.

'Don't finish it if you don't want.'

It was the kind of thing she used to say to him. She nodded. Drank water to clear her mouth.

'You were a bit tense yesterday,' he said. 'When you arrived, I mean.'

'Yes.'

'Well. You're on holiday. You can relax. You don't have to worry about anything.'

'I know.'

He pursed his lips.

'And let me know if you want to do anything, or if you want to do nothing, or if you want to . . . whatever.'

She smiled.

'I will.'

'Because you're to have a good time. Relax. Get your breath back.'

'From what?'

'You know. This week. You must be kind of rattled.'

She nodded quickly and tried to say thank you, but it got caught in his smoke and was lost somewhere. She did not think he heard it.

Philip joined them, sitting between them, brushing Grace's elbow with his own. They talked about Martin's house, about Henry. Philip talked about Henry as if Grace knew all about him, whereas Martin had actually told her very little. Almost nothing in fact. She did not really understand why he was away. She was too embarrassed to ask. It was something to do with his work – his job – but she didn't know what he did.

'Sean's in his element,' said Philip, and Grace stared at him.

'He is,' said Martin. 'We saw him last night, or heard him anyway.'

'Sean?'

Philip leaned forward and put the tips of his fingers on Grace's arm.

'Sean is a friend of ours,' he said. 'He's a journalist. He's busy chronicling our turbulent times. Scourge of politicians, unraveller of dark plots. Or so he'd have you think.' He sat back again. 'You'll meet him, I'm sure.'

She smiled. The name had startled her. They chatted on, and as they did so she became more relaxed and more talkative. She found out that Philip was actually a student and worked in the café only part-time. He was nineteen, he told her. It seemed so young. He chatted on, got them more coffee, seemed to like Grace. Soon he was talking just to her. He wanted to know about Martin as a boy. She told him small things. Walking over the hills. Martin's habit of

55

sucking his fingers and holding his mother's ear. Philip laughed loudly. Martin smiled.

Grace talked and while she talked she wondered. She could hide herself. She had not thought that she could do that. It had not occurred to her. But it seemed that she could smile and make jokes and cut through the world without cracking. She could glide. She could walk through the city. She could make people laugh.

'Will you come out with us?' Philip asked. Martin stared at him.

'Where?' asked Grace.

'To the pub, tonight. You can meet Sean. We go out most Saturday nights. Just for a couple of drinks. It'd be great if you came along.'

She was conscious of Martin looking at him intently.

'Well . . .'

'Go on.'

She thought of staying in on her own. It was something she had done enough of. She looked at Philip. He was young and handsome and he smiled at her as if it mattered what she did. As if he would be disappointed if she refused.

'All right.'

Philip smiled broadly. 'Great,' he said.

Martin shifted in his seat.

'Are you sure, mum? I mean, this week and . . .'

He trailed off. Grace became confused. Philip still smiled at her, but he scratched his head, and there was a small reddening in his cheeks.

'I meant to say,' he said quietly, 'I was so sorry to hear about your husband.'

Grace stared back at him blankly, unable to understand for a moment what he was talking about. His face was set in such a sorrowful and sympathetic mask that she was distracted by it. It was ridiculous. Without thinking she gave a burst of laughter, quickly clapped silent by a hand

56

over the mouth. But she could not really stop it, and felt her face redden and her shoulders shake. She removed her hand and emptied a long loud guffaw out of her chest, as impossible to suppress as a cough.

Both Philip and Martin looked at her with their mouths frozen in a perfect o-shaped caricature of surprise. The sight made Grace laugh again. Then she saw Martin look down, embarrassed, and her laughter slowly stopped.

'I'm so sorry,' she said. 'It's a nervous reaction. It's like laughing at funerals – that kind of thing. It's just that I was sitting here having such a nice time. It was almost as if I'd forgotten about it all.'

'I didn't mean to remind you,' said Philip. 'I'm sorry.'

'No, I mean, it was good of you to say it. It was just so unexpected, so out of the blue.'

Martin was looking at her, his face bright red, apparently unable to speak. Grace could not look back at him. She finished her coffee and smiled meekly at Philip, who smiled meekly back. The silence stretched out between them.

Grace thought of the road in Monaghan, and the still and breathing darkness of the place where she had stopped the car. She thought of the trees at its sides, the high dense hedges where noises created a mythology all of their own. She knew that she had not been seen, but she knew also that what she had done there had been somehow recorded, etched into the air on that stretch of roadway like words engraved on glass. She could not change that. Eventually someone would focus on the glass instead of looking through it, and they would see the words and read them. And then Grace would have to return to that place, and stay there.

The conversation did not recover.

MARTIN

Memory.

Walking.

They had walked together over the boggy ground and fought their way through the heather and the tangle by the lake. They had talked. Endlessly. About what he could not remember. He remembered only the progress that they made. They took steps and he remembered the steps – how his feet would move one after the other and take him to some different patch of ground, to the edge of water, to longer grass or shorter grass, or up the gentle slope of a hill, or through mud or across roads. He remembered that sense of distance travelled, that safe sensation of being a long way away from any other person, except his mother. As if they were escaping. As if they reeled in the horizon and for a moment had it in their grasp. Then they had to turn back. They shared a secret that they never spoke of, a secret that was only real because it was silent. It was in their eyes and their hands, in the routes they chose when they walked away.

He looked at her. Her embarrassment kept her silent. She sat at the kitchen table sipping tea, staring at a newspaper. She looked as if she had never laughed in her life.

Martin had always known something about his mother that nobody else knew. But he could not have said what it was. He was aware only that there remained something unspoken between them. Perhaps it was a simple thing. Common memories. Love. But Martin thought that it was something else. To do with their walking away and coming back. The risk in it. Like a dare. It played in her eyes. It had strength. It had stared out at him, and she had allowed no one else to see it but him. He remembered the strength of it. He looked for it now, but either it had gone, or he had forgotten how to see it.

The phone made a long, strange noise, as if engaged. Then there was a click, and a brief pause that crackled and filled with Henry's cheerful voice, speaking the fluent French that Martin hated. The answering machine. He cursed and hung up.

In the kitchen his mother stood by the sink in Henry's dressing-gown, just out of the shower. Martin had told her to use it, but the sight of it was unpleasant, somehow improper. He sighed, shook his head at her back.

'Did you get him?'

'He's not there. I'll try later.'

She went upstairs to dress, to get ready. He could not talk her out of it. She seemed to believe that going to the pub with them would make up for the earlier embarrassment. As if she had been misunderstood, and would have the chance later to explain herself. Her face was set, afraid even to smile. Martin felt half sorry for her and half angry. She was not herself.

He could think of nothing to do in the kitchen. He went back to the sitting room and dialled again. Still the machine. Perhaps something had happened. Saturday was the day he called. Teatime. It was arranged. The answering machine made for a gathering of things in Martin's chest. A dense compression of jealousies and static. Gravity. Left to its own devices there was only one way his imagination could go. He smiled at it and shook his head and bit his smile down. It wasn't funny. He wondered for a moment which would be worse – an accident, or Henry with someone else.

59

He had showered and was half shaved when the phone rang. He threw himself through the kitchen, past the still figure of his startled mother, and into the sitting room.

'Hello?' he yapped.

'Martin?'

'I rang, the machine was on.'

'I know, sorry, I had to go out and I was expecting one of the guys from the training course to ring so I had to leave it on.'

'What guy?'

Henry told him things in a lazy, clipped sort of way. It always made Martin feel that parts had been left out. He heard a few words now on the business of trading practices and computerised dealing, lightly populated by shadowy figures given no more substance than exotic sounding names. Martin was often unclear as to gender. This distracted him. He threw out experimental he's and she's and was corrected or not, and felt his mind and his heart rise and fall in a kind of self-generated graph of potential betrayals.

'How's your mother?'

'Oh God, she's coming out with us. I mean with Sean and Philip.'

Henry laughed, thought it was great. Martin made low noises, eyed the door.

'She's odd. I know she doesn't want to go really. She's trying to fit in. There's no fitting in. But I can't talk to her.'

He wanted to tell him about what had happened, about his mother laughing, but he did not know how to describe it. It would sound wrong.

'She's had a hell of a week,' said Henry.

'Yeah.'

'She's bound to be a bit stressed. A night out will do her good.'

'But Henry, Jesus.'

He laughed again. Martin tried to see him, put him in a

room, but he could not. He got stuck on his face. He wished he'd been to Paris. His neck burned from the incompleted shave. He put fingers to his throat.

'I miss you,' he said. His fingertips were speckled bloody.

'I miss you too,' came the reply. Martin put his fingers in his mouth, sucked at them. Coughed.

'Is she all right?'

'Who?'

'Has she talked about it – you know. How she is?'

Her hair was all grey. It had been brown, he thought. He could not remember. He remembered odd things. Memory.

'She doesn't talk. She seems confused. I don't know. I miss you properly.'

Henry sighed. Said nothing.

'When are you coming back?'

'You know that.'

Martin rocked back and forth. He had barged through the kitchen with just a towel wrapped around him. He felt suddenly that he should have put on his dressing-gown.

'You should bunk off. Come home.'

Henry made clicking noises in his mouth, hummed. Martin wondered what Henry would make of his mother. What she would make of him. How that would work. All he would get then, all he would hear, would be the little things, the strange sounds, of humming and laughing and the gaps between words.

Out in the hall Martin bumped into his mother. He held his towel. His arm moved across his chest. He smiled, half smiled, went to pass her.

'God,' she said, her hands coming up, stretching out towards Martin's face.

'What?'

'Blood. There's blood on you.'

GRACE

She must not laugh.

In the dark that flooded upwards from the black street to the still light sky, they moved through traffic that had halted at the head of the small hill, and Grace watched her son and his shoulders, his hunched shoulders, shrug at the cold and weave between the cars. He had suggested that they go somewhere other than their usual, but Philip had insisted, saying that Sean would not find them otherwise, and that Grace would love it. Martin was not happy. Grace did not know how to alter that. She glanced at the grey clouds that billowed from exhausts. Storms in small places. She smelled the fumes and the city damp and liked it.

She must not laugh.

'Over the river down there is Capel Street,' said Philip, and Grace looked. Street lights trickled away into the distance. She could not see any river.

Her body shuddered and her eyes were wide. She didn't know how she was meant to be. She had wanted to go out. But she had not understood Martin's wariness, his insistence that she should do whatever she wanted, and then his asking her constantly whether she was sure. She thought of saying to him that he did not have to introduce her as his mother. But she had not known how to put it.

As long as she did not laugh. She must not laugh.

She kept her head down as they went into the pub, conscious only of the warmth, and the low hum of voices.

She followed Philip down the length of the bar to a door. She did not understand. She turned and looked at Martin.

'We're going upstairs.'

They went up in silence. Philip was ahead of her. She watched his feet.

Wooden floor. Music. Voices. Not as loud as downstairs. Not as many people. She looked up a little. The light was reddish, glowing, indistinct. There were tables and stools and seats that lined the walls. A faint smell of beer. A bar ahead of her. Pictures. Photographs. Lots of them. Framed in thin black frames. Black and white and colour. Of men. Naked.

She laughed.

'What?' asked Martin, turning towards her. He was smiling, but in his eyes she saw a small fear. She coughed and shook her head.

They were young men, sleek, tanned, some were black. They stood in showers, in water, with towels draped around them, alone, in shadows and in light.

'Nothing,' she said, but Martin glanced at the walls and seemed to blush. He dropped his eyes and turned towards a free table. Philip caught on last. He laughed, nudged Grace.

'Subtle, isn't it?' he said.

She nodded, swallowed her laughter. It fell away inside her and her tension slipped with it and she breathed a little better and her head cleared. The pictures hung in rows all around the walls, so many of them that it was hard for her not to look at them. Her eyes darted and stretched.

It took time for the place to fill. Grace stared at everything – at the people who came in, at the men behind the bar, at the women who sat together and the single men who stood by the walls. She saw two boys kissing, and she stared at them until Martin coughed and Philip laughed and she found that her mouth was open and

63

closed it and looked away. She was astonished. Philip sat next to her. He talked, and did not mind that she didn't look at him. He described what she stared at, gave her a little running commentary. Told her some people's names, told her what they did, who they were going out with. Others he speculated on. Told her about types.

Martin said little. He drank fast and went back up to the bar before Grace or Philip was ready for a second. Grace watched him, and was happy with the look of him, happy that he was her son. Then that seemed a corny thing to feel, and she blushed. She turned to Philip.

'What age are you?'

'Nearly twenty.'

'How long have you known?'

'Always. I came out two, about three years ago.'

'How always?'

'I felt it. I knew. I don't know. I wanted to be closer.'

'Have you . . .'

'What?'

She shook her head, looked at Martin. Couldn't ask it.

'What?'

'Nothing.'

Philip followed her gaze. Martin leaned on the counter, his hands at his face, his eyes following the barman. She saw a part of her husband. She shook her head harder.

'Have you and Martin ever been together?'

Philip frowned, squinted at her, then understood.

'Oh. No. No, we haven't.' He coughed. 'Just friends.'

Grace felt her face light up. She held her nearly empty glass to her cheek. She could not look at him.

Martin came back to them with three drinks held out in front of him and a sheen on his forehead. A colour had risen in his cheeks. Grace thought he might have overheard, but knew that was impossible. He concentrated on the drinks. His hair was too short. He looked like his father. He had his shape. Not his eyes, but his shape. She squinted and saw her husband. She watched him sit down, sigh, and light a cigarette. His steady hands, his eyes, picking her out, his smile. She looked away.

Ahead of her she had the room. She watched the people expand, multiply, filling the gaps between them, turning the dull red walls with their photographs into a swell of smoky colour, hands and faces and eyes. Men, mostly. Young men. Aftershave hung in the air. It was not unpleasant, but she felt now that she had spoiled it.

'Here's Sean,' said Martin clearly, and Grace looked at him with her wide mouth, startled. But he nodded towards the door and she looked and saw a fleshy man with a small mouth bear down on them, shouldering sideways through the crowd. Sean. Martin's friend Sean.

He came to their table and gave a general wave and seemed to count the glasses. He glanced at Martin and Martin nodded, and said something to him, and Sean took off his coat and handed it to Philip and turned without a word towards the bar.

'Is that Sean?' Grace murmured, but nobody heard her.

'He's late,' Martin said, looking after him. 'Late and hassled.'

Philip smiled, leaned towards Grace.

'Sean has hassle down to a fine art,' he said. 'It's all bullshit of course. Journalism stuff. He's seen *All The President's Men* once too often. Looks busy, sleeps a lot. Shrewd though.'

Grace nodded. She could see him up at the bar, his round hunched shoulders risen above the smaller figures like a tooth pushed up. He was quickly served, and turned with three pint glasses clutched in his big hands. He shouted and smiled, and a path opened up before him, some men saying things to him, greeting him, joking. One of the drinks was for her, she was sure, and she stared now at the three-quarters-full glass still in front of her. It would be enough. She had not asked for another one. She remembered the smell of her husband in the bed, the sweet thick smell of his body, like a cloth soaked in the dead water of old flowers.

Sean sat beside her. His body dipped the seat and Grace's line of sight jumped an inch. He ignored Martin's attempt to introduce him and spoke his own name with gravity, his eyes on hers, and held out his hand, cold and loose.

'Ah, it's wonderful to meet you finally Mrs Quinn, after hearing so much, and I only wish it was better circumstances. My sympathies on your loss. I got you a drink.'

Grace nodded. 'Thank you.'

'I met your husband once. I covered his trouble last year for the paper. I was in court. Spoke to him briefly. He didn't want to talk. I can understand that, Mrs Quinn. I didn't mention I knew Martin. Wouldn't have made any sense really.'

His voice was quiet so that the others could not hear him.

'Have the police made any progress?'

He leaned towards her, his body inclined, the roll of his chin dipped to his chest, his big dog eyes a little bloodshot, his arm on the seat by her head, his blunt elbow filling her sight.

'No,' she said quietly, and he jerked his head a little and she said again, 'No,' and he nodded and gathered his lips and shrugged.

'Well. A hard thing to unravel. A tangle of things like that. They ask you a lot of questions?'

His voice rolled like the rest of him. A Dublin accent with a pitch that rang in her head.

'Who?'

'The police. Oh, they ask and ask and never answer.'

'No.'

He made a face, his mouth contracted, his eyebrows raised, and nodded, and brought his pint to his lips. As if this was surprising news.

'You're a journalist?'

'Yes. All over the house I'd imagine, were they?'

'No.'

'No?'

She shook her head. He made the same face a second time, took another drink. Grace asked him quickly how long he had known her son. He looked at her, took his time, considered.

'Years,' he said.

He talked to her for a while about newspapers and politicians and people he expected her to have heard of. He told her about Albert Reynolds, about what he would be like as Taoiseach, about who would be in the new cabinet. He was able to tell her who the TDs were for Cavan/Monaghan, who it was that they had supported, where they stayed when in Dublin. He did not stop. His hands flew, his voice rose and fell, his head rolled. He was like a treetop in a big wind.

She asked about the bathroom and felt foolish when Philip rose to go with her. He smiled, told her he wanted to go to the Gents anyway. It was through the door, off the stairwell. They cut together through the crowd.

She looked at herself in the stained mirror. She was doing all right. The music thudded from outside. A girl smiled at her. She could hold conversations, smile, be herself. Be most of herself. Here, of all places.

Philip had waited for her, was standing outside the door. She liked him. He was the age Martin had been when he had left. As she thought of that, as they crossed the small square of space between the door to the toilets and the door to the bar, Grace glanced down the stairs at the back of a boy descending; his hips, his waist. Then her mind, as if it knew, jerked her eyes upwards, sideways, at a face climbing towards her, or rather, a head climbing towards her, its face to the steps, its huge baldness like a fist. All

67

stopped. All came rushing quiet, all sense left her, all safety. She was scared as a child.

She turned, flung herself around, collided with Philip, and went back into the Ladies. Fast.

'Careful,' said a woman sternly as the door that Grace threw open hit her hand. Grace pushed past, put her back to a wall. For a moment, nothing. She was terrified that Philip would call her name, but he did not. His head appeared around the door. Puzzled, he glanced around and stepped in after her.

'Are you all right?'

'Yes, yes.'

The door was closed. He had not seen her, she had been too quick.

'Mrs Quinn?'

Philip spoke softly, looking into her face.

'I thought . . . I'm sorry. I thought I saw someone coming up the stairs.'

'Who?'

She could not get her mind to work. It trawled through possibilities, but her fear now was like a balloon inflating inside her.

'My husband,' she said, and looked at Philip in astonishment. He regarded her for a moment and his eyes flicked once or twice. They seemed to water. His face filled with pity. Sympathy. Those odd things.

'Oh, Mrs Quinn,' he said, and put his arms around her. Put his arms around her. She froze. He circled her neck with the warmth of his skin, and pressed his face into her shoulder and murmured something about getting over it eventually. But Grace only felt him, the grip of him like a memory, clinging to her solidly, pressing close to her, holding her. She lifted her arms and joined the embrace and her eyes burned but she held them closed.

MARTIN

Her face looked out at him from the Ladies, an eye in the crack of a door, an odd panic in her stare, her mouth a little open, as if to keep breathing.

He asked her what the matter was but she shook her head and took her coat and told him she was tired. She moved fast for a tired woman. She told Philip to stay put. Philip shrugged, patted Martin's shoulder, told him he'd ring.

'I'll see you during the week, Mrs Quinn,' he said. 'We'll meet up.'

Martin looked at him and wondered what the hell he was talking about. Jesus.

She led him down the stairs and out into the street by the side door, Martin skipping to keep up. He cursed beneath his breath, felt like shouting at her. But she slowed. And he just asked, 'What's wrong? What happened?'

Around the corner on Dame Street a crowd was spilling out of the Olympia Theatre, their breath rising in the air, cars and taxis pulling up and taking them away.

'I thought I saw your father.'

'In the pub?'

'Yes. It wasn't him.'

He smiled without thinking.

'Glad to hear it.'

He raised his hand and one of the taxis stopped in front of them. They climbed into the back seat.

As they drove away she looked out of the rear window.

'I embarrassed you. I'm sorry. I'm very sorry.'

He shook his head and tried to see her eyes, but they scanned the road behind them. He looked back. Nothing. Taxis, cars, the window clouded grey at the edges.

The driver turned up the volume on the radio. Music surrounded them. His mother turned in her seat, folded her arms. She did not look at him. She was turned instead to the side, towards the sight of the city going cold. Martin knew that he should talk to her, but the music stopped him. And if it had not been the music then it would have been the way she sat with her face pressed up against the glass, her eyes unfocused, looking not at the passing streets or the watery lights, but at her own reflection, framed in the window of the car like the moon on the surface of a black lake.

GRACE

It was not sleep.

She lay on her stomach in the dark, her face pressed flat to the mattress, her arm hanging loosely, chill, over the side of the bed. Her neck hurt.

Perhaps it had not been him.

She stared at the window, at the dim blue light that leaked through the curtains. She pretended she was paralysed, stuck to the bed, each muscle disconnected. But her mind drifted. Small things. And before she realised what she was doing she had moved, shifted her legs.

It had been him. Puncturing the noise of the pub. Letting in a silence. His head on the stairs, rising towards her like a stubby finger.

Small things.

She remembered her mother taking her to mass. She remembered the two of them kneeling together at the altar rail for the first time. Her mother had smiled at her, and whispered, but Grace could not remember what she had said. She remembered the priest, a plaster on his finger, saying 'Corpus Christi' and holding out the host in front of her mouth. Grace had hesitated then, looking up into the eyes of the old man whose breath smelled of apples and tea. He stared back at her, sternly, his lips puckered up like her father's always were for the noisy goodnight kiss. Her mother nudged her and she opened her mouth and closed her eyes and felt the host and the tip of the priest's finger touch her tongue. She remembered the dry feeling of the small white disc in her mouth, the way it sucked up all the moisture like an unbuttered cracker.

'You're supposed to say "Amen",' her mother whispered to her as they returned to their seats.

Her sister giggled.

'I forgot,' said Grace.

She had prayed very hard then. She imagined baby Jesus landing down in her tummy and climbing up into her heart and then into her soul and turning into the man Jesus with his beard and his eyes crying all the time, filling her with holy water that ran through all her veins. Then she imagined Jesus on the cross inside her soul, dying for her sins and turning the holy water into fire and making her a vessel for God.

It was better in the local church, with her mother, amongst their neighbours and all the families in their best clothes. In the school church where she had made her first Holy Communion she had not been able to pray properly – she had been too excited, too proud of her dress and her tiny white handbag.

But in the local church it was real. She was really praying. She said an extra Our Father to make up for not saying 'Amen'.

Her father did not know. Grace did not know how to tell him. He sat in the kitchen and shook his newspaper and grunted when they came in.

'Lot of nonsense,' he would say. 'Superstition and nonsense.'

Sometimes he walked the three of them to church. Grace and her sister and their mother. He would reach the church gate and tell them loudly to make their own way home, and he would walk on then, whistling, and people would stare at him a little. Mr Wilson. Not a Catholic. Not Irish.

Her mother died. He stood beside his daughters at the funeral and they showed him what to do. Stand now. Kneel. He cried and stumbled and gripped their hands.

The priest had come up to him afterwards and told him that he had known his wife well. Grace's father nodded and let him shake his hand, and said nothing.

'Every Sunday,' he said, 'nine o'clock mass, without fail. Herself and the children. She was a devout woman, your wife. Devout. It's funny, I thought she was a widow.'

'And why was that?'

'Because you were never with her.'

There was a dead moment then, when everything stopped moving and nothing made a sound and the priest's smile quietly faded. Grace watched her father as he raised a thick finger to the man's chin, so slowly and deliberately that Grace thought that he was going to say something about it. That the priest had cut himself shaving, that there was a spot or a dimple.

'Is that so?' he said, so quietly that Grace could hardly hear him. 'Is that the case, Father? So where were you over these last months while she lay dying?'

'I didn't know . . .'

'And where were you for the last thirty years? Where? While she struggled to bring up two daughters? You were telling her to have more and to hell with it, weren't you Father? And while I fought for this country, and she worked in the factories and ruined her health for this country? Where were you? You were with the other side from what I can see. Blessing the Fascists in Rome and Berlin. That's what I heard.'

He lowered his hand and half turned, but stopped then, thinking of something else.

'What's your name?'

'I don't see that . . .'

'What's your bloody name?'

'Father O'Malley.'

Her father laughed. He had not raised his voice, and now he continued, quietly, so quietly that other mourners had come over to him to pay their respects and had waited,

73

thinking that a conversation was in progress, and now stood, embarrassed, and listened, their heads down.

'O'Malley? Jesus. What did I expect? Irish priests. God save us from Irish priests. The Pope and De Valera, eh? Blessing the Nazis and mourning the Nazis. Mr De Valera signing the bloody book of condolences when Hitler died. And all in the name of a free Ireland that couldn't get up off its backside if it knew where to find it. Your church and your country, Father O'Malley, are a joke. A joke. And you might have seen my wife's face peering up at you for an hour on Sunday, but don't you dare tell me, don't you bloody well dare to think that you knew her. You did not. And nor did you matter.'

He had stormed off then, Grace running after him, wiping at the tears on her cheeks and feeling the heat of them. People stared and whispered. Grace's sister did not cry, but she was older. She sat in the car quietly, and Grace saw her lips move and guessed that she was praying. But Grace could not do that. She held her father's arm and felt the tremble.

She thought of prayer now. She could not remember having prayed since then. She had stopped going to mass. She found it hard to imagine what a prayer might consist of. She could not remember what it was for.

At midday a slammed door startled her, and she woke to brightness and cold and the sound of her son below.

He did not mention the previous night, her flight, the silence since. He talked about his job – about going back to it. He suggested things she might do in the daytime. He kept talking, did not ask her anything, moved from room to room as if he could not settle. Nothing happened. No one called. No one came to the door.

On the Monday morning she cooked a breakfast for him that made him smile. He rushed through it and winked at her. She felt strange as he left, once more like a mother, seeing her son off to school, though now he wore a suit and carried a briefcase and became embarrassed when she kissed him on the cheek. He joked about her standing on the doorstep and waving at him. But she did not do that. She did not even put her head out.

Alone in the house she became bored and tired. She stared at a light rain that flecked the windows and darkened the ground. The street was empty. The cars were empty. People walked by and did not linger or look up. She found an umbrella and wrapped a scarf around her head and slipped into the cold with a terror inside her that she could not shake off. She moved fast, and paused then at the corner and looked back. Nothing. She walked to the canal and over the bridge and into Rathmines. She swung around suddenly and walked the other way. No one looked at her. No one turned. At the bridge once more she waited for a while and looked into the green water, at the pockmarked surface and the collapsing edges, reeds and mud and the bright trail of litter. Nothing. No one noticed her.

In a shop in Rathmines she bought Martin a silver lighter in a presentation box. The girl wrapped it for her, and smiled.

She bought groceries in Dunnes, guessing at what was needed.

The rain stopped but she pretended not to have noticed and walked back to the house with the umbrella raised in front of her like a device to part the air. It restricted her view. Suddenly at her feet, cowering angrily in a doorway, a bottle clutched in her hand, was a woman with skin like leather. She was not old. Her feet were tucked beneath her and she whispered. Her eyes stuck to Grace, and followed her, and when Grace glanced back the woman spat something dark and thick on to the ground and said: 'You fuck off you. Pestilence.'

He did not like her buying groceries. She was his guest,

he said. He took his present and lit it once, twice. Leaned across the table to kiss her cheek, knocked the spoon out of the sugar, cursed. She watched him eat, putting his food into separate piles, working his way around the plate as if there was a way of doing it that was right. Sugar crackled beneath his feet.

Grace stood and looked at her reflection in the window.

'They must think I'm mad.'

'Who?'

'Your friends. Sean and Philip.'

'No,' he said. 'They understand.'

She did not know what he meant by that.

Tuesday was cold and windy, and small showers of rain raced through the streets, chasing people down. The ground felt oily, slick. Grace looked at her feet as she walked, careful of kerbs and steps. She stood at pedestrian crossings while the crowds streamed past her, her eye firmly fixed on the red man, waiting for him to change. She could not understand how people could race across the road like that, judging the gaps between cars, knowing when they could make it and when they could not.

She made her way to O'Connell Street, past the sound of the gulls on the river, and the wind that ripped across the bridge, snapping at her coat. She glanced up at the monument to Daniel O'Connell and the angels stared back at her, their wings unfolding. She felt the breath of the wind on her cheeks and the cold of the rain on her hands and she walked past Abbey Street and Easons to the GPO, where she stood for a moment in the shelter of the old stone.

There were marks, indentations in the columns. Years before, when they had passed through, between lives, her husband had told her that they were bullet holes, left unrepaired since 1916. Shrapnel and ricochets, the marks of missiles that might already have killed, that might already have cut through flesh and bone before pounding themselves into the pale stone. She had put her fingers in the hard wounds, felt the rough edges and the smooth shallow pits, but she had not believed him. And still she did not believe him.

Crowds moved through Henry Street, in and out of the shops, flowing like ashes through a grate. The cries of traders were bellowed through the clutter and the drizzle. Down Moore Street there was bad food in the gutters, and weighing scales and potato sacks and sawdust spilling out from the butchers and onto the paths. There was a smell which she did not like – food and perspiration and handled money and fresh baked bread, all washed in the sour rain. It was a city smell. A Dublin smell.

When the gunmen left the GPO they had made their way over here somewhere. Her husband had shown her the place. There had been a gun battle in the street. It had been raining. They had carried James Connolly, guns blazing, buildings on fire, blood on the walls where they crouched for cover. She looked around, but she could not remember where.

The rain became heavier as she walked quickly past the warmly lit windows of the department stores, to Mary Street and Bewleys, where Philip waited with his hands in his pockets and his eyes on the crowd, his face a shock to Grace, so unfamiliar and welcome. She felt a thrill that she knew who this was.

Martin had answered the telephone late on Monday night and had talked for a while before handing it to his mother. She had been so confused, so alarmed by the voice and by the invitation, that she had agreed to meet in Bewleys that morning without having an absolutely clear notion of who it was she was talking to.

'Well, you're certainly wrapped up,' he said. 'Who's this Muslim woman coming towards me, I thought.'

'What?'

'Your scarf. How are you?'

He led Grace along the food counter and ordered himself a large fried breakfast. Grace was not hungry. She took a coffee. Philip insisted on paying and they made their way upstairs and found a table near the front, beneath a big stained glass window.

The place was almost empty. A few shoppers taking shelter. Damp newspapers. Fires on either side of the room, orange and yellow, a single elderly man close to each like a reflection of the other.

'I'm glad you've come,' he said. 'I hope you didn't mind me asking. I thought you'd like the company while Martin's at work.'

She sipped her coffee and watched him try to gather scrambled egg on his fork. She cleared her throat. Steadied.

'I'm sorry about the other night,' she said.

He smiled at her, nodded.

'That's okay.'

'No. I embarrassed everyone. I was being stupid. You must have thought I was very rude.'

'No I didn't. Not at all. Sean thought he might have said something . . .'

'No . . .'

'I just, well, I explained to him that you hadn't felt very well and wanted to go home. Back to Martin's, I mean. That was okay, was it?'

'Yes, yes. Of course. Thank you.'

He smiled and resumed eating. Grace watched him and wondered whether he had really told Sean that, or whether he had told him the truth. Martin's mother's gone mad. Sees ghosts in pubs. Not that that was true either.

'Did you feel better when you got home?'

'Yes. I calmed down. Went to bed. I was just silly.'

'Well, you've had a terrible week. You're bound to feel a little raw.'

He ate normally, mixing things on his fork. She watched

78

his jaw at work, his clean hands handling knife and bread and serviette.

'My son is like my husband,' she said. 'He used to eat things on his plate one at a time. Martin does the same.'

'Does he?'

'I hope it's just small things that carry forward. Not . . . not the others.'

Philip nodded. She wondered how much he knew. How he knew it.

'How did you meet him?'

'My husband? God.'

She had to think. They had not really met, they had become aware of each other.

'I had a friend who was a nurse, training as a nurse, in a hospital in Manchester. He worked there as a porter. We met in a big group of people. The nurses, the porters, friends like me. We would meet in cafés and go to dances and they would all tell hospital stories. It seemed very glamorous to me. He was only a porter, but, well, he had a talent for making himself seem interesting. But really he was just another Irish immigrant. It seemed a little exotic to me. I was eighteen.'

'But your mother was Irish, wasn't she?'

'Both of my parents were Irish. My mother was from Clare. She went up to Dublin when she was very young and worked in a hotel and met my father. They were only about sixteen. They went to London together and got married and then my father joined the army and they ended up in Manchester somehow. He became very anti-Irish. I think it was in the army. I don't know why. It was up like a wall by the time my sister and I were born. He would hide the fact that he was Irish. He went through a big rigmarole resigning from the Catholic church and becoming a British citizen and changing his name from O'Brien to Wilson, of all things. I think he wanted to change it to Windsor, but my mother put him off.'

Philip laughed.

'But he could never get rid of his accent, not really. He always sounded like a Dubliner. And he would give out to my mother because of her accent. But at home, when they were relaxed, chatting to each other, they sounded like an ordinary Irish couple. He never quite managed to complete the transformation. And my mother always refused to give up the church. But you can see how exotic a real unashamed Irishman would have seemed to me.'

'Yes I can,' said Philip, smiling. 'And I suppose your father didn't approve. Makes it even more attractive.'

'He hated him. He refused to meet him.'

'Did he go to the wedding?'

'No.'

She wanted to tell him now. Tell him that her father had been right. Tell him about Monaghan, about Sean who had died, about Martin. But she hesitated, and looked down, and could not do it.

He finished eating, put his plate to the side, sipped his tea. His hands lay loose on the table. She looked at them and wanted him to talk to her, to tell her things, to map out the future. She could not think of a way in.

'Are you friendly with Sean?' she asked.

'Yes, I suppose. I don't know him as well as I know Martin. But he's all right. He can be a little overbearing at times.'

Her father had never liked Michael. He had snorted the name, repeating it over and over as if it was unbelievable.

'Michael Quinn. Quinn is it? Michael Quinn indeed.'

They had eyed each other up in silence, no more than two or three times. That was all.

'He loves to talk,' Philip said. 'He'll go on and on for hours if you let him. Bores me to death sometimes. And he's a shameless name-dropper. But he's all right underneath it all, I suppose.'

Grace had not protested. She had sulked through it,

telling her sister quietly, in front of their father, of how Michael had taken her to see the ships sail out of Liverpool, of how they had taken a packed and suffocating train to Blackpool, and of how he had asked her, finally, to marry him, as they walked on the moors in the rain one day in April.

Her father warned her not to marry Michael Quinn. He warned her earnestly, not scolding any more but serious, desperate. Don't go to Ireland. Do not go to Ireland. Behind her back he went to the hospital where Michael worked and asked questions about him. Without her knowledge he wrote to Michael's family in Monaghan, asking them to tell him something about themselves. Michael told Grace about it. She was embarrassed and angry. Her father was mad, obsessed with his birthplace, obsessed with his hatred of it. She shouted it at him and slammed the door and walked out of the house and did not go back. She stayed with a friend in the next street. Her sister brought her her clothes.

Then she married Michael Quinn. And she refused to do it in a register office. No. She wanted a church wedding. She scoured the city until she found a priest willing to marry a couple he had never set eyes on before. He assumed she was pregnant. There were few guests. No reception. Her father and her sister did not come. She had sent her father a letter. Times and directions. But she was given away by a hospital caretaker whose name she could not remember, and the church rang hollow with the voice of the priest. She had taken the boat with her new husband the very next day. A steward had told them that it was never as full going to Ireland as it was coming from it. He laughed at them. Heading in the wrong direction they were. There'd be no one left when they got there. She sent her father a postcard from Dublin. Honeymooning here. Going to live in Monaghan. Hope you are well.

'He's really Henry's friend, chiefly. Sean is. Henry is

great. You'll love Henry. Very funny, very nice. He can put Sean in his place when it's required.'

She had married Michael Quinn out of spite. Because she was angry at her father. She had been that stupid. She remembered waiting for months for a letter from him, an apology. She expected him to give in, to ask whether he could come and visit, to admit that he had no right to be so set against her marriage, to dislike her husband so much, particularly when he had known nothing about him. But no letter came, despite her increasingly frequent prompts in the form of postcards and letters to her sister. Then one day a telegram. And she had known without even looking at it. He was dead.

She missed the funeral. The ferry had been delayed for twelve hours, a storm pounding the water, a screaming wind pouring into the cold, bare waiting room in Dublin port where Grace spent a tearful, miserable night. She felt homeless.

She called her sister in the morning to say what had happened. Her sister was quiet, sullen. Formal. They agreed that there was little point in Grace getting the boat then. It would all be over by the time she arrived. Then suddenly, as if something had broken in the middle of the Irish sea, they cried at each other like children. They did not understand any of it.

Grace went back on the bus to Cootehill and walked the six miles to the farm. She remembered the feeling that she had in her then. It came as a taste in her mouth, a sensation in her feet as she put them down one in front of the other. It was like something inside of her had had its juice squeezed out. It was like an anger that makes itself foolish.

Philip stared at her. She had wanted to talk to him. He had said something. He coughed, glanced down, repeated it.

'Will you come out again?'

'To the pub? I don't know.'

'In a while. When you feel like it.'

He smiled. He looked at his watch.

'I'll have to go soon,' he said. 'I have a lecture at twelve.'

'You're very good to come and meet me.'

'Not at all. I've enjoyed it.'

'And I'm sorry again for Saturday night.'

'Oh, please forget about that. It really wasn't a problem. Even Sean got a bit of a fright when he saw the guy. It's bound to upset you seeing someone like your husband so soon after . . . well, afterwards.'

Grace stared at him. All the noise of the café seemed suddenly to be sucked through a small gap. She felt her face drain pale.

'Sean what?'

'Oh. Sean saw him too.'

'I thought you said you told him I didn't feel well.'

Philip hesitated and began to blush.

'I did, but . . . well, he asked. He leaves nothing alone. He asked me did you see someone, and so I told him that, yes, you had seen someone who looked like your husband, and then Sean understood because he'd seen him too.'

She bit her lip.

'I'm sorry. I didn't mean to embarrass you. But Sean understood what had happened. He saw the guy come in and go out again. He said he was the image of your husband. It's absolutely understandable, Mrs Quinn. I can imagine the shock of it. Seeing someone the image of your husband.'

They put their coats on and left, Grace pulling her scarf tight against the chill she felt, covering her face. The rain had stopped and a dilute sun brightened the city. They walked together slowly down Liffey Street to the river. She shivered and ducked her shoulders on the narrow, crowded pavement. Philip chatted about shops. They crossed the Ha'penny Bridge and went silently through the mist of people in Merchant's Arch, past a cold boy who played a guitar and sang loudly a song that Grace knew but could not have named.

Philip nodded at the Central Bank and said that it looked like a spring, a jack-in-the-box, held in place by the black metal straps that ran down its sides. He said that he wanted to cut the straps and see the building shoot up into the air and bounce softly like a toy. Beneath its shadow they paused and said goodbye, Philip surprising Grace with another hug. This time the cold was too much. She nodded and said something and walked away.

Traffic on Dame Street was stopped. The pedestrian lights were turning from orange to red as Grace left the kerb and began to run. A white van to her right moved towards her and then braked suddenly as Grace crossed in front of it. The driver blew the horn, loudly, and people looked at her.

Grace cursed beneath her breath.

'Fuck,' she said.

Brady looked nothing like her husband. Nothing at all.

TWO

SEAN

He sat at his desk drinking some kind of orange that had come out of the machine. It was lukewarm. Didn't help. He raised his arms and flapped them a little, and rolled up his shirtsleeves. It was close to freezing outside and he could see a sleety rain cut through the blackness of the windows. But he had walked from Leinster House in ten minutes flat and had run up the stairs until his calves ached, and he was sweating.

Something odd had been happening at the Four Courts. Sheridan had the blinds down, which was not in itself unusual, but he had the door closed too. Foster told Sean that the legal people were in, and that Moby, who'd spent the whole day in court, had come back to the office with a look on him. Like he was privy to something.

'What?' Sean asked, pressing his palm to his forehead. Foster shrugged.

He turned again to the screen and started to try and make sense of his notes. A stack of files sat on his desk, one for each of the new cabinet members. It would be a dull task.

He glanced again at Sheridan's closed door.

'What's going on in there?' he muttered.

'They want to run something,' said Foster.

'Yeah. But what?'

'I think it might be some rape case.'

'Is that a guess?'

'I don't know. I heard Kathy on about it. Maybe that's something else.'

Sean snapped up his phone and hit the buttons. He hit a two instead of a four, dropped his head, sighed, and did it again, slower.

'What?'

'Kathy, pet. What's Moby on?'

'What?'

'Foster says you said it was some rape thing.'

'Kind of.'

'And . . .?'

'It's in camera and they want to run it.'

'Can they?'

'Maybe. They can do the ruling anyway. Probably.'

'Why all the fuss?'

'Abortion.'

'What?'

'Abortion. Interim injunction granted stopping a rape victim leaving the country to obtain an abortion abroad.'

'Fuck off.'

'Fuck off yourself.'

She hung up.

'Christ.'

'What?' asked Foster.

Sean shook his head. He stared for a moment at the blank windows of Sheridan's office. Very still. He glanced at the screen in front of him.

'What?' asked Foster again.

'Big news day, boyo. And it's not the new fucking cabinet either.'

First thing Monday morning he had called Cavan garda station. They hadn't been very keen. Brady wasn't there, they said. Then nobody was there, then Brady was there but he'd call back. He didn't. On the second try Sean got him. He was in a hurry. He didn't seem to remember Sean's name.

'The hit and run. Michael Quinn.'

'We're following certain lines of enquiry.'

'Being?'

'Can't comment.'

'Are you hopeful of charges?'

'Hopeful.'

'When?'

'Can't comment.'

'How's Mrs Quinn doing?'

Pause.

'Fine, I believe.'

'Is she a suspect?'

There was a long pause. Then the line went dead.

Sean rang back, but he was told that Detective Brady had left, and had asked that all enquiries should be directed to the press office.

'You have a press office?'

Sheridan emerged and stood in his doorway. He nodded at Sean and Sean stood up, delighted with himself. Then Sheridan nodded at Foster and Conway and shouted at O'Kelly. Then Kathy and McMullen appeared. Moby hung at Sheridan's shoulder looking very serious and very pleased.

They all crowded into the office and there was silence. The legal guys had the chairs.

'For those of you who haven't heard, the High Court has granted an interim injunction to prevent the victim of a rape, alleged rape, from leaving the country to obtain an abortion.'

There were a couple of low whistles. Someone said, 'Jesus.'

'We're running it in the morning, but we're being cautious. The case was heard yesterday and today in camera, and the principal is being referred to only as "X". An interim injunction is not a ruling, so we're on slightly dodgy ground. But the Attorney General took the case, so I think it's very much our responsibility to go with it.'

There were nods.

'Who else is going with it?' asked Sean.

Sheridan smiled at him.

'They all are. The AG is looking for a restraining order on the grounds that the life of the unborn is protected in the constitution, and that once the state becomes aware that a . . . what do you all it . . .'

'Foetus.'

'Well, yeah, an unborn child, is at risk, then they have to step in. Dick here is doing the case, the bones of it, and that may well be all we bring out tomorrow, but we have to get moving on it anyway. I think it's safe to say that it's going to be story of the week, if not the month.'

'Fucking decade,' said Conway.

'Right. The full decision comes at the end of the week, or possibly Monday. The Cabinet haven't found their offices yet so they might be good for gut reactions. On the telephone please, Sean and Lisa, now. Kathy, I'd like something, probably for Saturday, on the boats to England, trail of tears, all that. Statistics. And Ciaran please, get in touch with the Pro Life people. I distinctly remember them being asked about this during the referendum. They said it could never happen. Dig that up. Dick is organising a legal trawl.'

Sheridan nodded at Moby. He took a breath. Scratched his nose. His voice was quiet, contained, about to burst with the excitement of it all.

'The parents of the girl went to the gardai themselves, to ask whether DNA material from an abortion could be used in evidence in a rape case. The gardai went to the AG and he's gone to the courts. We don't know who he asked in government before he did so. If anyone. Or in which government, the new one or the old one. So there's about twenty stories in there to be going on with.'

'You said parents,' said Kathy.

'Yes.' He looked around the room and he waited. He couldn't stop the smile. 'X,' he said, 'is fourteen.'

Sean wanted to tell someone about Grace Quinn.

He went for a late pint with Rita Conway and Kathy. They talked about the girl. They pondered the shock of it. The anger. Rita told them that she had had an abortion. They looked at her and said nothing. Sean changed the subject.

'Remember the guy last year, or more, who ran over the girl in Monaghan. Pissed stupid. Put her in the car.'

'Yeah.'

'He got six months,' said Kathy.

'Right. Same thing happened to him.'

'God, I heard about that. Was it the same guy?'

'Yeah. Same guy. Same place. Hit and run.'

'My arse,' said Rita.

'Exactly your arse.'

'Who then?'

'Her family,' said Kathy. 'Stands to reason. I know I'd have thought of it.'

'Or suicide,' said Rita. 'Punish himself.'

'Then where's the driver?' Sean asked.

'Scared shitless. Drunk himself. Knows it'll be his fault no matter what.'

'Maybe.'

'Well, whoever it was,' said Kathy, 'they did good.'

Sean drank and looked at them. They were not thinking it out. They didn't have the details.

'He was banned from driving,' he said. 'So he walked. His wife must be having a hell of a time.'

Rita stared at him.

'You know,' she said. 'You know what I think?'

91

'What?'

'She should just go. Her family should just take her and let her have the abortion. I mean, fuck it. What are they going to do – jail her?'

He couldn't get them back to it.

They went off together in a taxi and Sean walked to his car and drove slowly home. It was cold. The house had draughts through it that whistled when the wind was strong. In his kitchen he ate sandwiches and drank milk.

His room smelled odd. He hadn't opened the curtains all winter. He was never in it, except to sleep. He undressed and lay between the sheets and tried to remove from his mind all thoughts of Grace Quinn and Brady and Martin and the girl.

He was in an important place. A moment. On one side of him the X case. Sheridan was giving them a free hand, more or less. Do what you can. And on the other side a story all of his own. Fallen at his feet almost fully formed. He had access. He knew the background. He needed only to keep his head, to monitor, to wait for the inevitable. Brady would move on her, and Sean would be there, at Martin's side. As close as that.

All he needed was to keep his balance. Keep all of it steady. Adjust his position slightly. Check and adjust. Measure his words. Check and adjust. Make himself part of it. Naturally. Until they couldn't make sense of it without him. Balance. Steady.

Or else fall on his face.

MARTIN

He couldn't find the lighter. Anywhere. It wasn't in the kitchen. It wasn't in the front room. He pulled up the cushions and crouched on the floor and could think only that his mother had put it somewhere. He didn't want to ask her. In case she hadn't.

His hands were cold. He had dreamed of Henry the night before, and his day had filled like a flooded field, with bad thoughts and stutters. Henry in the distance, leaving.

He stood in the front room and tried to think. His mother was washing the dishes. He could hear the radio, her splashing, the clack of cups and saucers. His own place, not his own noise. And the missing gift – snagging his cold fingers on the claw feet of the armchair in the search for it, crushing the cigarettes in his pocket in the bending over.

In the kitchen his mother had her head to one side. A whimsical stance. Dreaming.

'Now, don't panic. I haven't lost it. I know it's here somewhere. I just can't see it. The lighter?'

She shook her head.

'You had it inside last night. You smoked nine cigarettes in front of the television.'

He glanced at her shoulders, her tilted head, the back of her. The space she took up was little, but it was not little.

He started on the kitchen again, looking on the floor, through the pile of newspapers in the corner.

'If my smoking bothers you then you should say so.'

'It doesn't.'

'Well then.'

She dropped something into the sink with a splash.

'Are you meeting Sean as well?'

'No. Just Philip.'

'Have you spoken to Sean since the weekend?'

'Yeah. On the phone.'

'How is he?'

Her voice was lower and she stood still. Martin knew what this was about.

'He's fine. He's caught up in this X case thing.' He opened presses. He saw the 'Henry' mug he had bought in Belfast. Henry hated it.

'Why?'

'Apologise for me when you do.'

There.

'God, Mother. Will you stop going on about that. No one minded.'

'Still.'

He looked behind the plants on the windowsill that were, he now noticed, dying.

'Shit', he said. 'Will you water those things if you get a chance? Henry usually does them.'

'Yes.'

She hunched up as he passed behind her.

'I'm sorry. I'm snapping. I just can't find this bloody lighter and I'm late.'

'You go on. I'll find it.'

She had a splash of soapsuds on her shoulder. He pointed at it.

'You're glistening. Are you sure you'll be all right here on your own?'

'Of course.' She wiped at her cardigan.

'Do you feel better? After last night, I mean.'

'Yes.'

He had come home to her crying in the kitchen. Standing at the sink like she was now, trying to hide it, telling him he was early when he was late. Frantic because she hadn't cooked anything. He had been embarrassed, had scooted up the stairs and waited.

'I'm sorry about that,' she said. 'I just . . . I just got to the point where I wasn't . . .'

He nodded. Looked at the window. Saw them in another room.

'Wasn't able . . .'

'It doesn't matter.'

'Wasn't able to be calm.'

Her eyes caught his and he was suddenly aware of her, definitely, without question, as the same woman he had walked with as a boy. The strength was back. The secret that he knew but could not explain, even to himself. She stared at him and he was startled by memory. His father. The smell of his father. The feel of the air on their faces as they ran. Her laugh. The lap of the water. Swimming in the lake in summer, hiding a whole life from his father. His father and the things he said to her. His hands.

That had been her. The same. And she knew it. It rang in her eyes now as surely as if she was seeing the same things he was. They had gone out together from the hub of that man, and they had got so far. Only so far. And then.

She had stayed. He had left her.

'Martin?'

'I have to go. I'm late already.'

'Will we not talk?'

She touched his arm.

'Yeah. I won't be late. Or tomorrow. Whatever.'

'I don't know what to do.'

He nodded and leaned forward and kissed her. She took him in her arms and embraced him with the strength. Used it on him. He patted her back and laughed. Laughed.

'I have to go, Mum. I'll see you later.'

She let him go. He walked through the house and in the hall he remembered where the lighter was. By his bed. The last cigarette had been smoked there, worrying about Henry, running his hand over the gap. He paused at the stairs but did not go up.

'Bye,' he called.

She was silent. She let him go.

GRACE

She did not want to weep. Weeping was open-ended; it welled up and gathered everything inside her and poured it out without discrimination. It died away and left her with more debris than she had started with, as if there was nothing in her but wreckage and confusion, down to a depth unimagined.

The water of it. It put her off. Everything floating.

He was only gone a couple of minutes when the doorbell rang. She had not heard it before and it took a still moment to work it out. She dried her hands on a tea towel and moved slowly to the hall.

It was not Martin. He had left with his keys. She had seen them in his hand, swinging at his side. She edged along the wall, peering at the door, listening. It rang again.

She crept past it and up the stairs, barely breathing. She went into Martin's room. It smelled of stale clothes and deodorant. Passing the bed she got her feet tangled in something, a shirt or a jumper. She kicked at it and reached the window and pushed back the edge of the curtain with a single finger.

The street was pooled by its lights and she saw parked cars and the road and the pavement and the edge of houses. The doorbell rang again. She could not see straight down.

'Baldy, baldy, who loves ya baldy.'

It came from the darkness on the other side. It was rasping and singsong, a woman's voice. Grace strained and saw her feet, pushed into the half light from the shadow of her doorway. The pestilence woman.

'Fuck off,' she roared.

Grace pushed her hair against the glass and then her cheek, hurting her eyes in the effort of looking down. She caught a glimpse of his head.

'Keep on knocking but ya can't come in. Who's who at the window?'

Grace pulled away, but he took a quick step back and looked up and saw her, stared at her, straight at her eyes, his face like a puddle in the yellow light. She stayed still and watched him.

'Can I come in?' he called, not loud. He pursed his lips and nodded. 'I'm on my own.'

Grace let the curtain fall. On the stairs she found herself rushing and paused, and went on then, slower. She walked to the door and watched it get bigger in front of her. She was a little dazed. The lock caught and her hand slipped. She gripped it more firmly.

He had his hands in his pockets and nodded at her again.

'Come in, Detective,' She said, and her voice was a shock to her.

'Thank you.'

She looked into the dark for the woman. It was very cold.

'Fuck off,' came the roar, with the barest shimmer of the black air.

'She's an odd creature,' he said as he brushed past Grace. He was no taller than she was. He shivered.

She closed the door and said to him, 'How can I help you', before realising that they were standing in an almost dark hallway, face to face in the gloom. She didn't wait for an answer but moved to the front room and went in and switched on the light and drew the curtains and felt him follow her. She stood and asked him to sit. He did not.

'You shouldn't have run off like that, Mrs Quinn.'

'I didn't.'

He sighed and sat now on the edge of the sofa and looked down.

'You never left word. It made things very difficult for me.'

She said nothing. He looked at her. His expression was one of mild hurt. She took it for a falsity, but she was not sure. He watched her carefully and seemed to be learning from what he saw. She tried to make her face go blank, but could not control it. She looked away.

'I have a boss, you know. I have to answer to others.'

'I don't understand.'

'You should have told me that you were coming up here. Instead I go up to your house last Friday and you're nowhere to be found. You be thankful that I went on my own.'

He coughed. His face reddened and he spluttered and Grace tried to see his eyes but they were squeezed shut.

'Excuse me. I think I've caught a cold.'

She thought of offering him something. A cup of tea. But she could not move. He pulled a handkerchief from his pocket and blew his nose.

'I guessed you'd come up here. Stay with your son. But I had to vouch for you without being sure. Caused me a few jitters, especially when I came up on Friday night, on my own time, and couldn't find you. Turned out the address I had for your son was an old one. I thought I was in big trouble.'

'What do you mean, "vouch for me"?'

He rolled his heavy frame to one side and stuffed the handkerchief back into his pocket.

'I said you'd told me where you were going. Told them I knew how to get in touch if need be. That you were in Dublin with your son. That you'd been cooperative. It raised a few eyebrows, but, well.'

It was not what she had expected. She lowered herself gently into the armchair and kept her eyes on him.

'Why?'

He ignored her.

'I had to race up here then, to make sure I was right. I was getting desperate by Saturday.'

'You were in the pub,' she interrupted.

He seemed surprised.

'You saw me?'

'Yes.'

'Well, well. I didn't see you. I wasn't looking for you, I suppose. I was looking for your son. Going to . . .' he hesitated, 'going to that pub,' coughed, 'was a real shot in the dark. But there he was. I couldn't believe it when you came out the door with him five minutes later. Didn't seem the type of place for you.'

He smiled as if was a great gas, to have seen her there, to have been there himself. Shook his head and half whistled.

'How did you know . . .'

'You hear all sorts,' he said. 'I know the Boltons well enough. It's not hard to get inside a family – not in our place.'

She did not want to think about it.

'You followed us here. I never saw you. I looked, but I never saw you.'

He smiled and winked.

'I know a few tricks still.'

He ran his hand over his head and Grace thought that it made a noise, but realised that it was his coat that rustled.

'That was fine then. I knew where you were. I wasn't telling little lies any more.'

She still did not understand, but she was conscious of a change in her fear. It was different now, differently directed. He was not going to arrest her. But that meant he was going to do something else.

'Did you have me followed?'

'No.'

'Why not?'

He smiled, and then coughed again.

'I've been telling everyone you're innocent, Mrs Quinn. Can't do that and then ask them to follow you.'

She opened her mouth to say something, but he raised his hand.

'I don't want to know. I really don't want to know. Anyway, all that is last week's news. The fact is that your leaving, and the absence of any other developments, has meant that your car's been sent to Forensics. I couldn't object too much. It's an obvious step. They do their bits and pieces and come up with an answer, yes or no, by next week.'

She had wiped the car, she had run mud over the metal. The damage had been there already.

'But you looked at it,' she said. 'The car. I saw you. With that other man. Outside the house.'

He nodded.

'He wanted to look it over. We couldn't see anything. It was a mess anyway. I don't know if it'll come to anything. Forensics, I mean. But you do. You know whether it'll link the car to your husband's death or not.'

She looked away. He dropped his head.

'I just wanted to tell you the situation. Early next week the results will be in. You know what those results are going to be. That's all. I'm not saying what you should do. I'm just telling you the situation.'

She kept her eyes to the floor and asked again the question he had not answered.

'Why?'

He sighed, and from the corner of her eye she saw him shake his head slowly.

'There's a lot of people locally who are putting two and two together and getting the same answer. I don't know if it's the right answer, but it's the one they're getting. And it hasn't escaped the attention of the papers either. Asking for your whereabouts.'

'Who?'

'They're all interested. A few have asked about you. It all just gathers. I thought no one would care. I thought your husband wouldn't be missed. But that was stupid.'

'You haven't answered my question. Why?'

'I have,' he said, and they looked at each other again. 'I have answered it.'

She didn't know what he meant.

'I knew him, Mrs Quinn. Your husband. I watched him sober up on a long night in Cavan station, talking us in circles, seeing our faces, going quiet on us then, turning hard. How long were you married?'

She had to think.

'Thirty-two years.'

'Christ. That's a hell of a long time. It's about two life sentences.'

He smiled. She thought it a clumsy comparison, and it made her wince a little. But she was astonished that he had made it. Something inside her was lit. Or put out.

'It wasn't all bad.'

He smiled.

'They all say that. "Made some good friends." "Learned a little woodwork." But they don't want to do it again. Would you do it again?'

'There was my . . . There's Martin.'

He nodded.

'Yes. There is. There's Martin. Would you do it again?'

She looked around the room. It was unfamiliar. Not hers. Cluttered with the stuff of lives other than her own. She had not had her own room since the days of her father and her mother and the small motions of living a child's life. Then nothing. Nothing of her own. What had she expected?

'No,' she said. 'No, I wouldn't.'

SEAN

Reynolds looked as if he might plunge the hook of his nose into Sean's face at any moment. His mouth was open, his eyes wide, his teeth hanging like little exclamation marks against the incredulous red of his tongue.

'I'm not saying that,' he said. 'I'm not saying that at all.' He paused and stared at Sean. Someone coughed. 'Don't tell me I'm saying one thing when I know I'm after saying something else entirely.' He shook his head. 'You people.'

'But Taoiseach . . .' started Sean.

'I've answered your question. Someone else now, please.'

Sean flinched as the man from RTE began to tickle him.

'We know who she is,' Kathy whispered as she passed him. Sean looked up at her and made a face. Big deal. It wasn't as if they could tell anybody.

There was a stack of memos on his desk, all cluttered with X's. He couldn't shake off the feeling that they'd been censored. There was a plan of action for the decision going against her, and a plan of action for the decision going for her. They were, as far as Sean could tell, the same. One quick, one slow.

'I believe we've adopted a position,' said Foster.

'You could say.'

He'd spent the day chasing down government back benchers, trying to get something out of them. They had been elusive, and when cornered, had been grumpy and nervous and generally pissed off. One had run away. Actually run; his little legs chopping over the pavements of Merrion Square, Sean following for a while, and gaining, but having to stop because he was laughing so much. The Attorney General, they all said. Go ask him. He did it.

He stepped off the pavement without looking and heard a sound that his mind identified, bizarrely, as a hot air balloon pierced and deflating on the spire of St Andrew's. It was not. It was a motorbike. Skidding on the sweaty ground for what seemed like an entire minute, then hitting the back of a car that was parked on the yellow line outside Combridge Fine Arts. Sean thought the impact had made the car's warning lights come on, but realised then that they had probably been flashing already.

He stood where he was and wondered whether it was his fault. He had not checked. He had been miles away. The bike had passed behind him, between him and the kerb, perhaps clipping a wheel against the old stone of the footpath – that smack that Sean had heard like a puncture in the sky above the church. He looked around, trotted across to the other side, could not see anybody looking at him.

The motorcyclist rolled backwards, one leg trapped beneath the bike, and sort of twitched, and lay still. There was a sizeable dent in the car and the bike was ruined. He had hit sideways on. Sean thought that he had probably broken his leg. People gathered. Traffic slowed to a crawl, and after making sure that there was nobody paying him any attention, Sean continued on his way, slowly, and then jogged around the corner to Dame Street.

He was a little shocked. At least as much by his flight as by the crash itself. He pondered it as he walked towards the pub. Leaving the scene of an accident, he supposed. At least technically. All because he knew Martin was meeting Philip and he wanted to have a look at him. Ask him politely how his mother was. Whether the police had made any progress. The irony troubled him. Notions flashed in his mind. Omen. Lesson. Warning. He could not dwell on it.

In the distance there was the frivolous din of an ambulance.

GRACE

She was to go. Leave. Disappear. He had not said it, not exactly. But it had been in the look he gave her when he told her about the car, about her husband in the small hours. It had been in the words he had used about him – words that had startled her, annoyed her. Talking about him like that. Her dead husband.

If you stay you'll be caught.

She sank her shoulders beneath the water, and opened her lips and blew, sending out ripples that caught the light and played with it, bouncing it away from her face in swift silver lines. She looked at her skin, at the slightly mottled paleness of it, the looseness that was beginning, exaggerated by the water. She would be old soon.

There had been nothing in his eyes to tell her where to go.

She put her feet up on the edge of the bath, on either side of the taps. Such a silence. Rich with warm water. Her nails needed cutting. They were grey and sharp like dead teeth, and they bit into her skin in places; they were painful in her good black shoes. If she left she would have sore feet at the end. Brady with his looks. His eyes. There would be a nail scissors somewhere, in a cupboard, amongst the bottles of thick liquids and sweet scents. Her son's bathroom was cluttered and curious, lit like an old shop, a pharmacy from a different age. Apothecary. Dim shadows and small mirrors and the drip drip and the smell of ginger.

Brady was like her husband. From the same place. He

had sat with him in the small hours and heard about the girl dying on the road. She could see the two of them in a damp cell, a rage between them, an anger that overlapped in the middle. Brady wanted him dead, was glad that he was dead, was inclined towards Grace like a father or a brother or a loving son. His soft words and his eyes.

He had no right.

She bent her legs and let her head slip beneath the water. The heat on her face hummed and was still. She thought about opening her eyes, of seeing the bathroom through the silver waves, seeing it swim and bend like a reflection, but she was afraid. She stayed under until her breath gave out and then pushed herself up, breaking the surface with a small roar of falling water, splashing the floor, rubbing her eyes with her knuckles.

Just go. As if there was nothing to hold her.

She wondered whether Monaghan still existed. She wondered if the farm still stood – the line of trees like broccoli that cut the sunset in two, the roll of the fields and the patch of blue water beyond. The ugly, grey, unpainted house that crumbled at the corners and let in only cold air. The barn the colour of dried blood, a hood against the rain. Did it still exist? Or had they come and taken it apart and put it away, piece by piece, like Christmas decorations. They would have watched from a different hill, waiting for her to leave.

She had not thought of it before. Now she knew that places were not constant. They were the inventions of minds that stayed still for a moment. They were a gathering of walls and shelters, and certain odours in the air, that served to divide and define and keep a person real.

She had left Monaghan forever. She would not go back. She had come to be with Martin, to make out of the space at his side a place of her own. It had been her one idea, her plan. There had been nothing else. But she had not thought it through.

he wondered whether her memories were wrong. She
remembered him following her around the house, smiling
all the time. He had talked, endlessly. She could not
remember ever having to make an effort with him, ever
having to coax or cajole or press, ever having to wonder
about what she could safely say. Maybe she had just forgotten. Now there was a silence that she could see him
prising off every time he talked. There was a new air
around him. He had learned a way of being in the world,
learned how to manage his progress, his breathing, his life.
Learned all of it without her.

She breathed across the water and the light breathed
back.

Martin belonged here. He had dug himself a dry pit,
cleared a space amongst the shadows of his growing up.
He had set himself against his past, and made his stand
on this cluttered ground by the river, where his friends
talked in a language that he had decided to understand.

She did not have it yet. Not yet. Still the dirt on her feet,
still the smell in her clothes. But she would have it some
day. She would get it right. There was nowhere else.

Grace moved her arms beneath the surface of the water,
creating waves that pushed against the smooth white sides
of the bath, billowing a gentle steam out over the room.
The night hung. Nothing moved but the water and the
steam and her arms; Grace's engine – her pale limbs
driving the yellow light and fading warmth and the dusk
of escaping.

She would stay where she was until the water was cold.

MARTIN

He shivered in the cold and coughed and listened to Philip's complaints. It was too early. It was too cold. For a while they were the only ones there, sitting at the same table as they had before, that night, with his mother.

She filled his mind. His mother. Rattling around their house, Henry's and Martin's house, with his past draped over her, his father in her eyes. All that. He drank a quick pint and nodded at Philip and shivered her away. He made himself worry instead about Henry.

Henry and his mother. As if they were a pair, a balance of faces, a small conspiracy. He felt flung backwards, toppled off his feet by the absence of one and the presence of the other. His life in reverse.

'What I can't understand,' Philip was saying now, as the bar filled, 'is why someone didn't think of this in 1983. If it could happen like this, then why did nobody think of it? Because even my parents, who are as anti-abortion as they are anti everything else, are shocked by it. Although my grandmother thinks it's great. She says the Virgin Mary was raped by the Holy Spirit and she thinks, what would have happened if Mary had been allowed to have an abortion?'

Martin nodded.

'There's a logic to it.'

'Isn't there?'

Martin drank. He listened and drank. Eyed the men who stood around the bar, thought about fidelity and about sex.

He saw great shadows on the floor. And on the ceiling. He let his knee touch Philip's and concentrated on that. He smoked. Henry ran amok in his mind like a man with a short time left. A man living a lifetime in a single evening, in a single week, in a matter of months. Martin imagined all the damage that could be done to him. Felt it as low blows and crouched over the wet table and the tapped ash.

'What's wrong with you?'

'Nothing.'

He drank. Clung to his measure of self-pity. It was only fair, he thought, given the situation. He allowed it to flood him, safe in the knowledge that he was protected by the filling room and the music and the noise, and the sound of Philip's gentle questions, gentle jokes. He looked at a man he fancied, stared at him for a while. Watched him stare back and then fall into conversation with a moustached teenager from Cork with whom Philip had once spent a night. Martin was about to point them out when Sean arrived in a flurry of white raincoat, throwing an umbrella on the floor as if sick of it, and glaring at them wide eyed.

'Drinking behind my back like a couple of faggots.'

'I told you we'd be here,' said Philip.

'So you did.' He spun and jostled his way towards the bar.

'Fuck,' breathed Martin.

'What?'

He shook his head. Got up to go the bathroom. Philip might allow him a little self-indulgence, but not Sean. He would be nagged, prodded and bullied out of it. The good-looking man glanced at him over the teenager's shoulder and smiled. Bored, thought Martin, then stood at the urinal with one eye on the door and a weight in the pit of himself where hard thoughts had gathered.

Sean was quiet, for Sean. He answered Philip's questions

about the X case, but did not elaborate, did not seem interested. He sipped his pint and eyed Martin.

'How's your mother?'

'She's fine.'

'She didn't want to come out?'

'No.'

He nodded.

'Did you see Reynolds?' asked Philip.

'Oh yes. Doesn't like me at all at all.'

'He knows you then?'

'He knows the face. Knows he doesn't like me.'

'What did he say?'

'Nothing. Is your mother going to stay with you much longer?'

'I don't know,' sighed Martin. 'I hope not.'

'Why?'

'She's driving me crazy.'

They looked at him. He shrugged, smiled.

'She just doesn't know what to do with herself.'

He ran his eyes over the crowd by the bar. Groups of men stood and drank and talked. At the counter there was a line two deep. He couldn't see the man anywhere. He craned his neck.

'You know that lanky Cork guy, Philip?'

'Who?'

'The guy with the moustache you went out with last year.'

'Thomas? I didn't go out with him.'

'Well.'

'What about him?'

'He's an awful bollox, isn't he?'

They talked to each other and let him alone and he drank too much. He watched the blur of heads until he was sick of them all, and looked then at the grid of hips and crotches at eye level, a tangle of conjunctions like the hooves of a herd and him lying on the ground regarding them, restless.

The warmth of the place became brazen. He thought he saw someone come in with snow on their coat, but he didn't want to mention it because he knew he was drunk and wasn't sure, and thought that he might have been seeing things, and thought that perhaps the cold he felt pressed up against the walls of the pub like the whole building had slipped into the river, might just have been his imagination.

Sean left. He put his hands on Martin's shoulders and whispered something in his ear that Martin could not make out.

'What?'

'I'll call over tomorrow.'

'For what?'

'Say hello.'

He ducked out though the wall of shoulders and disappeared. Philip laughed.

'He just invited himself over to your place.'

'Did he now? The fucker.'

Philip smiled at him.

'I'm going to the bar. Think you can stay here and not fall over?'

'Fuck off. Get me a gin and tonic, will you?'

'No.'

'A double.'

'No.'

'I'm giving you the fucking money for Christ's sake, what do you mean no?'

Philip snatched the note from his hand and went off, shouting 'Excuse me,' gone a little camp from annoyance. Martin lit a cigarette.

Henry like a ghost, drifting across his mind. A Paris bar. Sober. Staring.

*

There was no snow. But the cold of the street hit them full on while they were still trying to close their coats. Martin looked up and saw stars.

'It snowed upwards,' he said, but Philip did not hear him.

They stuck their hands deep into their pockets and walked briskly to Dame Street, bumping into each other at the corner and laughing. Philip refused Martin's suggestion that they go on to a club. Or that he go home with Martin. Where would he sleep? he wanted to know. Martin had forgotten about his mother. They parted outside the Central Bank, swaying. Philip kissed Martin's cheek and jogged away for his bus, his solid strides making Martin dizzy.

He crossed the road and ducked into the tiny laneway that led to the Stag's Head. He had a piss in the half alcove, and his legs cracked and groaned and his head was confounded by the cold. Outside the pub he paused and watched the crowd spill out. He had had a row there once with Henry. Had walked out on him and headed home, before stopping, and turning, and walking back.

He walked down Dame Lane, remembering that night, remembering what he had done, suspecting now, one eye closed, his mouth puckered up, that he was about to do it again. He coughed and spat and strained for a blank mind.

He crossed through the paused traffic of George's Street to where Dame Lane continued, running along the walls of the castle. He resisted the urge to stop at the corner, to wait and think and weigh things up. He was pleased to discover that the part of his brain that did that was congealed in drink and the miles to Paris. Stalled with distance.

He strode into the darkness, avoiding the light that spilled from the open doorways of restaurant kitchens. A Chinese waiter in a white shirt and black waistcoat stood smoking a cigarette, watching Martin as he passed by with his hands in his pockets, his head down. He felt very cold. Cold in his stomach. He had the hiccups.

Halfway down the lane there was a grey door lit from above, the entrance to the sauna club, the small way in to a large space. As he pushed open the door Martin glanced back. The cars passed by on George's Street. People scurried along the pavement in the distance, crossing the gap in an instant without looking down. In the shadows closer to him he could see the orange dot of light rising and falling, where the waiter stood and watched him.

Inside, everything was painted a battleship grey. The walls and ceiling of the stairwell as grey as sky. Cement sky. He thought it might have something to do with reassurance. This is a grey area. Leave your scruples at the door. Leave your panic and your guilt and your fear at the door. Pick them up on the way out. Martin's hiccups had stopped.

At the top of the stairs he paid the man and scrawled a name on the sheet of paper that was thrust in front of him. He was given a locker key. A buzzer sounded and he pushed open another, heavier door with his shoulder.

There was a thick heat, and a sweet, vague scent. Two men with towels held around their waists looked down from the narrow stairs. Martin glanced up at them and then ducked his head and turned the corner into the changing room. It was empty and he breathed, breathed in again, a muscle in his hand twitching, his feet catching awkwardly on the thin dark carpet.

He was very drunk. The change in the temperature had his head spinning. He sat on a bench and scanned the lockers for his number.

Three times a week sometimes, in his first days in Dublin. Then less and less as he had met more people in the pubs. By the time he had met Henry he had not been in six months or more. And since then only that one time. Falling over in the showers. Spilling a bottle of poppers in one of the tiny mattress rooms with two other men about whom he could remember absolutely nothing. Telling himself that it was despair when it was not. It was less than that.

He had trouble getting the key into the lock and then almost fell over while trying to untie his shoelaces. He took a ragged, pale blue towel from the locker and stuffed his coat into the small space, patting it down and putting his shoes on top of it. He took off his jumper and his shirt. He stood for a moment in his jeans, running his hand gently over his chest.

The temperature suited bare skin. The air clung to him so that he could not feel it. He swam in the heat. He took off his jeans, pulling them inside out over the obstruction of his socks. Then his socks. He slipped his underpants down to his ankles and kicked them up into the air with one foot and caught them.

'Cool,' he muttered, and saw a dripping man, paunch, grey hair, rolling towards him with a smile.

'There's a trick,' he said.

'Fuck off.'

He picked up his towel and slammed the locker door and it bounced out again. He closed it and locked it and scratched his head.

'Sorry,' he said, and touched the man's shoulder in passing.

'That's all right.'

He walked unsteadily from the room and past another room where men watched television. There was the sound of gunfire and explosions. One man was black. Another drank from a plastic cup. He went into the next room where the man who had let him in stood behind a counter dispensing tea and coffee and sandwiches and chocolate. Martin handed in his key, saying the number in his head over and over, glancing at a big bowl of condoms and a big bowl of mints and at a man who sat on a stool reading

115

a newspaper. The black man came in and asked for tea. Martin took two mints and brushed past him and went out slowly, pulling his towel tight. Carefully, one narrow foot after another, like the long hands of a climber, he went upstairs.

It was crowded. All eyes. They were all ages, walking to and fro, naked but for their towels, some carrying keys, some cigarette boxes, all with the same look. Just eyes. Martin smiled. They looked like men given some terrible task. They wanted it over with. They wanted it done right.

A line of towels hung on hooks outside the steam room. As Martin passed the door it opened and two young, good-looking men emerged, naked, their cocks sticking out from them like arrows shot in. They took their towels and moved awkwardly away, the one in front checking that the other followed, towards the next flight of stairs.

He thought of going in there but he put it off. He thought of Henry and shook his head. His towel slipped and he caught it. A blond guy who looked too young smiled at him. He went to the video room and stood in the doorway. The two tiers of seats, just wide ledges really with thin black plastic mattresses, were full. In one corner sat a fat boy with a bottle of poppers pressed to his nostril. Beside him a bald man moved a hand up and down beneath his towel. On the bottom tier, in the corner, a man with a moustache, his eyes half closed, his head lolling on his shoulders, his towel on the floor, masturbated as if he'd been doing it for days. An asylum scene. Martin turned away.

On screen there was something happening in what looked like an African hut, with reed mats and a veiled bed and a fire in the middle of the floor. One black man and two white. Something was said and Martin thought there was something wrong with the sound until something else was said and he realised that they were speaking French. French. He turned away.

At the end of the corridor was a toilet and the showers. He watched a man washing his hair. He watched suds run over his back and tried to see his face but it was scrunched up and anyway, he decided, the body was just a little too good. He said 'overdressed' to himself and laughed. He stopped laughing when he felt the return of his hiccups. He bent over the sink outside the toilet and cupped his hands and drank tepid water and caught a bad smell and moved away, brushing slightly against the warm walls, stared at by an elderly man with hair like his father's.

He rubbed his eyes and saw parts of Henry spin around in front of him like branches broken off in a storm.

At the door to the steam room he hung his towel over another and glanced back up the corridor and saw the man from the shower look at him. Inside there were grey bodies piled in a corner and the smell of poppers was like a gas leak, and almost immediately his cock was in somebody's hand. He pushed him away, tried to get his bearings. Sweat started on his forehead. The man from the shower came in and stood beside him. Martin found the bench and sat down. The man sat down too, thigh against thigh. He put his hand on Martin's balls, very gently, and leaned in close as if to kiss him. Martin stood, turned, faced the guy, pointed his cock at him, tried to hold his head. Half heartedly, the man kissed Martin's stomach and Martin sighed as loudly as he could, and coughed, and went out.

Downstairs there was the type of telephone that allowed you to dial and wait until your call was answered before you had to put in any money. He poked at the numbers and heard the sound they made and heard the familiar clicks and the odd tone that he always mistook for engaged, but which was not engaged. It was like a hospital machine, tethered to a death-bed. He let it ring until it rang out.

Upstairs he decided to limit himself to men who had poppers.

He moved to the video room. French was fitting. There was no space to sit down. The fat boy was still there, but the man beside him was now the man from the shower and the steam room. On screen the two white boys ran, chasing each other, through a shallow stream, their shorts and their T-shirts stuck to their skin like bandages. They wrestled and rolled in the water, laughing. It wouldn't last.

He looked into the corner behind him. A man smoked and drank from a mug. Beside him the drunk, still wanking. Behind them the very young looking blond guy, intent on the screen. Beside him, pressed into the corner, a man stared at Martin and smiled. Martin squinted. The man waved. Lifted up his hand and waved, as if it were the middle of the street. His smile in the darkness was like an electric shock. Jolting.

Sean.

SEAN

The first he saw of him was out of the corner of his eye, a blur that was the right height, the right shape, the right dimensions for a small kick of recognition. He shifted his unfocused gaze from the screen to the doorway, just missing him, catching only the dull glint of television light on shoulder blades as he disappeared. Sean was tired. He yawned widely, glancing at the others on the seats, their odd motions and the shallow glow suggesting an aquarium, a line-up of fishes.

He thought he had imagined it. He had been thinking of Martin. Mind's eye. Next he'd be seeing his mother. They were bigger in his mind than anything else, blocking out his view of things, sending him dazed into reveries, people snapping their fingers at him – Sean, hey Sean, anybody there?

Then a while later he saw him again, and squinted and stared and couldn't believe it. He smiled and waved. Martin turned away. Sean stood and stepped down from the seats and went to him, touched him on the arm, looked into his eyes as he turned. He was drunk. Embarrassed. More than that.

'Sean,' he said. 'Jesus. Wait till I tell you,' but he just stared and nothing came to him, and Sean saw a flicker, his eyes in a panic, and stopped smiling and nodded. He said nothing, but led his friend across the corridor to the stairs and up to the third floor.

Three or four men stood by open doors. Music played.

Some rooms were taken, their doors closed. Others were empty. They were really nothing more than cubicles, the space to lie down. The music was not loud, but thumping, full of bass. The light was low, the air still and serious.

Sean peered into the rooms until he found one that looked civilised. Martin, whom he now held by the wrist, was swaying, bumping into things. He sat him down on the edge of the bunk, closed the door and adjusted the light. Martin's head fell forward on to his chest. Sean sat beside him.

'You all right?'

'Now?'

Sean leaned towards him, tried to see his face.

'Now, any time you like.'

'I'm an awful fucker.'

'Why?'

He said nothing. Sean thought he might like a cigarette, but he didn't seem to have any with him. He looked around the waistband of his towel. No bulges. There was a damp sheen on his skin. He ran a finger along the line of his shoulder and Martin shook it off.

'For being here?'

He made a noise and for a second Sean thought he was crying. But he sniffed loudly and raised his head, his eyes closed, and sighed.

'I rang Henry and he's not in.'

'No?'

'He's not at all there.'

'No.'

'So I thought I'd come here.'

Sean nodded. There was a silence. He could hear breathing, panting, through the thin wall behind him. He coughed.

'Why?'

'Because I can't tell the difference between the two.'

'What two?'

'Whether it's him or whether it's me. Or whether it's him first or me first or whether you just meet someone in a pub and have a night with him or you come somewhere here, like here, and pour yourself into it.'

Sean recognised that he was not as drunk as he was letting on.

'It's not a big deal, Martin. He won't hear about it from me.'

'You miss the point.'

'He's not being unfaithful.'

Martin opened his eyes and looked at him.

'How do you know?'

He did not know. He shrugged.

'He doesn't let things happen. He decides everything. He wouldn't decide to do that. It's not like him.'

Martin peered at him, frowning.

'What do you mean?'

'He's honourable.' He laughed. 'Neat. If he wanted to screw around in Paris he'd come back here first and break up with you properly. You know what he's like.'

Martin nodded.

'He has notions of good behaviour.'

Martin brushed a hand over his legs.

'I don't see what that has to do with it,' he said quietly, picking at the loose threads of his towel. 'You don't talk to him. I do. I can hear his voice. From his room. He speaks French. He says hello in French. He's doing something. I know he is.'

'No you don't.'

'I do.'

'You suspect.'

Martin was silent.

'You suspect. You think he might be because you think you would if you were him so you've decided to get in first. Pre-empt. Maybe he's stronger than you.'

Martin shifted his shoulders.

'I said it.'

'Said what?'

'I shouldn't be here. I'm fucking . . .'

'Oh Martin, it doesn't matter. It's really not a big deal. I don't think it is, anyway. Don't go guilty mad.'

'It's like a dream. There's shadows and heat and you try not to see faces but it's really all you see. Clouds of faces, and this silence full of people. No words, mouths.'

He rubbed his hands over his face, stretching his skin, and down over his chin to his neck, and around to the back of his neck.

'And the heat. It's like there's no air. It's like you're in water, warm water, so that you can't feel anything. And it's grey – have you noticed? And the smell and the eyes, everybody rotten in some way, rotting, as if we're thrown here, dead. I mean, a kind of dead, but seeing, like . . .'

'It's the sauna Martin, not Dante's fucking Inferno.'

Sean hated guilt. It was indulgence, it was lazy. Weighty and useless. A layer of fat. He came to the sauna to relax, to rest in the warmth, to wander through a gentle maze of possibilities. He slept well afterwards.

Martin sighed, slowly shook his head.

'It makes me sick, that's all.'

'Have you done anything yet?'

'No.'

Sean ran a finger down Martin's back.

'You've been in the steam room.'

'Not for very long. I didn't do anything.' He looked at Sean. 'I'd tell you if I had.'

'Well, go home then. Leave. If it bothers you. Have a shower, get dressed and leave.'

He nodded, and his head dropped again and he looked at his knees.

'If he hurts me I want to be able to hurt him back. I want to be able to tell him things. And if he doesn't then I will have this for myself. I mean to hurt myself.'

'Yeah, right. Nothing torments quite like a blow job in a warm dark room.'

'We're different.'

'We are. Maybe I'm just old fashioned.'

'Maybe.'

They went downstairs for coffee, Martin getting cigarettes from his locker, being sheepish. They sat in the shadows in the corner of the television room, Martin hunched over, his elbows on his knees. Sean looked at him, near naked, shamefaced. His short hair glistened, his skin slowly dried. It was as good a chance as he'd have. To find out how much he knew. How much he guessed.

'How's your mother?'

'Christ. What time is it?'

Sean nodded at a clock on the wall. It was just after half twelve.

'I hope she doesn't stay up.'

'Is she coping all right?'

Martin shrugged.

'She was crying yesterday,' he said. 'She seems sometimes to be ... elsewhere. I think I may be a disappointment.'

'We always are.'

'Yes.'

He drank his coffee and made a face. Grateful that the conversation had moved on. He smiled, looked at Sean.

'It's as if she's just dropped out of my head. You know, from where I remembered her. She's the same as I remember her, but she's not because everything else has changed. She's here, I'm different. She's in my house now. It's all wrong, out of place. And my father dead, all that.'

'Does she talk about that?'

'My father?'

'Yeah.'

'No. Maybe she wants to. I'm not very good with it. I'm preoccupied by Henry.'

'Henry isn't here.'

He nodded, blew smoke into his coffee, carelessly stroked a knee.

Sean looked at the door and saw a man he knew from another newspaper. He caught Sean's eye and looked away.

'I met the guy,' he said, and started again. 'I met the guy who's investigating it. I suppose he talked to you.'

'Investigating what?'

'Your father.'

'Investigating?'

'The hit-and-run.'

Martin squinted and frowned. It seemed to Sean that he was confused.

'They have to investigate a hit-and-run, Martin.'

'I know that. How did you meet him?'

Sean coughed. He had to keep a clear line in his head. Tell mostly the truth. Know when to make the switch.

'I knew him already. From the time your father . . . The thing with that girl.'

'Anne Killeen.'

'Yeah.'

Keep it close. Simple.

'His name is Brady. He's invest . . . he's in charge of it. I met him at the weekend, Saturday, after you'd gone home with your mother.'

He took a sip of his coffee, fixed his voice. Balance.

'He was on Dame Street. I think he must have been at the Olympia or something. It was around there. I introduced myself and he remembered me and we got chatting. He asked me a little about you.'

'About me?'

'Yeah.'

'What about me?'

'Just what you were like. How you were getting on, you know. All very conversational. Like, I believe you know

124

Martin Quinn, I believe his mother is staying with him now. You know. Making small talk.'

It might have happened. If Brady had seen him, had remembered him. Had they been in the street.

'Did he not go and see you?'

Martin gave him a look. Sean thought he'd blown it. But Martin blinked, and shook his head, open-mouthed, fascinated.

'No. Fuck. How did he know, you know, how, that you know me?'

'I don't know. He asked whether I'd met your mother as well.'

Martin lit a second cigarette.

'Maybe he talked to her. She never said.'

'I'm sure he did.'

'It's a bit odd having a fucking policeman going around asking questions about you.' He laughed. 'Hope I'm not a suspect.'

Sean smiled. Sipped his coffee. Ran one bare foot over the other on the cold rung of the stool.

God, but Martin was stupid.

He watched him smoke and eye up the men who passed the door until he was too tired to watch any more. All he could talk about was Henry. Every silence leading back to Henry. Every attempt by Sean to move the conversation on blocked by the great mystery of Henry, of what Henry might or might not be doing in Paris. And all the time, his eyes, passing over the overweight or older ones in a glance, struggling to focus the honey skin of others, staring at those who came in to sit down.

He did not seem to sober up. Instead he became more heavy-limbed, fixed on the one thought, grinding away at it until Sean began to realise that Martin was waiting for him to leave.

As he dressed he remembered the motor bike crash. The

quick sparks of the exhaust scraping the ground. The hiss of leather. His fault. It was as if his power to influence events had been used up in a single random incident. Irrelevant. Drained from him without his consent by a speeding courier and a parked car. He was powerless now. Idling.

He kissed Martin on the cheek and told him to be good. Martin nodded seriously.

'One last smoke,' he said.

At the door Sean stopped to wait and see how long it would take before Martin ventured upstairs again. But after a few seconds he shook his head and turned away and went down to the street. It would not be fair. It would unbalance things. It would lose him his status. Keeper of secrets. Trustee.

The cold air was a shock to him. He walked to his car with his arms clenched to his body, his legs close together, careful not to clip one ankle against another.

Foot after foot, short strides, straight line.

GRACE

Her father had atlases and encyclopaedias and maps on the wall with the British Empire pink. At breakfast he read to her from the *Sunday Times*. In the evening it was Jane Austen or Churchill's *Marlborough*, or sometimes, if she was giddy, he would read the horrible parts of Dickens. He recited Tennyson with a booming voice and made her mother laugh. He bought expensive prints of strange paintings. Cleopatra carried on her chair by black slave boys with bare shoulders and shaved heads. Ophelia drowned. A portrait of Keats reading. He made her learn Shakespeare's sonnets and she spoke them for visitors who did not know when she made a mistake. Once he quietly gave her a book of poems by Wilfred Owen. She had not liked them.

He wanted her to sing. She did not have a voice for it. He wanted her to act. But her eyes were always wide with the terror of being watched, and he gave up his encouragement. Her sister was better at it. She was in *The Mikado*.

Grace's father would sit for hours in the small room he called his study, surrounded by second-hand books, writing in his huge leather-bound, yellow-paged diary. He kept it locked in a drawer. When he died, Grace's sister had forced the drawer open and read it. She said she couldn't understand most of it. She had it still, kept somewhere safe, waiting for Grace to come and turn the pages and hear her father's voice again, wooden with the effort of being English.

She would write to her sister. Ask her to send it over.

She could not sleep.

She had held Sean in her arms and pointed at the stars and named the shapes she knew. The plough. That was the only shape she knew. And then she had put him down so that she could take the clothes from the line. She threw them over her arm. She took each of them down and threw them over her arm. Then she had turned and looked into the darkness, and she had known almost immediately that he was in the ditch. It was easy. She looked at the clean clothes and turned again and draped them carefully over the line, knowing that some of them would fall and be dirtied, but knowing that some of them would stay where they were and that she wouldn't have to do them again. Then she went and took her drowned son's body from the shallow water and carried it into the house and sat with it in her arms until her husband came in. He hit her. He hit her and tore her clothes and dragged her out and threw her in the ditch and left her there. She had tried to drown. She had tried to lose consciousness, with her head under the water. But she could not. She could not stop herself from breathing, from gasping and sucking in the air in cold dark mouthfuls. When she climbed up out of the ditch she saw all the clean clothes lying on the ground – all of them, muddied and strewn. She sat on the grass and stared at them for a long time. It stayed with her more than anything else. Those clean clothes lying in the mud.

In the early hours, the dead black, the front door slammed and Grace sat up in bed. There was a minute's silence, a waiting silence, before footsteps started – the creak of floorboards and the squeal of the kitchen door opening and the click of the light switch.

For some reason, she thought it was Henry. He had come home. He would creep silently up the stairs and past her door and into the other room. He would slide into bed beside Martin and put his arms around him. He had missed her son too much.

She heard the tap, the splash of water in the sink. Then there was another short silence. The bathroom door opened and closed and she thought she heard a whispering. Words. The toilet was flushed and the bathroom door was opened and closed again. There were indistinct sounds, impossible for her to interpret, like old machinery ticking over quietly in a basement. Still there was the whispering, a soft trickle of syllables that she could not make out.

She wondered whether it was possible for her to hear someone whispering in the kitchen. She thought she might be too far away. Perhaps she was imagining it, giving a voice to the silence. It was not Henry.

A glass smashed. The whispering stopped. Grace sat still, a hand stuck in mid air. There was quiet for a moment before she heard a curse, hissed out in a drunken Monaghan accent. Then the curse came again, a little louder. And then a third time, almost shouted. She let her hand fall gently on to her lap and she made herself quiet and listened to the noiseless gap that lay between her and the kitchen.

A foot kicked at shards of broken glass; a dull tinkling sound. Then there were footsteps, and the flick of the light switch and the closing of the door and the footsteps started on the stairs, irregular gaps between each step. Grace slid down in the bed and lay still. She could hear the swish of a shoulder against the wallpaper, and the wooden clatter of pictures being knocked sideways, and the hand squeaking on the bannisters. She could hear the breathing.

She turned on to her side and pulled her legs up and and got her knees in front of her chest. She could hear him outside her door, pausing, regaining his balance. She wrapped her arms around her shins and ducked her head between her knees and felt the tiny flutter of calm that came to her always, settling somewhere between her shoulder-blades like a hand; a moment of warmth and clarity and reassurance that had her father's face. It never stayed for long. She heard the door open and she held her breath. She tried to make her muscles relax.

There was a noise. She thought it was footsteps. Feet, walking across the room, coming towards her. She thought it was that, because that is what she expected. But the noise was utterly different, and for a moment she could not understand it. It was alien and confusing and frightening. But then she realised that it was the door closing. It was Martin. Turning in the tiny space of the landing and opening the door to his own room. It was the sound of her son going to bed. That was all.

She stayed still for a while. Then slowly she released her body and allowed it to stretch out in the bed. She opened her eyes and searched the darkness and saw the shapes of the room in Martin's house, the calm shadows that surrounded her.

She remembered. She knew the words that described it. She said them to herself quietly, slowly, like a child's prayer. She allowed herself to think about what it was that she had done.

She remembered the cold that night – the way the car had started first time. She remembered thinking that it was a good omen. She wondered now what business she had thinking about omens. She wondered what pain he had felt. She wondered whether the cold would have made the pain better or worse. She wondered why she had not cried, and then she wondered whether she might have, driving home, with the car not right, and the cold black sky and the thought of it all, the whole crooked mess.

She remembered his thin hair in the moonlight. She remembered his grey head bowed in the moonlight, his pale hands clasped together in the moonlight. Then she squinted in the darkness and bit her thumb. She wasn't sure. She couldn't remember. Had there been a moon?

At breakfast Martin was quiet, sickly. Hung-over. He apologised for the broken glass he had left on the floor. He was confused. She watched him push his plate away, and then pick at his food as he drank cup after cup of tea. His face was pale, his eyes turned down. He buttered some toast and left it. When the letter-box rattled he jumped, and closed his eyes then and sighed. And when the radio beeped the time signal for eight o'clock and the presenter introduced the news, he frowned as if trying to remember something.
'What's today's date?'
Grace shook her head.
'I don't know.'
'He just said it.'
'I didn't hear.'
He went out of the room then and was gone for twenty minutes or more. When he looked in again it was to say goodbye. Grace listened to the front door slam and thought for a moment about what she could do with the uneaten sausages and eggs and potato cakes. She drank another cup of tea and listened to the politicians on the radio discuss the X case. She threw the food in the bin.

It might snow. The air pressed up against her roughly and her cheeks hurt. The grey sky seemed solid.
She wandered through the city centre. She found herself in the art departments of big book shops, flicking through heavy hardbacks with shining pages, looking for something. She could not find it.
She bought a second-hand copy of *Hard Times* – there seemed to be hundreds of them – and went into a small coffee shop on Dawson Street. The afternoon was flooding

nto evening, the sky darkening, a shadow cast on it, a blossom of black cloud like ink in water. She read a little, and looked out on the street at a small boy in a blue anorak and cropped hair. He held a shallow cardboard box and though it was clear that he was begging, holding the box out to passers-by, Grace thought that had you not known, you might have assumed that he was offering them something, holding out a gift, presenting something of himself to strangers.

She finished her coffee and stepped out into the cold. The boy had moved to the other side of the street, his round, cut face turned upwards, his jeans holed at the knees. She paused, wanting to cross and give him some money, but stopped herself. He was saying something to people, and no one stopped. No one gave him anything. She turned towards St Stephen's Green. Dark now. She glanced back and saw him still, bobbing in the throng of pedestrians, interloping, odd, speaking the words of a spell, offering, holding out. His blessing rising in the cold air.

Walking on. Up towards the Green.

Her mother praying. Sending up words. Her husband, huddled at the side of things. Sending up prayers.

She did not like to think of him. It had become a single picture, clouding her eyes. It had become a blur of trees and black sky and cold road and a dump of old clothes caught in the headlights. It came into her mind and it stayed there, crawling slowly, a damaged animal. It was as if she had not killed him. Not the first time. It was as if she had turned the car around and had driven back and had found him alive still; breathing painfully, a rasp of cold air through his bloody mouth, his ribs crushed and his hand outstretched to her, cut and patterned by the pebbles of the road.

At the corner of Cuffe Street she stopped at the lights,

pulling her scarf tight around her neck, gritting her teeth a little.

She thought of what she would have done then. She would have had to drive over him again. Crush another part of him, send him off. Would it hurt more the first time or the second? She knew that she would have swallowed hard and cried, and she knew that she would have had to force her foot to the pedal. She knew she would have screamed if she had had to do it a second time. She would have screamed and twisted the wheel out of shape with her fingers, and hurtled on into the ditch, snapping to a stop against the bushes and the trees, her head against the glass, feeling the cold outside the car and the trickle that was the hard part of dying. She understood that.

Up Camden Street.

Her book. She had left her book in the coffee shop. Hardly started. The One Needful Thing. She stopped and stamped a foot, and went on.

His prayer. What had he prayed? Something formal perhaps; a decade of the rosary. She could not remember what a rosary consisted of. She could remember the Our Father. Now I lay me down to sleep. Hail Mary full of grace. She had always laughed at that. Bless us oh Lord. Bless me Father. Bless me.

Now I lay me down to sleep I give my soul to God to keep and if I die before I wake I give my soul to God to take.

Was this praying? Saying it in her head, thinking of her husband, shrunk from the beams of light, kneeling by the dark flowers, the hard road. Was she praying now? And thinking of him. Was she praying for him so?

So. At the end of a sentence. I'm off out so. He would nod his head as if acknowledging himself. I'm away now so.

She walked up Richmond Street and saw the traffic steaming at the lights. There was snow in the air, falling slowly on to the concrete, and dissolving gently, disappearing somewhere. She stopped at the corner and stared up into the blackness, her head tilted back so far that her neck hurt. She saw tiny white specks fluttering down, falling softly towards her. She thought of Monaghan, covered by snow. She thought of the narrow part of the road where the flowers were propped up against the hedge. She pictured them, the snow resting on the bright petals and the green stems, melting into the colour, confusing the brightness and the dark, making a mixture of them, a damaged halfway shade that fell pure, and rested in stained patches on the grey ground.

Her eyes had closed. She opened them, and lowered her head, and turned for the door of her son's home.

He was later than he had been all week. He kissed her cheek and then put a cold hand to her face and she shuddered.

She had not prepared a meal for him. He preferred to make his own.

'Do you know what day it is?' he asked.

'No.'

'St Valentine's Day,' he said, and he smiled and handed her a pink carnation.

'Martin.'

She sat in the kitchen while he cooked. He was cheerful, but she was not convinced. He talked on, slicing tomatoes, beating eggs, peeling potatoes. He wore a pale beige shirt, the sleeves rolled up, a blue tie tightly knotted hanging on his chest.

'I got a card from Henry and of course forgot to send him one, so I'll have to ring him before he rings me. I was trying to think of something to do today, you know, something that he'd get today. I even priced having flowers delivered in Paris. It'd be cheaper to fly over and deliver them myself. Would you like an omelette?'

134

'No, thank you.'

'I rang him at lunchtime on the off chance that he might be there, but he wasn't. I think Friday is a long day for him too. He usually rings me because he can be in quite late, but I think I'll try. Actually, will you watch this and I'll try now?'

She stood by the heat of the rings and poked at his food. She was sure that he had not boiled the potatoes for long enough. They sizzled now, cubed, white islands in the pale yellow.

She wanted to tell him about Brady.

'No answer,' he said.

'How was last night?'

'Fine.'

'Did you meet Sean?'

He looked at her.

'Yes.'

'How is he?'

'He's fine. Do you know – you've been here a week today?'

'Oh. Have I? Seems like longer.'

He laughed, and loosened his tie and took it off, draping it over the back of a chair.

'The policeman who's . . .' she began.

'Brady,' he said, his back to her again.

'Yes. How did you know?'

'Sean met him.'

She stared at his shoulder-blades, pressed against the thin material as he leaned forward.

'Last night?'

'No, no. Last weekend. Saturday.'

She brought her hands together.

'What did he say?'

Martin had raised his head. He was looking into the black window. She thought for a second that he was

135

looking at her reflection, but she could not see his face. He was still.

'What did who say?'

'Sean. About Brady.'

'Nothing really. He knows him you see, vaguely. He just introduced himself, asked him how things were going, I suppose. Brady didn't say anything much. Asked about me. How Sean knew me. How you were, that kind of thing.'

'Last Saturday?'

'Apparently.'

He had not moved. She could not tell if he was looking at himself, or staring into space.

'What about him, anyway?'

'What?'

'Brady. Was he in touch?'

She watched his head drop again, looking down at the pan, his elbow moving in and out as he prodded the sides of his omelette.

'Yes.' She spoke very slowly. 'He came here. Last night.'

Martin swung on his hips and looked at her. His face was red from the heat. She saw the skin of his neck fold upon itself.

'Any news?'

She held his eyes. They did not flinch.

'No,' she said.

His eyes. Passive. They regarded her for a moment and he nodded then and turned away. He had changed. She could no longer tell if he was lying.

He rang Henry. Grace stayed in the kitchen making tea. She listened to the hum of her son's voice, but could not make out the words.

It occurred to her that everybody might know and not mind. That Sean had guessed and did not care. That he had told Martin and Martin did not care either. He had

136

given her a flower. She glanced at it, sitting in a black vase against the black window like the last of the sky. She could not decide now which would be worse – her son knowing that she had killed his father and not caring; or her son suspicious, trying to scare from her an admission with talk of Brady. Or Sean. Lying to him, seeing what he knew. Testing her from a distance. The name of her son.

Martin put the phone down and Grace re-boiled the kettle.

'Henry says hello.'

'How is he?'

'Tired.'

As they watched television, drinking tea, the X case dominating the news even on the BBC, Martin asked her occasional, casual, questions about Brady. About what he was doing, what he thought. Whether she had told him where she was staying. She had, she said. Whether they had a lead. He used that word – 'lead'. She told him that Brady hadn't said.

'What do you think happened?' he asked, his eyes on the screen, his hands around his mug, slumped in his chair as though sleeping.

'I don't know.'

He looked over at her.

'Will you stay here?'

'Yes.'

He nodded.

'I will sell the farm and stay in Dublin. Get a small flat or something. Is that all right?'

He paused, and turned then towards the television.

'Of course.'

The screen light mapped his features in lines and splashes. She could not tell what his expression was. She could not decide if he was smiling or frowning or blank. She could not tell what he thought, or what he knew, or what it was that connected them. He changed stations with

137

the remote control, coughed, crossed his legs. She watched him move and not move, heard his breath. She could find no key to him.

She thought of Sean. The name of her dead son. She wondered for the first time what that meant.

MARTIN

On Saturday he slept late, as did his mother. They met each other in the kitchen just after midday, dressing-gowned and slippered, hugging their coffee mugs and sitting close to the heater. The snow had not stuck. There were patches of dirty frost in the corners of the yard, ice on the concrete. The heavy grey sky hung low, pressing the cold into the ground.

She was watching him. He could see her without looking, feel her gaze. He cut bread and buttered toast and scratched at the stubble on his cheek. He was conscious of his breath and coughed a harsh cough that had her alert, head slightly tilted, worrying.

'What?' he barked, not meaning to bark at all.

'Nothing.'

He chewed, and sipped at his coffee and looked at her. He asked her what she wanted to do. She shrugged.

All day, as if waiting, she stayed in the kitchen. He went out to the shops and came back to find her washing up. After his shower he found her washing the floor. He told her not to bother, but she shrugged again, and Martin began to worry that they would have an argument. When he was dressed he read the paper in the front room until he caught the smell of baking bread and went into the kitchen to find her doing the crossword from the previous week's Sunday paper.

'You can win whiskey,' she said, and he stared at her.

'You don't drink whiskey.'

'I could learn.'

He smiled at that, but later, when the bread was cooling on the table, he found her standing on a chair, a yellow cloth tied around the end of the sweeping brush, poking dust and webs from the corners of the ceiling.

'Jesus, Mother. You'll break your neck.'

'Cover the bread, Martin, will you please?'

He threw a tea towel over the loaves and sighed.

'It's a pity the snow all melted,' she said. He stood beneath her and put his hand on the back of the chair. She ran the brush along the lip of the doorway.

'Do you remember going out walking at home, in the snow. You used to trip me up on slopes and go diving after me. It's a wonder we weren't killed on a covered rock.'

'I only did it when I knew it was safe.'

'And then trying to dry off before we got home. Flapping our coats, and the clouds of snow we'd blow up. Like sending smoke signals, you said. Your cowboy and Indian days. Do you remember?'

'Yeah. I do.'

She smiled fully and stepped down, her hand on his shoulder for balance.

'Pity it all melted.'

He took the sweeping brush from her.

For the rest of the day he stayed away from the kitchen. Until later, when they sat down for their tea, and he cut the bread and talked so that she would not talk. He spoke as if silence cost him money, as if a word from his mother might break some spell. He prattled on, without pause, afraid that if she started talking she would undo the present, take it apart piece by piece, make it disappear. He galloped through words, tripping over the sense of things, stumbling on names, stuttering, all the time convincing himself more and more that his mother could expose him with a story, pull him back to himself, reduce his life to the few square miles of his childhood. He thought that if she wanted to, she could kill him. Tell him where he'd come from. Unlace his life like a shoe and shake it off. Kill him dead.

GRACE

She waited until he had gone out for the evening, his steps moving away from the house. She listened, expected a rap at the door, tensed and strained. Without Martin in it, with the dark down, the house was like an open place, a shadow on the ground. She crouched. She moved to the front room and rummaged through the small notebook of telephone numbers until she found Sean's.

There was no answer.

She waited and tried again. Then she put on her coat and slipped out on to the black streets.

For a long time she walked in circles, coming upon the house many times from different directions, different angles, trying to see something welcoming in it, trying to catch it by surprise so that it would take her in. But it stayed the same. She tried Sean again from a pay phone outside the bank. Still nothing. He would be with Martin by now. They would be drinking together in the pub. Talking. Grace knew their plans.

She went to the city.

Cars hummed and crouched close to the ground. The lights were like punctures in the darkness that seemed to let in some warmth, but did not.

In the lobby of the Shelbourne Hotel she drank coffee and then made an effort at a small whiskey and watched selfconsciously the spinning doors and the rich crowd. She walked around St Stephen's Green twice, looking for a way in. She checked the time too often, so that it seemed to stall. She sat for a while on a bench. Back in the Shelbourne to use the Ladies, she bumped into a woman who asked for a cigarette.

'Give me one.'

'I don't smoke.'

'Bitch.'

She waited at a bus stop and counted nine buses past her. At half eleven, as people streamed out of pubs, she made her way off the Green towards the gay nightclub where Martin had said he was going with his friends. With Sean. The place where they would be, the place where she would see them, see them go in.

She could tell which building it was by the dull thud of music and by the pale reddish glow from the basement. A small neat sign by the door gave its name. There was no one around. She was early.

She had no clear idea of what she would do. She stood in the shadows across the street, close to the wall and the columns of a porch, and looked at the club, feeling furtive and foolish. She could not approach them. She could not let Martin see her. She thought that she might let them go in and then have Sean paged. She thought that she might be able to do that.

It was a good five minutes before anyone arrived, a group of young men who laughed and stamped their feet as they waited for the door to open. The doorman wore an anorak over a dress suit. He looked across the street but did not seem to see her.

For nearly an hour men arrived in couples, groups, sometimes alone. They were mostly young. She huddled, pulling her coat close and folding her arms. They laughed and were loud.

· She was very cold and thinking of leaving when a small car pulled up at the kerb, and Martin jumped out of the front door and Philip jumped out of the back, and the car moved away again with a clipped squeal. She caught a glimpse of Sean in the driver's seat, squinting. She pressed herself into the doorway and followed him with her eyes. He drove up the street, past the turnoff where the other traffic disappeared back towards the Green, and on into the dead end, slowing down. He reversed awkwardly into a large space.

Martin and Philip were already up the steps. They did not look round. Philip seemed to have met someone he knew. Martin's shoulders were hunched, his head pulled low, his hands thrust into his jacket. They moved through the door and Grace waited until she could not see them any more before stepping out of the shadow and down the two steps and into the street. She crossed the road at an angle, the thud of the music and the noise of people loud and solid like a wind against her, pushing her sideways, up on to the pavement, towards the quieter places where Sean had gone.

The shape of him appeared on the footpath and walked briskly towards her. He glanced back at his car and closed his coat, looking up at Grace but not recognising her. She stood and faced him and he looked up again, this time hesitating, stopping. Then he looked around, and approached her slowly.

'Mrs Quinn?'

'I'm glad I got you out here. Before you went inside, I mean.'

He glanced behind him again, cleared his throat.

'Are you all right?' He raised a hand to his mouth, glanced over her shoulder, seemed bewildered.

'I tried to ring you but you'd left to meet Martin. He told me he'd be meeting you. That you'd be coming here. I wanted to talk to you.'

'He's just gone in. Just now.'

She nodded. Sean's breath was grey on the air.

'Did he not see you?'

'No. It was you I wanted to talk to.'

144

There was a pause and Grace waited to be asked what she wanted to talk about. But Sean simply looked at her, and said nothing, and over the minute that they stood like that his nerves seemed to leave him and a half smile formed, and he made a gesture with his arms that invited her to say whatever she wanted.

'You talked to Brady?' she asked, her voice quieter than she had hoped.

'Brady?'

'The policeman. His name is Brady.'

Sean simply nodded.

'When?'

'When?' He scratched his cheek. 'Monday. On the phone. He wouldn't tell me anything.'

'Did you tell Martin that you'd met him?'

He frowned, apologetic.

'Well, yeah, I did. Sorry about that. I didn't want to tell him I'd rung him. He'd have asked why.'

She sniffed. He sniffed. She was too cold – it was not good for her.

'Why?'

He was quiet. Grace looked up at him. He scratched his cheek again.

'Listen,' he said. 'Why don't we go somewhere for a chat? It's cold here. We could drive somewhere else, have a coffee. Actually, why don't we go to my house? We'd be comfortable there, no interruptions. I could make you something to eat and we could have a chat.'

She glanced towards the club. There were still people going in, bunched at the door, a faint steam rising from them, a reddish glow.

'Will they not be expecting you inside?'

'No. They won't even notice.'

'You saw Brady in the pub, didn't you?'

'Yes.'

'You think you know.'

145

He looked at the ground as if embarrassed.

'Come back with me. I'll make something to eat. We can talk. I can drive you home then. Come on.'

Grace paused for a moment and then followed him slowly to his car. He glanced at her every now and then, as if afraid that she would change her mind.

They passed beneath the dark arch of Christ Church and down to the river, and they drove through streets on the north side that Grace did not know. There was a skin on the ground, a thin veil of reflected light and old water, like sweat gone cold in a breeze. They crossed the greasy cobbles of a large square where shattered fruit boxes lay strewn and a group of boys stood at a corner drinking from a brown plastic bottle. Two girls in track suits, their hair bubbling down to their shoulders in dyed ringlets, ran alongside the car for a while. Grace did not understand what they were doing. Then they disappeared.

Sean drove in such a way that Grace asked him whether he'd been drinking.

'No,' he laughed. 'I'm just not very good.'

They came to a red light which he didn't see until the last moment. He braked violently, lurching Grace against her seat belt and stopping the car a good ten yards from the junction. He apologised. Laughed.

There were few cars. They passed the black shadow of a church set back from the road. Grace crouched to see it better, looking across Sean's chest, trying to see the height of the steeples, the top of the stained glass windows. She could not. It rose up too far, the scale of it lost somewhere in the darkness.

'Nearly there,' said Sean. They turned on to a long, undulating tree lined road of large shabby houses and orange lights.

'Where's this?'

'North Circular. It's just here.'

They turned into a crooked cul-de-sac with a cluster of big red-brick houses on either side. Sean pulled into the kerb and switched off the engine.

'Here we are,' he said. Laughed again. They got out of the car.

The garden was a tangle of weeds and rubbish, a small sickly patch that came as no surprise. He locked the car and led her quickly to the front door.

'I apologise if the place is a bit of a mess. I'm not all that domesticated, I do a big clean-up about once a month. I think I'm due one now.'

He hurried ahead of her, switching on lights to reveal a gloomy and rather sparse hall. It was not the house of a young man. A long narrow staircase rose up in front of her, its carpet discoloured and threadbare, and disappeared into a deep black darkness that made her uneasy.

He opened a door and Grace followed him into a small sitting room. There was a comfortable looking three-piece suite, a desk with a computer and piles of papers and books, and, set into a plain, marble fireplace, a television.

He switched on a couple of small lamps and some kind of heater, closed the curtains and took Grace's coat, only to drape it, not very carefully, over the back of a chair by the desk.

'I'll make some coffee, will I? Or tea?'

She shrugged.

'Coffee.'

'Right. You make yourself comfortable. I won't be a minute. Switch on the television or whatever.'

He turned off the main light and left.

Grace took a breath and looked around. Magazines and newspapers littered the floor. Mugs and cups and some plates sat on the desk and on the mantelpiece. There were video tapes lying by the television, but she could not see a video recorder. There was a faint smell of damp. Stale air.

147

She sat in the armchair closest to the heater and waited. It was quiet. Not even traffic. She couldn't hear him. She tried to make herself think about what might be said. What she wanted. But she could not make her mind settle on any one thing. She found herself looking critically at the curtains and wondering if he would bring food. She was hungry. She wondered would she get home before Martin.

He came back eventually, carrying a tray with a pot of coffee, cups and saucers, and a packet of digestive biscuits. He had taken off his coat and wore a tweed jacket that was a size too big for him.

'Here we are.'

He put the tray on the floor and fussed for a while with the cups before running back to the kitchen for spoons and a plate. Then he settled down into the armchair opposite Grace and smiled at her.

'Is it all right?'

'Yes, it's fine.'

'Help yourself to the biscuits.'

'Thank you.'

They sat in silence. Grace decided that she would not be the first to speak. She could not think of what to say. Sean sipped his coffee and did not take his eyes off her. He smiled. He ignored the biscuits. They sat like that for minutes, but Grace did not become uncomfortable. She felt only curious and patient. She was intrigued, fascinated by what might happen, by what might be said. It was as if it was a game. She was infected by his smile and mirrored it. Eventually he sighed.

'Well,' he said. 'I suppose I should tell you about Brady.'

Grace said nothing. She nodded slightly.

'It's nothing, really. I knew him because I'd covered your husband's court case that time. I'd talked to him then. I remembered him. He doesn't remember me, of course. That night in the pub, I saw him come in. I saw him come in, look around, lay eyes on Martin, and turn and go out again. I wasn't absolutely sure. I was about to say it to Martin, but then Philip came rushing back saying you'd gone all funny in the Ladies. Then that thing about thinking you'd seen your husband. That was too odd.'

He paused. Took a sip.

'I didn't believe it.'

'No.'

'So I just started wondering. Why he'd be there. Why you'd react like that.'

'Did you say anything to Martin?'

'No. I didn't. I rang Brady on the Monday. Last Monday.' He smiled. 'He was awful cagey. Wouldn't tell me anything. Hung up when I asked whether you were a suspect.'

Her head lifted a fraction and she could not stop it. Suspect. The word. She flexed her shoulders.

'And that's all, really.'

She nodded.

'Why did you tell Martin that you'd met him?'

'I wanted to bring it up. I don't know. Curiosity. I wanted to know whether he knew anything.'

'Does he?'

Sean tilted his head, hummed out a low noise.

'I don't know what there is to know. He didn't say anything about you, or about Brady. He didn't seem to think about it much. It didn't really register.'

Grace looked at the biscuits. She picked one up and put it down again. She sighed. She could leave. Her back had begun to ache, a twitching somewhere in her shoulder tensed the muscles of her upper body.

'What makes you think I might have been a suspect?'

'Aren't you?'

She wondered whether Martin had told him that Brady had been to see her. What could she tell him of that? Nothing. She could not say that Brady knew and did not want her to be caught. She could not tell him that. It would make him her only enemy.

149

'No.'

Sean frowned, and sat back in his chair.

'Well. Should you be? Did you run over your husband?'

'Oh no.'

She took a sip of her coffee and some of it dribbled down her chin and she wiped at it and smiled. In her back she felt a curious tightening, as if a spring was wound, a small force gathered.

'Did you know,' she said, 'that I had a son called Sean?'

'Really?'

'Yes. He died. He drowned. He was only three at the time.'

'I'm sorry.'

'He drowned out the back, in about two inches of rain water at the bottom of a ditch. My husband took his body and put it in the back of the car and drove away. I don't know where he went. To the doctor, I suppose.'

She thought for a moment.

'It was a different car then, of course,' she said.

Sean looked at her and looked away. She was talking about the wrong thing.

'My son would have been about your age probably. By now.'

'How did he drown?'

She twisted the cup in the saucer, making a scraping squeal that she felt in her teeth. She grimaced.

'Oh, I don't like that,' she laughed.

'Did you kill your husband?'

'Which question do you want me to answer?'

'Whichever one you like.'

His eyes stayed on her, but she could meet them for only a moment. She looked down at her coffee. She swirled it around a little and watched it come close to the lip of the cup.

'Sean drowned by accident. It wasn't my fault. My husband blamed me, but it wasn't my fault. Sean just came

150

out to the line when I went to get the clothes. It was dark. He fell into the ditch and I didn't notice until it was too late. Every mother takes risks like that, a hundred times a day. Don't they? They go to answer the phone, or they leave the cooker alone and they go to set the table. It was an accident.'

She took a breath and scratched her forehead. She knew that she would tell him now. She could think of no reason not to. He sat in front of her, his eyes unblinking, his elbows on his knees, leaning towards her, his strange tweed jacket bunched at the shoulders, waiting for her to tell him. He had guessed. He would not let it go. She thought that perhaps he would nod, and be happy to have his suspicions confirmed, and leave it at that. If she told it well. Her back hurt.

'My husband took it badly. He changed after it. He lost interest in things. He began to sell the land, small bits of it, to our neighbours. He sold off machinery too, and I thought for a while that he was going to sell the lot of it, but he didn't. He kept enough to make it worth while passing on. But he hadn't the heart for it. He started drinking. He had drunk before of course, but he took to it now – it was what he did. Over the years he seemed to just forget about me. It was as if I wasn't there. Sometimes he noticed.'

She paused.

Sean began to say something, but had to stop and clear his throat.

'Did he beat you?' he asked her, very quietly.

'Yes, but that's not an excuse.'

'For what?'

'He would beat me when he drank. Not much at first, just a slap or a push. But it got worse as time went on. It would stop for a while, when something good happened, or something bad. A friend of his died. They'd been close as boys. He was fine then, like someone who had got a shock, who was recovering from something. He would bring home cakes and make tea for the three of us and we would sit and watch the television. It was like he was sorry. But he never said so. He never talked about it. Then eventually one night he went out and got drunk and came home and beat me. It was as if he had spent a long time trying to stop himself, but once it had started again he couldn't stop it. After Martin told him, told him about himself, and left, then he began to beat me very badly, drunk or sober. He would punch, and he would throw me. He could pick me up and throw me.'

She stopped and remembered it, flying through the air of the house like a tiny ghost, feeling the brief safety of not being touched.

'God,' breathed Sean. 'Did you not get help?'

Grace looked at him and smiled. She did not know what he was thinking of. She was afraid to answer him. She did not want to hear now that there was something she could have done to make everything all right. She could not bear to hear that. She waited to be asked why she hadn't left him. She tried to think of answers but there was only a muddle of different things. Because of Martin. And after Martin had gone? But he did not ask her.

'Go on,' he said.

'Well. It just went on and on. After Martin had left he sold off more land. There's barely nothing left now. Then he killed the girl. You know about that.'

'Yes. He should have got a longer sentence.'

She nodded.

'A lot of people hated him then. He got rid of the phone. They would ring up at all hours and say things to him. Then when he came out of prison he got rid of the television as well. I think it was because of the adverts. The drink driving adverts. I don't know.'

She sipped from her coffee but it had gone cold. She put the cup and saucer down on the table and sat back into the armchair. She tried to think of what to tell him next. It seemed remarkably simple now, not at all complicated, as if it had somehow been exaggerated in her mind. It embarrassed her slightly. There should have been more to it.

'He began to hit me again. He started to kick.'

She stopped, unsure how relevant this was. It was no excuse.

'Go on,' said Sean again. Still sitting forward, looking at her.

'He would get me on the floor and kick at me with his boots. Not in the face, or at least, he would try to avoid my face. He would aim for my stomach and my chest. It was the same thing, you see. He came out of prison and tried to stop himself, and for a couple of months he didn't go near me. But I could see the tension building up in him. I could see it in his face, in the way he came into the room at night and got into the bed. It was something in his silence. Then one night he broke something in the kitchen and it was as if that was the end of the silence. He came in and kicked me. It was worse than before. Maybe if he had beaten me all the time – not tried to stop himself – maybe then it would never have become so bad. But he was fighting with himself and he was losing, and it made him angry. It made him angry that he beat me and that made him beat me more.'

She smiled.

'He was one of those men,' she said. 'Everybody's heard about them by now. For a long time I thought he was the only one in the world. But there are thousands of them. Thousands.'

She looked at Sean and he nodded and coughed slightly.

'Did you kill him?' he asked her.

She met his gaze and nodded slowly.

'Did you?' he asked again.

She nodded.

'Say it, Mrs Quinn.'

She wanted to laugh at that. He sounded like a chat show host. His face was a battle between concern and horror, but his voice was thrilled.

'Yes,' she said, looking away. 'It was the same place where he killed the girl. I drove the car at him.'

She was quiet for a moment, and she could hear Sean's breathing. She felt almost giddy. Her back had relaxed. She was afraid that she wanted to laugh out loud. She fought it, aware that it must have looked as if she was fighting back tears. She didn't know which it was. She managed a deep breath and looked up.

Sean was pale. He stared at her. His forehead was damp.

'Jesus.'

'You knew.'

'They'll know by the car. They'll do tests on it.'

'It was ruined before. It was the same car as he drove at the girl. It might not give me up.'

'Mrs Quinn,' he said. 'They'll tear it apart. It'll give you up.'

She shrugged.

'There's nothing I can do about it.'

She had relaxed. Her back was easy, she could not feel it. Her steady hands were linked together. She breathed and regarded him. He had not thought this far ahead. He fiddled with a spoon in the sugar and seemed to be trying to think of what to say.

'Tell me about that night.'

Grace frowned. She did not want to.

'Did you leave the house with the intention of killing him?'

'Yes.' She looked down at her hands.

'How long had you planned it?'

'I don't know. I thought of it months before. But I don't know when I started to think that I might actually do it. Maybe just that night.'

154

'Did something happen that night?'

'No. It was cold and clear. I don't know.'

'Why didn't you just leave him?'

'He was useless on his own. He couldn't do a thing for himself.'

She heard the breath of Sean and looked up to find him staring at her, his mouth open, looking at her as if she was mad. She began to redden. She should not be telling him. It was wrong. It was none of his business. She found herself suddenly thinking how bad she would be under police questioning. She would make a fool of herself.

She was about to say something by way of a correction, to clarify. She nearly said 'No, seriously . . .', but stopped herself and tried to think of something else. Then, in the silence, still, her eyes unfocused on the space between them, Grace heard a sudden, sharp, metallic click.

She looked at Sean. He coughed and reached inside his jacket somewhere.

'Do you want more coffee?' he asked, nervously, pulling his hand out of his jacket with a jerk, and standing up.

Grace sought his eyes.

'Are you taping me?'

He bit his lip and looked down at her, hesitated.

'I'm sorry,' he said. 'I should have asked. It's a habit really. I promise I won't write a word without your permission. And it'd be from your point of view. Sympathetic. I promise.'

Grace stood up. She wanted to hit him.

'Give me the tape.'

'Please, Mrs Quinn. Let me do this for you. It's such a great story. People would see it your way, really they would. You said there were thousands of men like your husband. That means that there's thousands of women who know exactly what it is you've had to go through.'

'Give me the tape.' She put out her hand.

155

'The paper would pay for your story. You need that now.'

'I want the tape.'

He turned and walked to the door.

'You're going to be caught. You know that. The car. Why do you need the tape? It's a way of telling your own story. I can do that for you.'

His voice had changed slightly and Grace knew that he was nervous.

'It's not as if you're going to deny anything, is it? When Brady comes for you. Are you? If I gave you the tape then I'd be in an awkward position, Mrs Quinn. I'd know the truth. What would you have me do then? Forget about it? I'd have to protect myself, Mrs Quinn. Tell somebody. Do you see? I'd know that you've killed your husband and I'd feel obliged to report it, and that would mean that you'd have no time left. They'd arrest you immediately. Whereas if I keep the tape then you can decide yourself when to go to Brady. Do you see?'

She withdrew her hand and looked down at the floor. She didn't understand what he was saying. Her back was clamped with a presence. It bit into her. Her head reeled. She thought for a moment that she was in Martin's house. She was about to tell Sean to leave. Then she looked up and saw the computer screen and her coat on the chair, and the television in the fireplace, and for a moment she thought she imagined it, but no, it was there. She thought that if she smashed the screen he would let her go, that the sound of glass breaking would get her out. Like Martin in the kitchen. It had been her son she had heard at her door, not her husband. Her husband was dead in the ground near Sean. She looked up and it was Sean that she saw looking back at her. She had told him what she had done. She had wanted to say sorry to him for turning her back just for a moment. But this was a different Sean, who was interested in something else, who stared at her with a look that was not right.

She picked up her coat and walked past him out into the hall.

'Mrs Quinn, can we not talk some more?'

She looked at him blankly. She didn't know what he meant.

'Or will I drive you home?'

'No,' she whispered. 'Thank you.'

She could not understand it. She was in a house somewhere, with a friend of her son's. She did not remember how she had got there. There was a confusion in her. She had done something wrong. She had said something. She had said it to a stranger. She felt as if she had been robbed, or had stolen and been caught.

She fiddled with the front door, trying to get it open. The thing on her back slowed her. She tried to shake it off.

'Let me call you a taxi, please.'

He leaned over her and she ducked, and he withdrew his hand again.

'Sorry. Just let me call a taxi. It's freezing, Mrs Quinn.'

'No, I want to go.'

He opened the door and she walked out into the cold of the street. She clutched her coat to her chest. She could not put it on. She glanced back and saw him standing in the doorway, watching her. She hurried to the end of the road and out of sight before stopping, breathless, unable still to understand what had happened.

She could not clear her head, even though the cold hit her like thrown water. She was uncertain whether she had confessed or been found out; whether she had made a mistake herself, or had been tricked. Panic rang through her like a storm of bells and she could not stop it. She pressed her back to a wall and tried to rub off the machine that was attached to her, tried to break its grip. She watched the cars flash past, flinching at the noise of them and clenching herself against the silence that followed. She started to walk one way before turning and walking the other, stamping at the ground as if trying to put out flames, rushing past the dark windows of tall houses towards the smell of the river, wanting in her soul to be lost amongst the black streets and the yellow lights and the numb danger of the city.

She tried for wrong turns. She rushed into alleys and the still darkness of church grounds. She lingered by the loose bricks of derelict houses and the broken glass of empty sites where she could hear snoring and the rustle of dogs in the shadows. There were voices that called out to her as she made her way, appeals for the chance to do her harm. She did not flee them, but she strode on with her head down and used her mind like a tunnel of knives. She ran through it in the hope of emerging.

At junctions she would keep her blind eyes to the ground and step off the kerb and cross the road without looking, like one who was protected by her disbelief.

MARTIN

She watched him with a steady eye through the darkness, sitting on the steps of a bricked-up house across the street, her head level with his. He could see his own breath on the air, but hers was invisible. He could make out only her face, and a hand which held together the corners of a filthy blanket at her neck. A dark bottle stood on the step beside her feet. He returned her gaze and smiled at her. Poor woman. He raised his hand and gave a little wave. Something shook beneath the rags. She let out a roar that stopped him.

'Don't you wave your wanker's claw at me.'

'Christ,' Martin whispered, and stuck his head down and strode briskly towards the house.

'Fucker fucker fucker,' she shouted, her voice like boots on gravel. 'Fucker fucker fucker fucker.'

He was afraid that she would draw attention to him, but the street was empty. He opened the door and quickly glanced back at her hunched shadow before stepping into the warmth of the house. He stood in silence in the dark, listening for the rattle of her voice. She had stopped.

He was a little drunk. The silence was a buzzing sound that surrounded him and seemed to grow louder the longer he left it unbroken. In the kitchen he took a carton of orange juice from the fridge and sat at the table and drank.

Nothing was fixed. In his mind now he was able to think of Henry and not spin with it, not find his eyes closed and his hands open like a man falling, the ground coming up.

He was able just to think of him. Think of him and then turn to something else, no drag of notions, no flailing. He knew why too. He knew it was because of what he had done. A little guilty store to feed on.

They had talked on the telephone like ordinary people.

He knew it wouldn't last. He had known it as soon as he'd put the phone down. He'd known it all day long, his mother grating at him. He had known it when he went out to drink. He had gained a respite, that was all, in a way that he could not, would not, do again.

His mother grating. She was staying in Dublin. Staying for the long run, settling in, getting her own place. He felt it like sandpaper.

He wondered whether she doubted Henry's existence. Maybe she thought that Martin had made him up. Maybe he had. Parts of him. He would have to make it clear to her that she could not stay. That she would have to get her own place soon. He could not stand to have her beside him. She made him doubt. She unsettled him. She startled him with her very presence. Her unlikely life still linked to his. All that oddness and that awful love.

He finished the orange juice. Went to the bathroom. He might talk to her tomorrow. Spell it out. Now, he was drunk and he was tired. He could not think. Everything seemed stark. There was only the gap, and his mother upstairs with her future thrown out in front of her, surrounding him, encircling like a border. The hum in his head.

He stood by the sink and stared at himself. Cold water covered his hands. He had somehow become aware of the distance between love and hate, and of the shortest route from one to the other. Only months before, only weeks, he would have held up both Henry and his mother as the two people for whom his feelings were uncluttered, distinct, strong. He had loved them. And he could not have imagined any ordeal that could have changed that. He still loved them. But he had not imagined absence. And he had not imagined presence. They had swopped their allotted places and left him spinning.

The humming in his head would not die down.

SEAN

He drove slowly and the police stopped him, and the policeman leaned his head through the window and smelled his breath.

He shone the headlights slowly over the whole length of the North Circular Road. He edged down the quays, both ways, and thought he saw her once, on Aughrim Street, rattling the closed iron gates of the Church of the Holy Family. But when he got closer there was no one there.

He drove to Martin's house and rang the doorbell. Then he sat in the car and waited, and saw Martin stagger in, chased by the scream of a drunk hidden in the shadows. Eventually, he started the engine and crawled home, uncertain, blinking. He was stopped again on Dame Street – again the head in the window, the smell of sweat and hair oil.

He listened to the tape. Her voice – tinny and distant. Some words were lost to static and the rustling of his jacket. His own voice was obscene. Breathy and deep and the accent squeezed out. He sounded like a man twice his age. He sounded fat.

He copied it out, shorthand, into his notebook. Then he took the notebook into the front room and typed it all into the computer. He could use it. He knew he could use it. He could see the shape of the story. He thought of openers. He would string out some facts. Then a quote. Where she says that he threw her.

There was the question of what she would tell Martin. If she would tell him anything at all. If she was there. And there was the question of Martin's reaction. Sean knew that he would have to be honest now, whatever way it went. She had, after all, approached him. She had talked freely. He had not pressured her. You could hear it. It was on the tape. Tone of voice.

His fingers played on the keys, and her words appeared in front of him as if pressed out of the air. He closed his eyes and wondered what he was doing.

Later, lying awake on his bed, warm in the cold, he thought of Martin in the sauna, in his towel. He thought of Martin's world, pressed into the space between himself and Henry, no wider than a bad night, no worse than that. Sean decided that Martin would not believe what his mother had done. He would not believe it.

But he would understand, inside, deep inside, from where no voice reported, how it had happened.

GRACE

Grace stood in the shadow of the church, holding her coat close to her, keeping out the darkness and the cold. It was the darkness that she did not like.

Above her the steeple stretched to a point that she could imagine better than she could see. She wondered how small it was, how sharp, how still in the wind. She wondered how to get there. Not literally. In another way, the way in which the steeple got there, the evolving slate. The higher the smaller.

Her mind huddled next to the ideas of falling and rising. She could not gather in the edges of either. She could not put a value on her progress – could not tell which way she was heading. Falling or rising.

She closed her eyes and felt the cold air on her eyelids and saw the town of Cootehill stretched out below the church like the spill of a quarry. It was a trick of the night to make it so black; to give it a sound like an engine turning over, to rock it slightly back and forth like a tar boat in a still harbour. She could see the White Horse, could see the old Protestant church at the edge of the woods with Coote's Castle grey in the distance. She could see the length of Market Street rising to meet the road from Monaghan town.

Grace balanced on the steeple, the ball of her right foot stuck fast to the pin of God. She whirled like a weather vane in the black wind and saw Brady's Mart and the road home. She saw the lakes and the white houses and the narrow place where the world had become small and quick and marked on her mind like a scar. She fixed on that.

She could not bring back the sounds now. She could not hear the noise of the tyres or the clip of the exhaust on the cold ground. She could not hear that strange dull thud of the impact – the popping sound that had brought her to a halt by the side of the narrow road, with her husband dead behind her. Everything was quiet as she ran through it. She saw it all but heard nothing. Only the wind around her ears and the drum of her blood as it circled her.

Grace opened her eyes, and pressed her back against the door of the church, looking out at the Dublin street that glowed orange in the darkness.

Rain started slowly and she found that she was not sheltered. The wind carried it into her face, and as it became heavier she felt that she should move. She was not quite sure where she was. Somewhere near the river.

At the church gate she turned and looked back up at the stone and the slate and the shadow that had hauled her in. She did not understand why her mind was filled with churches. There was a connection that had been made somewhere inside her that she could not see. She was scared of it, afraid that it indicated desperation, afraid that she was losing all sense. People reach for God when they have nothing else to hold them. People in small boats. They throw a line out into the night, and they tell themselves that the blank expanse of water is really God and his mercy, and that the useless splash their line makes is really the sound of God clutching their prayers and turning his soft face towards them.

A drunk swayed at the corner, spitting into the rain. He eyed her as she passed him and seemed about to speak, but Grace moved on and left him where he was. She could feel him looking at her back, could hear the soft noise of his mouth as he hovered between speaking and spitting and settled in the end on a rattling cough.

'Good night now, darlin',' he called. 'Sweet dreams.'

Grace returned the wish beneath her breath and pushed herself on into the rain; on into the rain without turning.

Between the wind and the water there were times of great silence, when Grace settled herself, exhausted, against the warmth of wet trees. She found an expanse of parkland that seemed to stretch both away from her and towards her; that seemed to roll beneath her feet as she stood still. The night was not dark there, or rather it was a country darkness, all starlight and the spray of the moon.

There was nobody about.

She followed a road that rose and fell, staying high above the sound of the river, overlooking the rooftops at the edge of the city. Street lights pinned the ink of the ground to the ink of the sky, and in the distance the rain hid the mountains.

Grace heard her feet on the pavement, but she was tired now, and did not feel her footsteps. She carried on, unsure of where to go, and not really caring. There was a blank space in her mind. It was as if everything had been pushed into corners, away from the place of concentration, becoming hazy and unfamiliar, edges of a floor cleared to dance. And she danced. There was a tumbling of songs and a succession of memories that signified nothing. There were faces that swam into view, faces that she did not recognise until they had disappeared again. Her back was numb.

A car passed her by, slowing slightly as it drew level, then accelerating away again. She saw it turn at a cross-roads at the bottom of the hill and roar back towards her and past her, leaving her gasping at the sound of it and the flash of it and the spinning sensation it created in her head and her stomach and the tiny pause, the expectation, the bracing of the muscles that shuddered through her quickly and made her think of home.

On she went. Down the hill to a small dark valley. To her left she could see a closed iron gate and street lights beyond. To her right the road led into darkness. She moved ahead, upwards between steep hills, on a road that curled its way towards a patch of rushing sky.

She turned a corner and found herself on a slow incline cut into the side of a hill that seemed to overlook all the lights of the city that hovered and danced between Grace and the mountains. They were orange and white, clustered and scattered like sparks on an old fire. Street lights and house lights and a few creeping headlights that dipped and disappeared and re-emerged, shimmering. She watched it all for a while, thinking that perhaps she could pick out the river in the near distance. There was a sound like running water, or like tyres on a Tarmac road.

Another car passed her. It slowed down, and for a moment Grace thought that it was the same one as before, but it was not. It paused beside her and seemed to hesitate, before accelerating off down the hill and around the corner. Grace watched it go, saw the red lights pulse as the driver braked.

She walked on. The rain had stopped now and she could see the cloud thinning overhead as it raced towards the sea. It was cold, but she was still warm from walking and did not mind. She wondered how long it was before dawn. She wanted it to be a long time. She was disconnected here. Except for the cars. The cars shocked her. She thought she heard another. A slide of loose metal, kept from sparking the black ground by the spin of rubber, by rings of soft waste, four circles of skin. It was not good. The sound of a car coming towards her on a dark road under the stars. Not now.

She left the path and set off across a strip of black grass that rose through trees to a wide open space where she could feel the speed of the wind, the freshness of it. And she could feel the dampness spreading through her shoes, chilling her small feet. Her little feet. Her steps.

Her father took her by the hand and did not alter his pace. She had to jog every few yards to keep up with him. They passed the corner house where Mr Taylor was clipping the hedge, wearing a ragged straw hat that sat askew on his ginger hair like something that had fallen out of a tree and landed on him. Her father nodded, and Mr Taylor nodded back. He glanced at Grace and she looked away, jogging a little to hide behind her father's long legs.

'He's a demon,' said her father, and Grace looked back to see if Mr Taylor had heard, but he was back into the rhythm of his work, his mouth set in a grimace that tensed at every clip.

'Why?'

'Killed his wife.'

Her father did not look down at her, but straight ahead, his shoulders back and his chest thrust forward. Old soldier. He would shine his shoes every morning on the kitchen table. Her mother would tell him to do it some-where else, and he would promise to, but every morning Grace saw the tiny marks of black polish beside the teapot and the sugar bowl.

'Did he?'

'As good as. Might as well have taken those shears to her and bricked her up in the basement. A thousand bloody pieces. That's all she was at the end of it.'

'Why?'

'That's enough now, Grace.'

He stopped at the kerb and tightened his grip on her hand as he looked from left to right. She did the same, aware that he was keeping an eye on her.

'Is it all clear then, Grace?'

'All clear.'

'Off we go then.'

They crossed to the shops; the butcher's first for sausages, and then to the grocery for milk and butter and bread and *The Times*. Grace didn't like to hold the newspaper. It made her hands grubby. But her father insisted that she did. He said that if it went into the net bag with the groceries the print would be smudged and he wouldn't be able to read a word here and there and he'd be misinformed.

'Can't afford to be misinformed, Grace,' he'd say, shaking his head slowly. 'I can't afford to be thinking one thing while the world knows another, now, can I?'

Grace folded the newspaper carefully so that the masthead was halved, and then folded it again and held it between her outstretched hands as if she was measuring something. She kept it away from her dress and followed her father.

He teased her by walking past the cake shop, rubbing his chin, murmuring that he knew he'd forgotten something, what could it be, what on earth ... And then he would snap his fingers and smile at her and she would laugh. 'Cakes, Grace. Cakes! What kind of child are you, forgetting cakes? Your sister would have bawled us out if we'd gone home without cakes. Cakes it is.'

And he would let her choose, and she would always choose the cream pastries with strawberry jam. And Mrs Booth would chat to her father and always at the end ask how Mrs Wilson was. He would smile and tell her that Mrs Wilson was just fine, that she was well, and that he would give her Mrs Booth's regards.

Her father walked with the net bag in one hand and the cake box in the other, held out from him like a waiter's tray. They crossed the road again and passed by Mr Taylor's house at the corner. He was crouched down behind his hedge putting clippings into a sack. Grace looked at him, trying to see his face, but it was hidden from her. She saw the shears lying on the grass beside him and wondered if they were sharp enough.

Her mother lay in bed, dozing. She was propped up slightly on her pillows and her mouth was open. Her hands had fallen to her sides, leaving her book to close itself and lose her page. Grace watched her, stepping quietly into the room and pushing her feet slowly over the thin carpet until she was beside the bed, looking down at her mother and knowing that it was wrong to watch her sleeping. It was the wrong way round.

Her mother stirred and opened her eyes and smiled.

'Hello, Grace.'

'Hello.'

She sat up, knocking the prayer book to the floor. Grace picked it up and put it on the small table and handed her mother the glass of water and helped her hold it and took it away again when she had finished.

'Would you like a cup of tea? Daddy is making some.'

'No thank you, dear.'

'I could bring it up to you.'

'No, that's all right. I'll maybe have some later. Did you go to the shops?'

She patted the bed beside her and Grace sat up on it, leaning her head against her mother, feeling the delicate warmth and the weakness.

'Yes. We saw Mr Taylor.'

Her mother nodded but didn't say anything. Grace waited and listened to the air that came and went from her mother's tiny body, sensing again the backwards way that things had arranged themselves.

'What happened to Mrs Taylor?'

'Oh, she's dead now.'

'But how?'

She felt her mother move slightly, and thought that the question made her uncomfortable, but her mother sighed and answered in an easy voice.

'She had a bad heart, I think. She just collapsed one day, very suddenly.'

'Oh.'

Grace shifted, lifting her legs so that they rested on the edge of the bed, careful to leave her feet in mid air.

'Did Mr Taylor kill her?'

'Grace! What makes you ask that? Of course he didn't kill her.'

'Daddy said he did.'

There was an intake of breath and a short silence, and Grace felt her mother stiffen.

'That man!' she said, angrily. 'He doesn't know what he's talking about. Pay no attention to him, Grace. He imagines these things and then he says them and before he knows it he's got himself in trouble.'

'But why would he imagine that?'

'Because he's an old fool.'

Grace twisted her neck and looked up into her mother's face. Her lips were pressed together tightly and she was shaking her head.

'You don't mind him, dear.'

She looked down at her daughter.

'He's making it up. I promise. He doesn't like Mr Taylor. It's because Mrs Taylor went away and Mr Taylor went and got her back and there was a scene.'

'Where?'

'In the street.'

'What happened?'

'Oh Grace, really, it's not our business.'

'Did she die in the street?'

'No, no. She died later, about a month later. But it had nothing to do with anything. She had a bad heart. Poor woman.'

Grace thought for a moment. She imagined what a scene in the street might be like. She tried to picture Mrs Taylor

171

falling over and dying. There would have been no pieces then, her father had just made that up.

'You go and have your tea, dear. Come up and see me later. Tell your sister to come up as well. And tell your father he's an old fool.'

Grace stood up and walked away from the bed. At the door she stopped and looked back. Her mother smiled, pushing the hair away from her eyes. In the dim light she was like a painting. She seemed to shine out of the centre of the bed and the centre of the room, as if everything was within her grasp.

'Go on.'

'Daddy didn't get a cake for you.'

'That's all right, dear, I don't want a cake. You go and enjoy yours. And no more talk of the Taylors, do you hear?'

Grace nodded. On the stairs she remembered the times she had been sick in bed and her mother had come and sat with her. She remembered how it had felt to lie there and hear her mother going downstairs again, to hear her reach the hall and open the kitchen door; and then the silence that came next, like holding your hands against your ears. That had been the worst part.

Ahead of her it loomed up, grey in the darkness. She laughed. She stopped and stood and looked at it and laughed out loud, slapping her thigh like a clown. Wherever she went she could not get away from it. It followed her and mimicked the shape of her shadow, long on the grass and sharp-edged like a fallen fence.

Why?

It was huge. It seemed to cut the clouds that drifted overhead, seemed to hang stars from its arms, and seemed at times to move, as if it worked the wind. Grace tried for a while simply to look at it, confront it, take it in; without wondering what it was for, or why it had waited for her, or why it had dragged her through the cold air of morning and the wet streets and the wet grass, punctuating her progress.

It was a cross. It must have been eighty feet high, set into a shaped mound and overlooking the blank expanse of land as if the world was ordered by signs and symbols and by structures left in clearings. Why had they chosen the cross? Why not the chalice or the staff? Why not the stone rolled back from the tomb? Why not the temple curtain?

Smiling and shaking her head, Grace approached it, crossing the empty grey ribbon of a road and picking her way over the wet ground, her feet now sore and leaden. The cross was white, and plain and unadorned. Behind it there was a line of trees, but they were small and black and merged together and she could not tell what shape they were. The wind whistled slightly, hitting her from the left, from the west she thought.

There was a cross that marked her son's grave. She was sure of it. It was a small cross, a child's shape, a tiny marker in a throng of adult tombstones. She had never seen it, not yet. But it was building itself inside her, creating its own image from the smallest parts of the countless churches that had sprung up on her in the flight from home. Now here it was magnified in the darkness, held up before her, almost offered.

At the foot of the small grassy hill that held it, Grace sat on the ground and stared up at the right angles that spelled out her son's name on the rushing sky. She read the letters and thought of where she had come from and where she was and knew that where she belonged was the place in between. Caught in the gap. She would not escape it.

A light rain started, touching her cheeks and her hands. She stretched her legs out in front of her and prised off her shoes and felt the pain in her feet ease a little, seeping out into the dark air.

She remembered the first time they had made love. He

had taken her to a field, a building site, a cluttered space at the edge of the city. There had been a railway track close by. They had sat there in the cold for an hour or more, not really talking. He had put his arm around her then and kissed her and she had felt the strength of her own body as it rose to him. She had felt the stinging, shuddering sensation that ran through her like a sound. She had lifted herself to him. He fumbled with clothes and with a contraceptive, cursing in the darkness as she ran her hands over the silhouette of his face, her mouth open, her eyes open. He had come towards her then, a mask on his features like a white sheet, a blankness that was hard to the touch. She tried to kiss him but his mouth was closed. She had felt the small pain then, and the rushing of lights and the short absence of the world, the closing off of her life. And then the falling, the spinning down and the sudden stop.

She had stayed where she was, her back to the ground, unsure whether or not it was over. He had stood up and wiped himself with clumps of grass and laughed out loud and slapped his leg and told her he loved her and that she was a great girl.

Above her now there was the quick sky and the giant cross. She lay there, motionless, letting the rain find her open mouth, resting her hands on the cold earth.

She thought: If somebody comes and finds me and asks me who I am, I will tell them that my name is Grace and I have fallen off the cross.

She laughed at that.

The sky brightened in the east. There was a straight road that pointed towards the city, its way lined with pretty lights and fog in the trees. A few cars, taxis mostly, passed in either direction, some very slowly, others at speed.

Grace stumbled once, and was careful not to stumble again. She was very tired. Her hair and her clothes were wet, and she could feel that blisters had formed on her feet. The wind and rain had stopped, but the cold had sharpened. She watched frost form on the path where she walked.

She came eventually to the last of it, where stubby pillars marked the entrance, where the road fell into the city streets and the greenery stopped.

A short distance away there was a line of closed shops, and a small open café. There were taxis parked outside, and through the window she could see the drivers huddled over teas and newspapers in the warm light.

She went in and ordered a full breakfast and bought a paper and sat at a cramped table at the back. She sighed and eased her feet out of her shoes and her arms out of her coat. She closed her eyes briefly and knew that she would sleep if she let herself.

She ran her hands slowly through her hair, pushing it back off her face and squeezing water from it. She could feel the water trickle gently down her neck, tickling her, causing her to shiver and feel the ache in her shoulders. She needed a hot bath and a quiet bed. She needed to sleep. She could not go back to Martin's.

Her breakfast arrived and she poured herself tea and ate hungrily. She laid out the newspaper and saw the pages stamped with the letter X. It was everywhere. It looked strange to Grace, not like a letter at all. It was scattered through the text like a printing fault or a new symbol.

The words were cautious and slow, and Grace had soon lost the thread of them. It was not just her exhaustion. They were small and inadequate next to the enigmatic figure, the cross fallen sideways, the slanted silence of it. Nothing she read could tell her what had happened, or what would happen next. All was confusion. This shape had appeared amongst them, this hieroglyph. It was something discovered, revealed. Oddly familiar. There were no explanations.

She saw Sean's name and stiffened. She read the first

few lines and slowly relaxed. It was about politicians – about their reactions. She leafed through the rest of the paper to see if he had written anything else. There were two more articles, both on the X case. Certain words appalled her.

She searched for something about herself, about the death of her husband, about Detective Brady, about the thing she had done. There was nothing. She did not allow herself the illusion that it was forgotten. She ate her food and asked for more tea and tried to warm the chill inside her. She was afraid to think. She was tired. And there were things she could not remember about herself.

The X stared out at her from the folded newspaper. She closed her eyes and saw it still. Martin would be sleeping. He would be warm and sleeping. Or he would be awake, frantic, telephoning his friends. Telephoning Sean. She did not know what her son would do when he found out. She could not predict. It was pointless to try. She thought instead of him sleeping, of his silent body, snug, his gentle breath in the gentle light, the warmth of his room. She watched him, while her husband, behind her, walked through the house as if blind, his hands on the walls. She stood with folded arms and watched her son.

The noise of two men laughing snapped her awake. She shivered. The light had grown. She needed to sleep.

MARTIN

In the morning there was nothing to wake him until a car began to rev its engine in the street below. He rolled on to his back and took his time. He had escaped with a minor headache only. A dry mouth. The light in the room gave no trouble, and he lay for a while with his eyes on the clock until it reached midday.

He could not find his mother.

Her bed was made and her window closed and her room generally neat and undisturbed. She was not in the front room or the kitchen. He knocked lightly on the bathroom door, and called her before trying the handle. Unlocked, empty. He could not see her coat anywhere, or her handbag, or her keys.

He assumed that she had gone to buy a paper. There was a light rain falling, so he doubted that she would be long, but after a slow breakfast and a quick shower he remained on his own. There was no sign of her.

By half-past one he had begun to worry. He wondered what to do, what procedure to follow, and could think of nothing. His mother did not know anybody in Dublin, as far as he knew, so there was no one he could ring. He could not think of any single place where she was likely to be. He looked around the kitchen and the front room and the hall for a note. Perhaps she had left one and it had been blown under a chair. He looked in the kitchen bin in case he had thrown it out. He lifted the telephone.

In her bedroom her clothes still hung in the wardrobe, her suitcase was still under the bed.

He looked again for a note. For something. He moved as methodically as he could from the kitchen to the hall to the front room, trying all the time to think of her as he had last seen her – her words, her demeanour. There was something that eluded him.

As he stood by the telephone, looking at it distractedly, it rang. It made him jump.

'Hello?'

'Good morning Martin.'

'Sean?' He did not want to hear from Sean now.

'How are you?'

'Fine. Listen, I can't talk now, can I ring you back?'

'What's wrong?'

'Nothing. I'll ring you back, okay?'

'Is your Mum there?'

Martin thought for a moment.

'Why?' he asked.

'Can I talk to her?'

'About what?'

'Is she there?'

'Why?'

"Cos I want to talk to her.'

'Why do you want to talk to her?'

'Oh stop it, Martin. Is she there or isn't she?'

'Why wouldn't she be?'

'Well, can I talk to her then?'

He looked out through the window, leaning forward slightly to glance up the street, looking for his mother, half-expecting to see the beggar woman, or the drunk, or whatever she was, crouching in her doorway. He saw no one. The wind blew paper along the pavement.

'She isn't here, Sean.'

'Where is she?'

'At the shops.'

He could see Sean with his face scrunched up, suspicious.

'Did she go back there last night?'

'How do you know she was out?'

'Because I met her.'

'What? Where?'

'She didn't go back, sure she didn't?'

Martin had sat down without realising it. He found
himself now staring at the television screen, the colour of
wet concrete.

'I don't understand,' he said, very quietly. 'Where is she?'

'I'll come over, okay? Give me half an hour.'

Martin heard the phone go dead. He put back the
receiver and stared at it and wondered what he was supposed to be doing. He was aware, vaguely, that some kind
of crisis was occurring, but he did not know what it was
about. It was not simply that his mother was missing.
There was something going on that he could not quite see.
He felt like a child, unable to tell what was meant by
certain words. But he could hear the urgency in the voices.
The panic.

His mother was missing. That made no sense. It was not
among his list of things that could go wrong in life.

.

SEAN

He had slept well and it bothered him. Now he drove slowly for fear of driving fast, and regarded the streets with suspicion, checking faces, looking into lanes and grey doorways. What had he done?

Martin opened the door to him, pale and lips parted, wanting to rush him, asking him, 'What? What is it? What happened?', and Sean could not answer, could only move from room to room, checking, just in case.

Then he drank water and paced the kitchen and told Martin everything. About Brady being in the pub. About ringing Brady.

'You didn't meet him?'

'No.'

About Martin's mother in the street, about driving her to his place, about talking to her. Talking.

'About what?'

He was so pale Sean thought he was dying. His face like paper, only his darting eyes alive. How could he tell him this?

'Do you not know?'

Martin blinked. His hands fluttered.

'Did you not guess?'

'What?' he breathed, his lips not moving.

'About your father.'

He would not follow. He looked lost. Sean turned away from him because he thought it would be easier that way. He looked out of the window at the concrete that was slowly darkening in the rain. He could see the cold in the air. It was in the shape of the soil in the borders, lying like rubble against the grey walls.

'I thought of it first when I saw Brady in the pub. And saw how your mother reacted. She killed him. Your father. She ran him over.'

There wasn't a sound. He left it for a minute and then turned around. Martin stared at him, and then looked away. He looked at the table top, looked at the floor, started to say something, stopped. He half coughed, half laughed. Smiled. Stopped smiling.

'Are you all right?'

Martin put a finger to his eye and looked at it. He coughed fully, his face coloured suddenly red like blood in water. He lit a cigarette.

'What kind of stupid fucking question is that?'

MARTIN

His father looked at him from the doorway. He stood with his hands on his hips like a man shaping up for a fight. But his face was not angry, it was clouded and distant. He looked directly at Martin, but there was no recognition, no acknowledgement. He might have been gazing at a photograph.

Martin sat up slightly, leaning on his elbow, pulling a leg back beneath the sheets. He rubbed his eyes and glanced at the clock. It was nearly eight.

'Your breakfast is done,' said his father. 'It'll be cold.'

'Okay. I'll be there now.'

His father did not move, and Martin returned his gaze, and the two of them stretched out the moment uneasily until his father broke it, wiping his mouth suddenly and turning from the room.

Martin lay back on the pillow for a while, breathing. Then he threw himself out of the bed and into the still, stale air of his room. He pulled on a jumper, and a pair of jeans, and a pair of socks, and picked up his trainers and ran to the bathroom. He could hear the radio from the kitchen and could smell the fry that waited for him.

They sat in silence, listening to early mass on the radio. His father mouthed responses as he ate, while his mother looked at her plate and once or twice at Martin, looking away again if he caught her eye. She had not slept. She had that look, that slightly bewildered hesitation about her, that told Martin that she had been hit.

After breakfast he and his father drove to mass in Cootehill. As they passed the Boltons' place, Martin tried to see if their car was still there, but most of the farmyard was hidden from the road. He could not tell.

'What is it?' his father asked.

'Just trying to see if the Boltons are still there.'

'Of course they are. Bolton has his missus to hold him up, fixing her hair.'

As he always did, his father slipped into the pew nearest the door and went down on his knees. Martin followed suit, looking around the church over the top of his clasped hands. It was Pat Bolton he was looking for, but he was not there yet.

As they rose for the priest, the Boltons came in, Pat last. He glanced at Martin and Martin tried to smile, but it did not come out properly. Pat seemed to shake his head, but Martin wasn't sure. The family went up to the front of the church, splitting up to find seats, Mrs Bolton taking her youngest daughter with her into a space that was only big enough for one. Pat glanced back once more and caught Martin's eye. There was something wrong. It was in his face. He looked scared.

Martin went through the mass with a sick feeling in his stomach. A flurry of thoughts hit him. He could not help but think that they had been discovered. That Mr Bolton had seen them. That Mr Bolton had told his father in the pub the night before, that that was why his mother had been beaten and his father had stood in the doorway staring at him that morning. It came to him like scenes in a film.

After the blessing his father turned in the pew and waited for Martin to move. At the front of the church Pat Bolton genuflected, stood and turned. He looked at the ground. Martin was nudged by his father, and stepped out into the aisle. As he knelt and blessed himself he kept his eyes on Pat Bolton. But Pat did not look up.

Outside the church, Martin lingered while his father walked towards the car. He watched people emerge through the high arched doorway, forming queues at the fonts of holy water. They blessed themselves and glanced at the sky. Some stood in small groups and talked. Others scurried away quickly. The Bolton family came out together, Pat walking next to his mother and two of his sisters. An older brother saw Martin and walked over to him.

'Will you be at our place today, Martin?' he asked.

'I don't know. Do you need me?'

'We could use a hand with the rest of the silage. I want to try and do it today. I'll not be around for most of the week.'

Martin watched Pat as he walked by, keeping his eyes to the ground, talking quietly to his mother.

'So are you on?'

'If I can. I won't promise you.'

'Right.'

Martin walked beside him, behind Pat. They came to the church gate and had to slow down. Martin managed to get to Pat's shoulder.

'How are you?' he said, quietly.

'Fine.'

They got through the gate and emerged side by side on the footpath, Pat slowing down so that his family moved ahead of them.

'John asked me to come over today,' said Martin. 'So I'll probably see you later.'

Pat stopped and looked at him. He was very nervous. He checked to see where his family were.

'Don't. Don't come over.'

'Why not?'

Pat looked over his shoulder and leaned closer to Martin and whispered. 'I don't want to see you. It's not natural. What we did. We could get caught.'

Martin felt himself go pale. He leaned against the low wall and felt it press into his back. He pushed himself against it as hard as he could. The air became still. It was as if there was no noise other than Pat's breathing. It reminded him.

'It's wrong,' Pat hissed. 'My brother nearly caught us yesterday. He was outside. He might even have heard something.'

'Did he say anything?'

'No. But that doesn't mean he doesn't know.'

Martin glanced towards his father, who stood at the car waiting for him. The road was full of people. He could feel the sun hitting the back of his neck. Pat's face stayed close to his. His breathing whispered words that Martin could not hear like the sighing out of secrets from a deathbed. He knew that there was something he should understand, something in Pat's eyes, something in the way his mouth seemed to hover close to his own. But Martin could feel only the fear of losing what he had found, and the fear of being discovered.

'What can we do?' he asked, and was surprised that he had asked it out loud.

Pat seemed to shake his head, his eyes so unblinking that Martin thought for a moment that he might cry.

'Just don't come near me, okay?' he said, his voice angry. 'Don't come anywhere near me. If you do I'll tell everyone that you're a fucking queer. I swear I will. I swear to God.'

He stared for a moment longer, his breath on Martin's face like a dream of warm water. Then he swung round and walked to his family, his heels clipping the concrete.

His father did not speak on the way home, he looked at him out of the corner of his eye. Martin could feel his gaze. He knew that there would be no questions, not from his father. There would be assumptions. His father would assume whatever it was easiest to assume. As they stopped in front of the house and Martin made to open the door of the car, his father gripped his arm.

'There's four sons in that family, what do they want with you? Eh? They don't need you. You won't get any thanks from them. Just remember that. There's no point in you going over there to do their work. You'll get nothing for it. Just aggravation. That's all.'

He released Martin and they both got out of the car. Martin faced him over the roof.

'That's all they'll give you. That young one of them. Don't let him talk to you like that. He's no business. He goes near you again, you tell me.'

Martin said nothing and followed his father into the house. His mother saw him, saw his face.

'Are you going over to the Boltons' today, Martin?'

'No.'

He went to his room and sat on the bed, listening to the silence that settled on the house on Sundays. His father would sit in the front room reading the papers and sipping his stout. His mother worked quietly in the kitchen, preparing dinner. Sometimes she would call him to do something for her. Today she did not.

Martin lay on his bed and thought about Pat Bolton and about his father.

At dinner-time he went to the kitchen and sat at the table and ate without saying a word, ignoring his mother's efforts at conversation and his father's eyes. When his mother and himself had cleared the table he sat down again, opposite his father.

'Mum, will you sit down a minute, please?'

His father looked up at him and his mother hesitated before taking her chair. He looked at both of them. His mother was concerned, curious. His father looked puzzled and slightly disapproving. He didn't like surprises.

'What's wrong with you?'

186

'Nothing's wrong with me. I just want to tell you both something.'

'What?'

'I'm telling you because I think it's fair. When I've told you then I'll go away for a while if you like.'

His mother put her hand on his arm.

'Martin, what is it? What's happened?'

'Nothing's happened.'

He could not think which word to use.

'I'm homosexual. Gay, I mean.'

He was aware of his mother's hand, aware of how it left his arm for a moment and then returned. He glanced up at her and realised that it was her face that he wanted to see, her reaction that mattered. She looked into his eyes without hesitation, without blinking, without turning away. He could feel her sorrow fill the space between them.

'Why?' she asked quietly, almost whispering. 'Why are you telling him?'

Martin could not think of the answer. He knew it, but he could not think of it. It was lost to him. He saw his mother's face and felt only a great fear.

'What do you mean?' his father asked.

Martin looked at him and saw that he was pale.

'I mean that I'm gay.'

'Queer?'

'Gay.'

His father looked at his mother.

'Does he mean he's queer?'

She would not look at him. She kept her eyes on Martin, her hand on his arm. His father stood up slowly, pushing back his chair, scraping it along the floor. He wiped his mouth.

'Are you telling me that you're queer?'

'I'm gay.'

'There's no such word. Not that way. It's queer. What about them girls you went out with? Eh?'

187

'What about them? It doesn't make any difference. I know what I am.'

'Queer?'

'Gay.'

His father slammed his fist on the table and Martin jumped.

'Stop telling me you're gay. There's no such thing. It's queer. Are you queer?'

'Yes.'

There was a silence for a moment. His father did not move. Then slowly he raised his hands to his mouth and drew a deep breath.

'Jesus. Jesus Christ. I don't believe it.'

'Believe it,' whispered Martin, and he felt the grip of his mother's hand tighten slightly, as if trying to warn him.

His father looked as if he was not listening.

'The animals in the fields don't even do that.'

He looked at Martin's mother.

'How is he queer? How? That's your fault. That's what it is. All that mollycoddling him.'

'Don't blame her.'

'What?'

Martin heard what was in the voice and said nothing else.

'What did you say?'

His father walked around the table and stood behind him. He bent down and held his face next to Martin's ear. Martin could feel his breath, could feel the spittle hitting him.

'Did you talk to me? Did you open your mouth? Don't talk to me again. Do you hear? Don't let me see your mouth move. There's shite on your breath. The animals in the fields don't . . .'

He stood up again. Paced.

'I always knew there was something . . . Your mother killed the wrong fucking one, that's for sure.'

188

He stopped, and stared at him.

'That's the story of it. You'd be better off if it'd been you that she killed.'

'She killed no one.'

His father took a clump of his hair and pulled it tight. At first Martin thought that he was going to pull him backwards off the chair. But he did not. He changed direction, slamming Martin's face into the table top. Martin heard his mother scream before he felt the pain. Then he felt the blood, and then he tasted it.

'I told you not to talk to me.'

Martin tried to lift his head, but it felt unnaturally heavy. He tried to push himself up with his hands, but his father brought his fist down hard on his fingers and pushed Martin sideways so that he stumbled against his mother who could not hold him, and fell to the floor.

'Please, Michael,' said his mother. 'Leave him alone.'

'Shut up. You drowned the wrong one. It's your fault.'

From the floor Martin could see his mother fall to her knees and try to cover him. She got in the way of a punch, and Martin saw the pain of it on her face. But his own pain held him still. Pain and fear. He wanted to stand, but he could not.

His father didn't hit him again. He muttered and paced, and shouted once or twice. Then suddenly, as if it had been a natural thing, like a rain shower or a storm, it was over. He was gone.

Martin did not become aware that he was crying until his mother wiped his cheek, and held him. She helped him to his feet. She took him to the sink and tried to clean the blood. His nose was not broken. He had hit the table slightly sideways, and one eye was badly bruised and a tooth was loose. He could not understand how his nose had not been broken.

They heard the front door slam and the car start up.

'I should leave before he comes back,' said Martin,

leaning against the sink as his mother dabbed at his nose and held ice to his eye.

'Where will you go?'

'Dublin. I know a guy there who'll let me stay with him for a while.'

His mother was silent. He felt her fear.

'I'll be all right,' he said.

'You won't get a bus this evening, will you?'

'There's one leaves Cootehill at six. I can meet it on the Shercock road.'

'I have money I can give you.'

'No, it's all right.'

'It's not all right. You'll take the money. You'll need it.'

She helped him pack, folding his clothes for him, remembering things that he would have forgotten. There were things he had to leave – his stereo and his tapes, most of his winter clothes.

'Will you phone me? Tonight. Let me know you're all right?'

'I will. Don't worry.'

She gave him 150 pounds. They stood together at the door and hugged. His mother cried, and he did not mind that she saw him crying also. He felt only fear, and he could not pin it down, could not tell which way to turn in order to stop it.

He walked down to the road, afraid to look back. He decided that he would wait until he reached the gate, and turn then and wave at his mother. But when he got there, he could not make himself stop. He felt that he had already left, that he was already far away. He thought that if he stopped and looked back there would be nothing there.

He kept on walking, his eyes to the ground, shifting his bag from hand to hand, hoisting it on to one shoulder and then on to the other. He felt the sun hit his face, reflected by the white walls and the silver windows of small roadside houses. He walked by the edges of still lakes, where groups of anglers murmured to each other through the clouds of tiny flies. There was no traffic.

When he reached the main road, he walked for a while in the direction of Shercock so that he was out of sight of the turn-off, where his father might pass by on his way home. He put his bag on the ground and sat up on an old, crumbling wall and waited. He felt the silence instead of the warmth. He picked up small stones and threw them into the ditch opposite. When cars passed by he kept his head down.

In the sky he searched for a reflection of the world, but there was only an unbroken blue, a stillness. It seemed cold to him now, like the water of a lake in the early morning. He could see nothing in it but the difference between heaven and earth, between his heart and his home. It hovered over him like an old curse. He wanted to be out from under it; away from the strangeness of knowing that it could see him.

What scared him most was that he had not thought of it.

They waited in the house all day, mostly silent. Martin could not decide whether he was glad of Sean's presence or not. He didn't want to look at him. He didn't want to be asked questions. He didn't want to talk. But he guessed that without him he would be frantic. There was something at the back of his mind that simmered like anger or panic. He did not trust himself. He was afraid that perhaps it had not yet sunk in.

He thought of his mother hurt. Injured. Unconscious. Sean rang the hospitals. There was no word of her. Martin was aware that there was something horribly comic in the notion that she might have been hit by a car. A completed circle. He smiled at the idea, and Sean saw him smiling, and he stopped and felt sick. His hands kept on opening by themselves and he waited for words to form in his mind but they did not – his thoughts were at a lower level and he could not interpret them.

But he could not really picture her injured or lost. He could see her only at home in Monaghan, her muddy boots striding to or from the lake like a woman doing a chore. She had had such determination in her then. She gave off the sense that she was in the middle of something and she would not be distracted until it was done. She hid her bruises and carried on. She breathed deeply and stayed. He could not imagine her doing anything else.

The day darkened. They sat in the front room, the television blank and quiet. He wanted to turn it on. He was not used to silence in the house in the early evening. He could not focus on its cause. He felt as though there was something that was not working.

The rain came again, heavier. He tried to read signs in the noise of the water, the cold in the house; tilting his head like a dog, listening and sniffing, unable ultimately to imagine what it was that he was trying to discern. He thought that he might reach some kind of understanding, if he could only remain still enough and quiet enough, generating his own warmth. But he was unsure what it was that he was trying to understand. He thought of the clairvoyants who circled the families of the missing, mumbling unfinished sentences and gently rubbing a finger on the side of their head. They were driven through hushed streets in the back of police cars. They held photographs to their chests.

Sean distracted him with questions, comments, useless little sentences that Martin did not understand. He drifted off – thought of his father. His father's face was unclear, faded. No words came. He didn't know himself.

Then Sean went for food and cigarettes, and Martin turned on the television and turned it off again. He struggled for something still. Some clarity.

He thought of Henry. He stared at their room. He held

192

his breath and thought of it suddenly, as if he had not thought of it before. He glanced at his watch and exhaled, and shrugged as if it was nothing.

He knew the number by heart. He had thought of it more times than he had dialled it. He heard that strange ringing tone and thought for a moment that it was not going to be answered. But it was.

'Henry?'

'Oh, hi. How are you?'

'Not good.'

He left a pause.

'What's up?' There was a hint of impatience in Henry's voice, making it clear that he did not want to hear the things that he had heard before. He was expecting suspicion. He was expecting the usual rant. The desperate words. Martin found himself smiling. It was nothing like that. It was something entirely different now.

'It's my mother, Henry. She murdered him.'

There was a huge silence, a gap in which Martin saw Henry sitting down, his face changing, a hand raised to his temple perhaps.

'Who?'

'My father. It was her. She ran over him in the car.'

'Oh, Jesus.'

Silence

'Oh, Jesus. Did she tell you?'

'No.'

Martin had to put his hand over the mouthpiece. He was afraid that he would laugh. He clenched his eyes shut and bit his cheeks and it passed.

'She's gone missing. She told Sean last night and then walked out of his place and she hasn't been seen since. She's disappeared.'

There was another gap.

'You're not serious.'

'I swear.'

193

'Oh, God. I don't believe it.'

'I don't know what I'm going to do. I don't know where she is. I can't call the police. Don't you see?'

'Christ.'

Martin could not help it. He began to snigger. He started to rock back and forth. He held the phone away from him, but it did not work.

'Oh shit, Martin, don't cry. Please.'

Martin hunched over, doubled up, his mouth stretched, his eyes puckered closed, a riot beginning in his guts.

'I'll come home.'

Martin stopped laughing. He sniffed a couple of times. He had not even had to suggest it.

'But what about work?'

Henry became efficient, calm, organised. He told Martin that he'd look after everything and be back by morning. He'd get the first flight he could. There wasn't even hesitation in his voice. He was returning. Martin listened open-mouthed.

'I'll call when I have a flight number. Okay?'

'Are you sure?'

Henry said yes. He said yes to everything. Martin replaced the receiver as if it might explode. He sat there and did not move. His face had relaxed. He was still. He sniffed again and rubbed his chin. A smile began slowly to form and he could do nothing to stop it.

'Yes.' he said. 'Yes.'

He hoped his mother would not turn up before Henry. He hoped she wouldn't embarrass him like that.

SEAN

He drove to his home and went to his computer and switched it on and deleted some files. He went to the bathroom and was sick. He tore pages from his notebook and flushed them after his own vomit. He took the tiny cassette from his small machine and pulled the tape from it quickly, watching it ribbon through the air and gather in a dead tangle on the kitchen floor. He stamped on it, crushed the plastic case beneath his foot.

There were messages on his answering machine about the X case. He listened to them and breathed. He drank cold water.

Before leaving to return to Martin's house he stood bewildered in the room where he had talked to Grace. He was suddenly astounded at how easy it was to end things. To kill or destroy or unhinge a life. It happened all the time.

He walked unsteadily back to his car. He weaved away from certainty. Wanted now to be an outsider, a chronicler of things already done. No more than that. Any more than that was not him.

He drove so slowly that other drivers blew horns and sped past. He held the wheel and concentrated. There was nothing easy.

THREE

MRS TALBOT

What was she like? Something toppled. Barely eight o'clock on a Sunday morning, a face cut out of candle-wax, alert and nervous, creamy white, eyes on fire. Her hair all wet, strands of it stuck to her forehead. At first glance she was like a girl in trouble, after a night in the great outdoors with the wrong fella. Stumbled in the muddy green. But when you looked at her a bit closer, peered, she was older, mid-fifties maybe, scared stiff, a bit of a tremor in her arms. Her handbag an old-fashioned thing, with a long thin strap cutting into the shoulder of her coat, and those little gold handles like you'd get on a chest of drawers.

'Hello,' said Mrs Talbot, not opening the door fully, taking a quick glance behind the woman, into the street. Quiet as it should be.

'Hello,' she said, and gave a little smile, apologetic. 'I was told that you might have a room.' She looked up towards Parkgate Street; the side of her face pale, her tapering lips dry, flecked with white, bitten. 'They gave me directions in the café. I'm sorry to be disturbing you so early.'

Mrs Talbot kept her face in check. A room, at eight o'clock on a Sunday morning? She smiled.

'From now, is it, dear?'

Her shoes were a state. Mud and God knows. Her coat had a big rusty leaf stuck to it at the side. Down through the trees. Just the handbag. Nothing else.

'Yes.'

Almost an English accent. Northern. But not pure. She'd come home, maybe.

'Well, come in, dear. Will you be having breakfast?'

She came past her, fiercely wiping her shoes on the mat and looking down as if embarrassed.

'No, I've had breakfast. Thank you.'

'There's a cup of tea if you feel the need. Cold morning.'

She thought about it, standing there holding her handbag in front of her, sniffing once, pressing her forehead with the tips of her fingers, pushing back her hair.

'Yes. Yes please. I'd love a cup of tea.'

Mrs Talbot nodded, and led her down the corridor to the breakfast room. There was only Myles there, still working his way though his eggs and bacon, a newspaper propped up against the teapot. He looked her up and down and glanced at Mrs Talbot with his fat cheeks working and a squint.

'Hello,' said the woman. Myles swallowed, his whole head involved.

'You take a seat, dear,' said Mrs Talbot. 'I'll be with you in a minute.'

'Hello,' said Myles, cheerfully.

From the kitchen she could hear him ask her was she off the ferry. Her voice was low, she hesitated. No she said. Just no. Then Myles on about his trains. She asked him something and he said, 'No, the guard. Tickets please.' And then silence.

She took a cup of tea through the swing doors.

'I still think of trains with a poor soot-black fellow shovelling coal into a whadyamacallit and pulling a whistle. There's none of that, of course. It's all diesel and a dead man's handle. That's what they call it, isn't it, Myles – a dead man's handle. It's the thing the driver holds and if he has a heart attack or what have you and drops dead then the handle is let go of and the train stops. Had you heard of that? Though Myles tells me that sometimes now they prop up the handle with a stick or a newspaper or what have you so that they can, well, I don't know what they'd want to be doing.'

She laughed. 'Dead man's handle. What a name.'

Myles laughed too. He glanced at his watch. He was late, she knew that. He gulped back his tea but made no move.

'Here you are, dear.'

'Thank you.'

'Of course, the name is wrong,' said Myles. 'Because if the driver dies he lets it go. So it's a live man's handle, not a dead man's handle. If you follow.'

The woman nodded to keep her eyes open.

'Are you sure you won't have something to eat, dear?'

'No, thank you. I've been travelling all night. I'm quite tired. Can I take this to my room?'

'And there are deaths when the muscles tense. When a body goes stiff as a board. The train wouldn't stop then. You'd have a dead man's handle then all right.'

He sighed and shook his head as if grieved by the inaccuracy of certain words, and Mrs Talbot thought that he looked like her late husband when he did it – sorry with the world, used to it. Failing. But her husband died. Now Myles bucked himself up and smiled at them and rose stiffly.

'I must be off now, Mrs Talbot. It's time I was off.'

He rubbed his hands together and shuffled past them, bowing slightly to the woman, winking at Mrs Talbot.

'See you Thursday, love,' she said.

The woman looked tilted, half collapsed.

'I'll show you your room, dear. I'll put you in a quiet one at the back.'

She led her out through the hall and up the stairs. She did not like going first. She was conscious of her size. She brushed both the bannister and the wall.

'This house, dear, was built by a skinny man. Tiny

en, tiny bathrooms, big bedrooms. And a man who
 stairs. This is one of four, would you believe. It's a
 er to me that I'm not as skinny as he was, the amount
 ⌐ ⌐mes I'm up and down them.'

She took her to number four, overlooking the garden
and the river beyond, and then the dull sheds and the
factory buildings up the slope into the sky.

'Is this all right? The bathroom is just outside, the first
on your left.'

'It's fine.'

Her smile was odd. She'd left her tea downstairs.

Mrs Talbot rummaged in her apron and came up with
the key.

'Here we are. Now, if you think you're going to be out
late I can give you a front door key, but I don't like to do
that really, as you can imagine. I'm here until half ten in
the evenings – that's my bedtime and wild horses wouldn't
keep me from it. I don't do an evening meal, but if you
can find me during the day I'm willing to make a sandwich
or what have you. There's a sitting room downstairs, off
the corridor to your right, where you're welcome to watch
television and the rule on that is that the majority gets
what the majority wants, and as my clientele is mostly CIE
men then I'm afraid you're most likely to be watching
sport of some description. I'm not responsible for their
language and if they invite you to play cards with them
then don't let it be said that I didn't warn you. The room
plus breakfast is fifteen pounds a night – I don't do
room only. Breakfast is from six thirty to eight thirty. Tell
me if you want it later and that can be arranged. If you
want it earlier then you're not human and I'll ask you to
leave. I don't take cheques or credit cards or foreign money
and what I do take I take one night in advance.'

The woman smiled again, better this time. She took notes
directly from her handbag, a tenner and a fiver. They were
cold, clammy.

'Thank you very much, Mrs . . .'

Oh, but there was hesitation now. An open mouth closed again, a glance at the window, the eyes suddenly a little more focused. What would come to her?

'Wilson,' she said. That was a first.

'Mrs Wilson. That's fine. Sleep well now. Sundays are quiet enough so you shouldn't be disturbed.'

She closed the door on her and stuck her hands in her apron and squinted at the morning light coming up from the hall. Wilson. It was a quick name, nothing hung to it. Mrs Talbot stepped to the stairs and eased herself down like the launch of a lifeboat. What class of disaster was this, she wondered. She ran a house for overnighting train men and bus drivers and the odd ill-directed tourist. Not women on their own without baggage. Not wet-haired women flung down through the trees, fiery-eyed, eyelids melting, ashy lips. There'd been none of that. None at all. Surprising really – that there hadn't, given everything else. Given the usual way of things in Mrs Talbot's life. Given the marvels.

There were little crusts of mud on the carpet. They bled black in the palm of her hand.

She went to the kitchen and cleaned up and took an apple from the basket. In the breakfast room she sat and peered out towards the Liffey looking for swans. The noise of her bite was startling.

GRACE

She did not dream. There was only her slow breath, the light trailing the width of her face. Still.

Her waking was a strange thing. It came to her slowly, with a gathering in of facts – where she was; how she had got there; what had happened. She wondered whether the numbness of her body had flowed upwards to her mind. There was a change in her. No panic. No unease. A calm had come, and she was unsure of it, as if it was improper. She felt that she had forgotten a detail. For a long time she did not move.

It was early evening. She had slept the day.

Eventually, a shift of a lower leg into a cold part of the bed reminded her that she was naked. She stretched, made a sound like a door. Her muscles ached, but the sensation was not unpleasant. It made her feel strong; it ran signals down her limbs, lighting her sinews like electricity. She thought of walking, of striding.

The room was in darkness. She had not closed the curtains, and through the window she could see orange lights in the distance, and the glow of roadways and traffic. She eased herself into the chill air, her bones cracking into place, her hair a presence about her head, a weight. Her feet on the carpet slid a tingling heat through her skin. She could see the glint of the river through the trees. Beneath her the garden was cluttered. She saw the shape of what might have been a children's swing. There was a shed as well, a flat black roof with a puddle of water, poked by slow rain. A new place now. Another layer.

She cleaned her shoes with tissues at the wash-basin. She dressed in her damp clothes, throwing her ruined tights in the bin, and found the bathroom. There she undressed again, as if she had come a distance, and showered. She made the water as hot as she could bear, and rubbed at her skin, trying to wake herself, trying to scratch some urgency back into her blood.

The fat woman sat amongst men. She balanced a cat on her thigh, a length of fur that she stroked with a fat hand. Grace asked about a place to eat. The men were dressed in blue. They debated the question, smiled at her politely, called the fat woman Mrs Talbot. Mrs Talbot shook her head and said she knew of nowhere, and complained of never having been taken out for a meal in all her years of feeding the men in blue. They laughed. One winked at another. They gave Grace directions. Go here, go there.

She walked carefully, slowly, trying to look at things in the dark and trying not to think. She found the restaurant and ate stringy steak that caught in her throat. She watched people, wished she had a book, a newspaper. She thought of her son.

She considered how she had come to be afraid of him. Of his reaction, his words. She was frightened. She knew it was her own fault for not telling him, but at the same time knew that she had no language for telling him. Had no place, no setting, no words to begin it, no words to end it. So she had told him sideways. She had told Sean, and taken off. So that Martin would know and it would be up to him, not her. She was a coward.

Red wine burned her.

He would think now that she had taken her chances, as if she was a criminal, as if she was on the run, looking for the best option, the safest route – as if it was her plan to get away with it. She had no plan. Trust Brady not to change his mind. Hope the car reveals nothing. That is not a plan.

She asked for ice cream and they offered her coffee. She walked back towards the guest house through a mist. In the morning she would have to decide what risk to take. To go to him or not. She grimaced at the size of the choice, at the puny way it formed itself and sat in her mind like a question of routes, of directions, a disjunction on a petty map.

A boat to England. Not Manchester. Not London. Scotland maybe. Up through the middle into a smaller place, a town, a village, where she would not be swallowed – would not disappear even from herself. Where she might find people to speak to, a room, a job. Just that.

Mrs Talbot fussed at her, fussed about the rain, offered her tea, stared at her a little. With curiosity. Agreed to call her in the morning early. Told her that Monday mornings were a curse. Grace nodded, felt something at the sound of her old name. Mrs Wilson. She could not tell what it meant to her.

In her room she quickly undressed and slipped again into the chill of the bedclothes. She had left the curtains open and for a while stared out at the rain and the lights that seemed smudged behind the wet glass. She could not tell the sky from solid things. There were no stars. She lay still and tested herself with the idea of never seeing Martin again. Of never being part of her own life, of always living out another. In her drowsing mind, with the night a jumble of shadows, the rain falling, she built herself a room in a northern city where she would understand the people and work quietly and well in a cake shop or a sweet shop or some shop of the past. Where she would walk home through a gentle park, a small lake beside her, a high sky, a pale blue world. Friends. Folk who came to tea. As she slipped towards sleep and past the point where she might have stopped herself, barred his entry, censored his eyes, she saw Martin. Martin up to visit.

On the window the rain made a noise like a stampede of tiny feet. Grace imagined her son with his arm in hers, walking slowly through the park. His head inclined, listening to her.

She fell asleep to the sound of running, and the dream of walking.

MRS TALBOT

When CIE men arrived before noon and took to their rooms she charged them for the previous night. It didn't bother them. The company never queried it. Mrs Talbot felt that it was fair practice. Every month she'd send off her bill, and they'd pay it all, even the little extras. She charged for breakages, for unreasonable laundry, for the time the two women had been sneaked in, for trouble, noise, complaints from other guests. Double breakfasts. She put everything down in the book in the kitchen, then copied it out, item by item, on to the stationery that Arthur had ordered too much of. There were still seven bundles as high as her waist downstairs in Paula's old bedroom. It might have killed him. He'd carried them down there and dropped dead a week later. Bent over in the garden to pick a pebble from the lawn and just toppled, crumbled, face down in a heap, his bum in the air like a toddler asleep in a cot. At the hospital they'd handed her the pebble, thinking it might have meant something, clutched so tightly. She wished now that she'd kept it, but she'd thought then that it would be a bad memory and had dropped it in the gravel by the hospital door.

'River View,' said the stationery in the top middle, with the address then, and the telephone number. She put the extra digit in front of it. When they'd changed the number she'd called them and asked about compensation. A roomful of stationery with the wrong telephone number. They told her that they were sympathetic but couldn't give her anything. They said they'd leave a message on the old number for longer than was normal – give her a chance to change her stationery. Mrs Talbot wrote the extra digit in a small hand with a green pen and she'd got so good at it now that you'd hardly notice it was different at all.

'Mrs Wilson,' she wrote. '16/2/1992. Bed and Breakfast. £15 recieved with thanks.'

She would buy a typewriter soon. Handwritten it looked a little, well, amateur. Arthur had done them before, in his beautiful script, and had stamped them too. She wasn't sure if he'd stamped these ones. They didn't need it really, with the address on top. Anyway, the stamp had disappeared.

She took down the book and found the page. She wrote:

'16/2/92. Room 4. Mrs Wilson(?) Arr. 8a.m.(!). Dishevelled. No br. Slept all day, English accent. Only chrg. Sunday. Not happy person. No baggage. Same clothes in evening. Out to eat. Did not mix. Leaves tomorrow. Am uneasy for her. In some trouble. She's panicked like a cat.'

She put the book back on the shelf and left the receipt on table four in the breakfast room. Wilma followed her, trying to catch her bare ankles, purring.

'Yes, pet, yes. Bedtime. Bedtime for Wilma.'

Mrs Wilson, she decided, was the type of woman Arthur would have flirted with. She had that face. Startled.

MARTIN

He slept sitting, his neck creased on the soft edge of the front room armchair, his breathing noisy, his dreams all water and country air. And small dark spaces. Waking, his first thoughts were for Henry. The impending Henry. The returning, homecoming Henry. Then the noise of Sean coughing from upstairs reminded him of his mother, her cold skin missing, her crime.

He staggered to the bathroom, showered, carefully shaved, lingered until Sean started rattling the door. Sean had not slept. He looked ill. His hands shook slightly.

'I made your bed,' he said. 'I tidied.'

Martin looked at him. Nodded.

'Will you not pick up Henry?'

Sean seemed to grimace.

'I told you. I can't. I have to go to work. I don't want to be . . .'

'What?'

'Nothing. I have to work.'

'I think you could at least go and pick him up. He's had to get up at all hours. He'll be knackered. A taxi will cost him a fortune.'

'He earns a fortune. I'm sorry.'

He left without eating. He promised to call.

Martin put his breakfast on a tray and took it to the sitting room. He turned on the television and watched the English stations' bright colours, their wide-awake sets. He watched their Dublin correspondents talk about the X case, about the decision that was expected that day. One of them stood outside the Four Courts in the gloom. At least it had stopped raining. Another predicted with some confidence that the judge would grant the injunction and stop the girl from travelling. Martin did not believe him.

He ate his toast, wiped his chin, and watched cartoons. The rigor in his neck receded.

He arrived earlier than Martin had expected. The noise of a car pulling up. The slamming of doors. He hit the remote control and flung it on the sofa behind him and raced through the kitchen and into the bathroom and looked at himself in the mirror and washed his hands and raced out again, casting an eye over everything quickly, knowing that he should have swept the floor. He stood in the hall waiting for the door to open. Nothing happened. Perhaps it had not been him. He was making his way back to the sitting room to look out of the window when the knocker sounded loudly, two short cracks like footsteps on a cold floor.

Martin smiled and could not get rid of it. He rubbed at his mouth as he reached out, but the smile stayed put. He could feel it splitting his face, could feel his cheeks bulge and the air on his teeth. He turned the lock and opened the door, slowly at first, as if afraid, then all in a rush, letting in the light with a tumble of colours. The sun had come out.

In front of him stood Henry, lifting his head to look. He had not been smiling, but he did when his eyes met Martin's. He stood there alone, wearing a three-quarter length leather coat that Martin had never seen before. His hair was shorter. There were dark circles under his eyes, but he was clean-shaven, his skin with the sun upon it.

'I can't find my key,' he said.

He had a small suitcase at his feet and a bag slung from his shoulder, but it was not what he had left with. The shoulder bag was new, and there had been another suit-case, a bigger one, as well. Martin took all of this in before he could say anything. Then he said:

'God. You look great. Come in. How are you?'

His grin was still there. Bigger than his face. He felt that Henry was smiling at it rather than at him. He stood aside and Henry brushed past, the suitcase held out in front, stepping up, his head level, an echo of aftershave, his shirt collar open, clean white.

'I'm fine. How are you?'

'Great. Okay.'

He dropped the suitcase at the foot of the stairs and looked around him. He took a deep breath.

'I feel like I've been away for years. Is there any news?'

'No, nothing.'

They looked at each other. Martin expected a wet, snorting laugh to burst through the stretched features of his idiot face at any moment. At the base of his vision he could make out the fat humps of his cheeks. Behind his nose and his eyes there was a tingling that brought to mind sneezing and laughing and coughing and other explosions. He ran a hand across his chin.

'Are you okay?' Henry said, walking to him.

'Yes. Just good to see you. Glad, I mean.'

He laughed then, putting his head down, gripping his mouth with his hand, bending his knees. He arched up again, wiping what he was sure was a bubble away from his nose.

'Sorry.'

Henry put his arms around him and they stood for a moment, embracing, swinging slightly back and forth. Martin buried his face in Henry's shoulder, rubbed his nose on the leather. He kissed Henry's neck, and then found his cheek, and his mouth. They kissed for a long time, gently, clinging to each other, Martin measuring every response that Henry gave him, opening his eyes once to check that Henry's were closed, moving his feet slightly to see if Henry would follow, observing and recording everything like a delicate device thrown up in the wind to gauge the weather, until eventually, reassured, he relaxed. It was the same as it had been.

'Christ, I missed you.'

'I missed you too,' Henry whispered, and they held each other together at the waist and leaned back slightly and stared at each other's face.

'Are you okay? Did you get any sleep?'

'No. No.' His neck twinged. 'Sean stayed. Bastard wouldn't collect you.'

They kissed again and let go at last and Henry ran upstairs with his bags while Martin put on the kettle. They sat together then in the kitchen, drinking coffee. Henry opened a window.

Martin asked him where he had got the leather jacket and the bag. He had bought the jacket second-hand, he said. And the bag was borrowed. Martin was about to ask who it was borrowed from but Henry cut him off.

'Tell me what happened.'

'I told you.'

'Everything?'

He nodded, but Henry looked at him, waited. Martin tried to remember, tried to form it into words. What Sean had told him. All those things. He didn't want to talk about it.

'She killed him.' He shrugged.

Henry nodded, looked at the table. Martin worried that it was not enough. It wouldn't keep him.

'Apparently there's this policeman.'

'What policeman?'

Then Martin had to remember what Sean had told him about that – about the policeman – and he told Henry about that, and about the policeman calling to see his mother and what she had said about it, or hadn't said. He became confused. He could not concentrate. He paused and stuttered.

'It's all right,' said Henry, touching his hand, thinking he was upset. Martin coughed.

'Can we . . .?' he started, and stopped.

'What?'

Martin put his head to one side, tilted it. Said nothing.

'Why hasn't he arrested her?' Henry asked.

'Yeah.'

'Why didn't he arrest her if he knows?'

'Yeah.'

'And why did she go to Sean? Why did she tell him?'

Martin shook his head, moved his hand out from under Henry's, reached for Henry's face, for his cheek, for that place where his skin disappeared beneath the collar of his shirt.

'Yeah,' he said.

GRACE

She did not sleep. In the weak light she sat up in the bed and waited for the knock. She was cold and hugged her knees. Her muscles were painless and her eyes were clear, as if she had in fact slept. But she was not rested. In her mind there was a sound like the ghost of rattling, as if voices had been speaking and had stopped when she listened.

The knock came loud and startled her, Mrs Talbot's voice ringing out words that Grace could not make sense of. She mumbled, put her feet on the floor.

'Okay.'

She rushed herself into her clothes, ignoring the staleness and the damp, one eye nervously scanning the window. Condensation kept her hidden.

Downstairs the dining room was almost empty. Two men sat at small tables eating. They glanced at her and nodded. She could not tell if she had seen them before. The grey cat was stretched out on the windowsill and eyed her lazily as she took a seat.

'Not there, dear,' came Mrs Talbot's voice. Grace could not see her. 'You're table four, same as your room, over there by the side.' Her head was barely visible over the top of the swing doors that led to the kitchen. A fuzz of grey.

She appeared fully after a while and persuaded Grace that she was hungry. A breakfast appeared that Grace could only stare at. Mrs Talbot smiled.

'No one leaves here hungry. Not a soul.'

She did the best she could. She left only a little. As she ate she watched the two men go, smiling silently at her, and others come in, and also smile at her. All men. Mrs Talbot moved amongst them, laughing and scolding. They chatted with her easily, even those who seemed most dour and reticent. She spoke to each of them in the same joky way, and they seemed to enjoy it, to smile in anticipation as she approached them, to glance at each other furtively like schoolboys. None of them, as far as Grace could see, were given helpings that in any way matched hers.

When she had eaten all she could she waited for Mrs Talbot to reappear and thanked her.

'Will you be staying again tonight?'

'I won't, no. I'm going to be travelling on. To Scotland.'

As soon as she had said it she realised that she should not have. Mrs Talbot, however, seemed not to pay it any attention.

'Well, I hope you've enjoyed staying here. You'll be welcome back. There's a receipt there somewhere.'

She lifted the bread-basket.

'There you are. It has the number. Any time you want to, just give a ring.'

She cleared some of Grace's things and went off again, and Grace went to her room. She spent some time looking around to make sure there was nothing she had forgotten. But there was not. There was only her coat.

At the bottom of the stairs Mrs Talbot was waiting. In her thick arms the cat rested, its glassy eyes peeping out from the crook of her elbow, its ears gently stroked by short, round fingers. Grace realised that she had not seen the cat walking. It occurred to her suddenly that the animal was legless, no more than a belly of fur and the head of a doll.

'I'll say goodbye, Mrs Wilson. I hope your journey goes well for you.'

Grace smiled and handed her the key.

'Thank you. It's been very nice here.'

Mrs Talbot stood aside, clutching the cat to her breast, and put her hand up to open the front door. A cat leg appeared, hanging lifeless over the curve of Mrs Talbot's stomach. Grace paused as she looked at it, and Mrs Talbot seemed to catch the pause and extend it. Her hand dropped from the door and gathered in the loose limb. She turned to Grace.

'This is none of my business. It really isn't. But if I don't say something I'll regret it after.'

She bit her lip and looked at the cat.

'I hope you see how it's intended. My late husband would have always said that you can't offer hospitality and then not care. That way is hotels. And those American places, motels, where people die in their rooms and nobody knows.'

She looked up again. Grace was frowning. She tried to change her face.

'You arrived without any luggage, you see, without even a change of clothes. I couldn't help but notice. And it's not usual. As I said, I got it from my late husband. I can't let somebody pass through here that looks like they could do with my help, and then not offer it to them. You look, Mrs Wilson, if you don't mind me saying it, like a woman who's left somewhere in a hurry. That can't be good. I'm not prying. I don't want to know. But I want to offer any help I can.'

The smile had left her, and she looked at Grace with a worried squint and a busy mouth, chewing at her lips. She seemed embarrassed. Grace did not know what to say and there was a long silence. The cat purred gently between them and Mrs Talbot looked down and concentrated on her stroking.

'I'm sorry, Mrs Wilson,' she said, quietly. 'I've an awful

big mouth. It's gotten me in more trouble than you can fit in a single lifetime.'

'No, it's all right.'

Grace let her eyes settle on the grey fur, seeing it gently move.

'It's good of you to be concerned, but really there's no need. It's all a mix up actually. I came up from, from the country, expecting to meet my son, and unfortunately he's away and so I couldn't stay with him, and all my things are in his house. His home. So I haven't had a chance to change. He's back now. Well, today. So I'll get my things and I'll be able to change my clothes and I can travel then. Leave.'

There was a silence and Grace watched the cat breathing, its small body like a heart in a grey purse. The round fingers kept up their tiny massage, and the cat's eyes squeezed shut for a moment at the touch that started each stroke.

'Well, there you are,' said Mrs Talbot eventually. 'There you are.'

The cat shifted suddenly and Mrs Talbot bent down a little and held out her arms and let it jump to the floor. It purred and rubbed its back along the bannister and crept quickly down the hallway and out of sight.

'No offence taken, I hope?'

'Oh no,' said Grace, as brightly as she could. 'Not at all.'

'Well then, I'll let you go.' She opened the door. 'All the best. See you again maybe.'

'Goodbye. And thank you.'

Grace walked up the steps to the pavement and turned to wave, but the door was closing and Mrs Talbot was out of sight.

On the street the traffic was heavy, heading towards the city. There was the faint smell of the river, an abstract of food, a fondness for rust. The grey sky again, with pale bruises like clouds punched upon it. A wind that pressed her back, a cold hand in the small of her back, this way please missus, this way please. Grace put her head down and started walking.

She noticed first the wigs and gowns and thought that she had stumbled on some ceremony in the street. But they were lawyers, and they carried reams of files and papers, and briefcases like doctors' bags. And the crowds were made up of people carrying signs and banners, and people with their hands in their pockets and their heads to one side. There were television cameras and men and women with mobile phones and microphones. They talked to each other in quiet voices and stamped their feet. Then Grace recognised the Four Courts.

She stood at the corner and scanned the crowd for Sean. She could not see him. Then she crossed the road and walked by the river wall. At the corner of the courts a small group of people held handwritten placards and walked quietly in a circle. 'The Rapist Is The Criminal', 'Justice For Women', 'Protect The Right To Travel'.

Beyond them there was a smaller group who stood still and defiant. One of their number held aloft a picture of the Virgin Mary, another held a printed sign that read 'Abortion Is Murder'. Others held rosary beads, and Grace perceived that they were praying.

Between these two groups, and scattered around the edges of the general crowd, were uniformed policemen, casting nervous glances at everybody. Grace stood by the river and stared for a while. She watched small conversations start up and quickly finish. People moved about as if unsure of their footing. They were waiting.

In the end, she could no longer watch. She did up the buttons on her coat and turned her head away and walked. She had her own business to be about. There was enough in that.

She had told Mrs Talbot that she was going to Scotland and wondered whether that meant that it was true. She had tried to make a plan of it, plot it out. Sneak back to the house, retrieve her clothes, and her bank book, and maybe leave a letter, or maybe not, and go then, head for the ferry. But all the time there had been the suspicion, the knowledge, that Martin would not have gone out to work. That he would wait for her, desperate, his hands on the table top, restless as children, his head full of thoughts of her, his senses straining for her return. And it was like a hope. And she did not trust herself or her motives. She was afraid that it was what she wanted. To be gathered in and forgiven, as if their roles were reversed, as if she was the child.

She had to collect her things. She could do nothing without them.

She paused at the corner of the street. She looked up its length and saw nothing. She made her way towards the house on the wrong side. It was easier to see. As she got closer she walked more slowly. She could see nothing. The curtains were open. The windows were closed. She drew level and stood in the doorway where she had seen the beggar woman crouch.

Nothing moved. In the street there was a silence that waited for her. She rummaged in her coat and found the keys. As she walked towards the door she scanned the windows for anything, anything at all. She peered, as best she could, into the sitting room. It was empty. What would that be like, if he was not there?

The key went into the lock and she quietly pushed the door open with her shoulder. First looking, and then stepping inside, she was embraced by the sight of it. It seemed so familiar. It was her son's home and it was filled with him. All the air, all the space, filled with him. She put her hands to her mouth.

MARTIN

Making love. For Martin it was loaded. It was heavy with a weight that he thought peculiar to himself. He suspected that it did not mean as much to other people. That no one but he felt defined by it. It was what he was. The circumstances of his life had flowed from the way he wished to make love. From that clumsy declaration. I am what I want. I am this.

They left themselves no space. It was as if they rushed together down a narrow corridor with nothing at the end but a white light that wrestled through them and left them weak.

In the bedroom Martin kissed him first, then worked at his clothes like a thief. Henry allowed himself to be stripped bare, as if he was helpless, a passenger. Martin marvelled at it, thought it generosity, and just as he began to feel that maybe it was not that, but something else, something cold, he was thrown backwards – Henry's hands going at buttons and buckles with useless fingers, laughing a little, before they fell together on the bed with a crash, all limbs and quick eyes with the laughter stopped.

Martin looked. He stared with a kind of disbelief at Henry's neat waist and at the dark line that led from his navel to the thick shock of pubic hair, distinct, like a patch of burnt ground.

Then he continued, and he felt the progress of things mostly in his heart, which was strange. His body was disconnected, distant. It raced to catch up with him; it could not quite manage what Martin asked of it; at times it misunderstood, and did something that was all right, but was not what he wanted, was too superficial, too quick, too instant. He wanted to stand on the bed over Henry's body and execute a dive of some kind that would take him beneath the skin, into the dark warmth where he would be covered and included and could not escape. But he could not do that.

Henry too. He gripped Martin and left marks in his skin. He kissed him, and Martin felt as if bruises were forming – small pools of sensation all over him as if he was out in the rain. Their mouths met again when the lengths of their bodies were pressed against each other as close as two hands praying, and their mouths could not open far enough, and the only sounds they made were close and silent and formed from colours and Martin told himself that it was the sound of one heart speaking to another. It was what he thought of.

Then as all this gathered, and narrowed, it became a calmer kind of lovemaking. Sentimental. That was the word that came to Martin. Sentimental. He didn't quite know what it was he meant. It was strange the way he watched himself, and watched Henry, the way he held his head and considered it all. It was not cold. It was not that kind of distance. But it was distance nonetheless, a space in which Martin measured what was happening and found himself in two places at once – in the pleasure of his body, the warm mix of senses that stretched his skin and blinded him; and in the calm concentration of his mind, the quiet, watchful space from where he considered all of this – all of this – and called it love, and weighed it then and decided in its favour, as if it was a picture of the future or the past, and not now, not real, not available to him but offered only – his if he was careful, his if he was good, his if he did it right. He closed his eyes and let the silence in him melt away into the noise that they made. There was nothing more for him to think about. It was all contained in that sound, in that rising pulse of sound that built itself around them like a cage, a house of cards, a pyramid of sticks, a height of half-words, becoming taller and taller and harder to hear, a structure that they could not see, so that they did not know it was there until the second before it collapsed, until the instant when its height towered over them and wavered at its smallest point, high in the distance, and then tumbled towards them and from them and through them and left them covered by the parts of it, panting out the evidence of a distance travelled, like two birds crashed upon a beach, the sea behind them, and the echo of the sea still ringing, clarion, crossed.

The silence moved back slowly into the space it had cleared.

They lay for a long time together. Then Martin laughed, and Henry laughed also, and they looked at each other and laughed again.

'I think we needed that,' said Henry. 'Both of us.'

After a while he slid from the bed and tiptoed through the scattered clothes to the door. Martin watched him go, smiling to himself, gently rolling his head on a cold pillow, happy, still, for the first time in days.

He listened to the breath of the city as it came back to him. Distant traffic, a low hum like fast water. Through the window he saw that it had clouded over again. He could see the bright edges of rain clouds race past chimney tops and slates that shared their colour. He felt his body cool and began to feel the air against his skin. He enjoyed the sensation, running his hand over the taut chill of his chest and his stomach.

From downstairs suddenly he heard a tiny gasp from Henry, a short exclamation of surprise. Then he heard him say something. Then Henry's feet were on the stairs, noisily racing back to the bedroom.

'Martin,' he hissed, bouncing into the room and immediately reaching for clothes. 'Your mother is here.'

Martin sat up slowly, staring at Henry carefully, checking him for a joke. It was not there.

'Are you serious?'

'She's in the front room. I thought I heard something and looked in and she was just sitting there.'

'Christ.' Martin got off the bed and joined Henry in the scramble. They hit against each other.

'Did she see you?'

'Oh course she saw me. I said hello. She must think I'm mad. I just ran.'

'Did she see all of you?'

Henry paused with his jeans halfway up his legs and looked at Martin and frowned.

'She saw my head. I don't think she saw anything else. She smiled at me. She must have come in while we were . . . Christ, Martin, this is too embarrassing.'

Martin flushed red. His T-shirt was inside out, rolled into a rope as if he had been peeled out of it. He thought of Pat Bolton, the cracked light in the shed, the hurry.

He had forgotten. She had slipped out of his present while he and Henry had made love, and she had disappeared into his past. And afterwards he had lain there for a moment and he had been in a new place. He had forgotten. And now this. As if she had waited in the street for the right moment. As if she knew. There was a speeding up in his brain. He saw Henry's ribs disappear behind the buttons of his shirt. He could not find first his sock and then his shoe. All the time he saw in his mind the shape of his mother, sitting primly downstairs, a look on her. This was not her house.

Henry found his shoe for him and stood by the door smoothing his hair and waiting.

'What'll we say?'

'About what?'

'This. What we were doing.'

'We'll say nothing,' Martin said, louder than he had intended.

He fumbled with his shoelaces, putting a knot in one that he knew he would be unable to untie. He stood up and looked at the bed, at the tossed covers and the creases in the sheets.

'Are you right?'

He couldn't fix her face in his mind. It came to him as it had been, raw in the open places. Not in city rooms.

'Yes.'

He did not look at Henry as he walked past him and started down the stairs. A silence met him that he did not like and he filled it with the sound of his feet and his hands on the bannisters and a cough that he summoned from a dry throat. He could feel Henry behind him and he wanted him gone, but could not say it. At the door to the sitting room he thought about pausing, but he did not, knowing that it would change him. He walked straight in and stood where he found himself and stared down at his mother. Her eyes met his. All wrong. Eyes from elsewhere. All wrong. The silence filled out. The doors had all been open. She would have heard them. Their racket. He set his face against the thought of that.

'Why did you kill my father?'

His voice came out in a rasp and startled him, and startled Henry too, who stood at his shoulder and turned and looked at the side of his face.

'Martin!' he said, quietly.

But Martin kept his eyes on his mother, and she held his gaze for a moment before looking down at her hands and turning them over slowly as if examining them.

'You know why.'

He did not think on that. He hardly let her finish saying it.

'Why did you come back here?'

Again Henry hissed his name at him, louder this time. His mother looked up.

'To get my things. I won't stay.'

'Dead right you won't.'

'For God's sake, Martin,' said Henry, taking a step towards him and putting out a hand which Martin shook off. He kept looking at his mother's face, waiting for a change to appear. But she did not change her expression or her colour or the line of her mouth.

'Are you not going to say anything, then? Not going to tell me how thick I am to have missed it? How stupid?' She didn't move. She was like a point, the claw of a hammer on the lip of the chair. 'What's wrong with you? Are you menopausal? Is that it?'

'Jesus, Martin.' Henry heaved his head to one side.

His mother seemed to half-smile. Her eyes shifted slightly, then back again, her face back to still, nothing in it, just a look, a stare.

'Like some women go shoplifting and you decide to run your husband over in the fucking car. Then forget about it. As if it's a thing you barely thought of. Laughing at Philip like that. That wasn't funny.'

She nodded.

'What?' he said.

She looked away. Shrugged.

'What did you say?'

She did not move.

'That wasn't funny,' Martin repeated.

'No.' Hollow voice.

She stood up. She took a step towards him. Her mouth opened. Martin thought she was going to say something and he made a noise, like a dismissal, a grunt to cut her off, his head going sideways away from her, and he looked back then and her mouth had closed and he wondered what she might have said. She stared at him. She glanced at Henry.

'I'll go upstairs and get my things so. I won't be long. Then I'll leave. You must be Henry. I'm sorry that we couldn't have met at a better time, but there you are.'

She walked towards them slowly and Henry stood back to let her pass. Martin hesitated. She would go now and he would be left with what he had said to her. But he could say nothing more. He moved aside. She stopped next to him and before he could back away she gripped his arms tight enough to cause him pain and she leaned forward and stretched upwards and kissed him with hard lips on his cheek.

'You have not hurt me.'

She let him go and he wiped at his cheek where the kiss had hit him.

'You have not hurt me.'

He wanted to say something. Nothing came. She disappeared out the door and started up the stairs.

Henry had his eyes on him now. 'Fuck's sake,' he said, quietly, and turned away. He followed her. He went upstairs. Henry went upstairs.

'Tell her she can go stay with Sean. He'll make a story of it. Get her off. Everybody loves a battered wife.' He shouted. 'That's all you have to tell them. He hit me. So I murdered him. Oh, that's all right, missus, on your way now, there's a good woman.' He paced and turned and came back. His hand gripped the bannister. 'He was my father. He was my fucking father.'

Without any warning Martin began to cry. The shouting stopped and he pushed himself away from the stairs as if he was burned, and he stormed into the kitchen, filling the air with a flurry of arms and angles of his head and weird little noises that he tried to understand, as if they came from someone else. He cried like a child. He could not stop. He sat down and rocked back and forth and it occurred to him that he had seen people do it, rock back and forth like

227

that, and he wondered whether it was learned or natural, and he muttered a debate and his hands were wet.

Henry came and sat by him and put his arms around him and whispered, and Martin could not hear what he was saying. He heard only the sound of his own sobbing, and his mother's footsteps overhead, and his voice not talking, but making a noise like talking, and the footsteps on the stairs, and the small pause then, and the front door closing. He did not hear it opening. Just closing. And then he heard the howl that came out of him and he made it louder to try and cover up the thought that brushed through him like barbed wire – that Henry would stay with him now. That at least there was that.

GRACE

She ran at first, her suitcase knocking her sideways, her shoulder brushing railings, her feet on the ground like hammers, her legs going, buckling. She went the wrong way. She was sure he would call the police. Sure that they would come and find her, her plastic bag of shoes ripped open on the gravel, her hands red and her eyes gone. Just gone.

She looked for a taxi but her eyes were gone.

She was on through the streets then, off the small back lanes and alleys and the quiet routes, and into the recognisable places, again, rushing as if chased. It was not wise to be there. She stopped in the doorway of a pizza restaurant. Let her bags down. Behind the glass a girl in a green apron wiping tables, looked over at her. Did not smile. Went off towards the kitchens, her shoulders sideways. Grace picked up her bags again, turned the corner, sought out narrow fissures in the great blank surface, darted down the smallest kind of crevice she could find, came to a closed gate in a high wall, put her back to it, watched the flash of traffic cross the gap of the world.

Don't hate him. Stop that.

There were rubbish bins against brick, a spill of peels, a sweet smell. She looked at the sky. Something was wrong in her understanding. The sky was empty, ghosted over with absence, the lack of things. She did not understand it. A rectangle, long and distant like the shape of a grave with her in it. Like him in it. Martin had told her what she had done. Killed her husband. His father. As if she had needed telling. She had.

A boy peered in at her from the street. He was small. His hair stood up. He scratched.

'Hello,' said Grace, her voice out of her like a breeze, her breath awful. Had Martin smelled that?

The boy looked away, then back at her. He wore a little earring. He was gone. She lifted her head and ran her tongue around her teeth. She needed toothpaste. Money and toothpaste and a boat to England and a train to Scotland and a job and a place to live. Just that. She must be careful.

Martin with his hair like the little boy's. His voice straight from his father's mouth. The ring of words in his mouth like the ring of rain in a steel bucket on a concrete yard in a cold place in the shadow of a hill. All that. His eyes flashing like traffic, one way and the other, never still for a second, giving her no chance, no chance, to see him, to find him. Gone. All gone.

There was a door in the wall on her left. It opened. A man lifted out a black plastic sack. He looked at her. 'Hello,' he said, and Grace nodded, the gate at her back pressing into her, making her think of a grill. 'All right?' he was saying, a smile on his face. He was her age, grey, greasy black trousers, a white shirt, a barman.

'I'm fine, thank you. Could you call me a taxi?'

He laughed.

'You're a taxi.'

He slammed the door. Grace shivered. For a while she did not understand the joke.

She looked over her shoulder, strained to see, and turned. Through the bars was a small space filled with kegs and crates of empty bottles. That was all. She stared at it for a while, and turned again, the street ahead of her, the shape of a window, its edges clear.

She could just stay where she was. Not move. Let the

light arc over her, its colour changing, her in the shoebox of a lane, still as this. Still.

It would rain. It was there. In the air. She could feel it.

She picked up her bags, her suitcase heavier now than it had been earlier. She looked at it, expecting to see something hanging on to the base, some creature stowing away in the bulges. Her bag of shoes was obscene.

The steps she took towards the street with her bad breath and the smell of her clothes and the sound of her feet unable to lift fully – her steps were not steps. They were measures, like marking out a distance with a blunt ink. She looked behind for the marks. She saw a clutter of similars. As if the lane was a place much used for this kind of thing. This kind of thing.

What was she doing?

The street was bustling, busy, looking the other way. She stayed close to the wall and went towards the river, her head down, her luggage difficult. She watched for a taxi, but furtively, and when she saw one, she did not hail it. She thought he would not stop. And she watched for police cars, especially unmarked police cars, and she saw one of them too, and stepped into a jeweller's windowed entrance and grew dizzy with gold until sure that they had passed. She knew they were police because it was a blue car and it moved slowly.

Every fifty yards she stopped and let those who walked behind her overtake, and she remembered their faces and looked carefully at those who appeared in their stead, and watched for any sign, any hint. There would be more than one. They would have radios, odd machines, techniques.

In front of her a boy ran across the road without looking and a car screeched loudly to a halt, its horn sounding furiously, though the boy had disappeared, running. The driver shook his fist at everything and pulled away with a squeal of tyres like the sound of the boy had he been hit. How did she know that?

'Christ,' said Grace out loud, and a woman looked at her sideways.

She saw the headlines on the evening papers as she passed the vendors in their small metal boxes. X. All they said was X.

What was she now? A murderer?

She was near O'Connell Street. By its side. She had crossed the river then and had not noticed. That was impossible. She looked behind her and caught the figure of a man ducking into a shop. There was a bridge down there, around the corner, the way she had come. The hump-backed bridge. She had clambered across and not seen.

She had to stop. She did not know where she was going. She could see O'Connell's statue, the giant angels, their wings unfolding. Above them, there was a circle of people, clamouring, she supposed. Then O'Connell himself, standing on the top, his face to the river, a stocky little man.

Behind her a woman dropped an umbrella and picked it up again.

She needed to get to a bank. That was it. She needed money. Then she could plan, then she could think. She needed to get to Dun Laoghaire. There would be a ferry that night and she could be on it, watching the water and the cold waves and the birds. She would be on it because that was her plan, Scotland, and she could not change it now. But she needed time to think.

She frowned and felt a drop of rain.

She gathered her bags and turned her back on the angels and her back on Daniel's back, and bowed her head and stayed close to the wall and watched the line of skeletal trees up the centre of the street go by her slowly. Light bulbs. She passed the bullet holes, the wounds, the statues, the place where the pillar had been, the monuments and the plaques. The pattern of past things was not hers. None of it hers.

She was not from here. She was foreign. Her father had wanted her to be English, and English she was. But he had meant her to be English in England.

The rain came down. Grace could feel a chill come into her shoulders. She could sense also the damp smell, the soft odour of the clothes she had been wearing for over two days. Had Martin smelled that? Her bag hit against her legs and she knew what she must look like, smell like.

She was coming near to the top of the street. Around the corner, over there, was the place where the bus had delivered her and she had met Martin and he had taken her bag and walked with her and they had caught that taxi while the tramp had shouted at them and they had driven through the streets to Martin's house. A mistake.

Where was she going?

At the corner there was a bank.

She came up to it slowly, pausing by windows, watching across the road, checking the passing faces. A man turned the corner, away from her, and a woman came around the other way, as if he'd sent her. She walked by Grace and kept on walking. They'd have her trapped inside, if they wanted her, if they saw her go in. She went in. No choice. She needed the money.

She checked her reflection in the tinted glass of the inner door. There was a security guard who looked at her. His shirt very white. She went to the counter by the wall and put down her bags, having to jiggle the shoes so they stood up and did not spill, having to concentrate to stop her hands going, having to be careful. She took a withdrawal slip and filled it in. She wasn't sure of her balance, so she left the amount blank. She looked in her bag for her bank things. Her account number. She still had the keys. The keys to Martin's house. She still had them.

She joined the queue clutching everything, pushing her

suitcase along the floor. In the round eye of the security mirror, hung high over the counter, she saw a man in a suit talk into a mobile phone. He looked familiar. A woman said something to the security guard. He looked at something in her hand. In the queue in front of her a gap opened up as people moved forward and she stood still. In the mirror the bodies seemed misshapen, upper halves too big for thin legs. The security guard smiled. Behind Grace someone coughed. She was holding them up, her body was stiff and breathless. She shook. Then she moved forward.

She lost the mirror. She tried to turn. Too many people.

At the counter the young man smiled at her and called up the balance of her account on the computer screen in front of him. He wrote it on a piece of paper and handed it to her and she subtracted ten pounds from it and wrote the remainder into the box on the withdrawal slip and gave it to him. He frowned and tapped at his keyboard.

'Do you have some identification?'

'I have my card.'

He smiled again and took the card and passed it through a device at his elbow and pointed out to her the small keypad like a calculator on the counter beside her.

'Just press in your pin number there, please.'

Grace looked at him blankly.

'The code,' he said. 'The code number you got with your card.'

She fished around in her bag and found the envelope that the number had arrived in, and squinted at it. It was hard to read because it was written against a blue web of lines and spaces. She watched him. He kept his hands in sight. Behind her there were voices.

'You should really memorise it, you know,' the young man smiled.

Grace nodded.

'I have a terrible memory,' she said.

234

She pressed in the numbers and looked up at the young man.

'That's fine,' he said.

He compared the signature on the back of the card to the one on the slip and then handed the card back to her. Then he opened a deep drawer full of money and counted the notes into his hand and then again on to the counter. She glanced behind her. The doorway empty. The security guard gone. They would wait for her in the street so as not to start a panic. So as to avoid the impression that a robbery was under way.

'Thank you,' she said. 'Is there a back door out of here?'

He raised his eyebrows, but he smiled all the same.

'Pardon?'

'A back door.'

He considered her curiously for a moment.

'There's a staff door, yes. Why?'

'Well, I wonder could I use it?'

He seemed at a loss.

'I'm sorry to have to ask,' Grace continued. 'I wouldn't if it wasn't very important.'

He looked around and scratched his head and peered over Grace's shoulder.

'Can I ask you why?'

Grace sighed and considered him carefully. She had bags with her. She carried her code number around with her card. Because of her memory. She smelled slightly and her hair was wet with rain.

'Well,' she said, quietly, leaning forward so that he leant forward to hear her. 'My husband is waiting outside. I need to get away from him. If I go out there he will only take the money and I'll be left with nothing. Again.'

The young man seemed to tilt his head to one side and become embarrassed.

'I'm sorry,' he said.

'Thank you. He drinks.'

'You wait there. No, actually, go to the end of the counter, over here, I'll let you in.'

Grace slung her handbag, gathered the plastic that held her shoes, picked the suitcase from the floor. She turned and followed the counter and kept her head down. The young man met her and led her through to the far side where the men and women looked up from their desks and watched as she passed them, her head down, her arm held by the young man, smelling slightly, rain in her hair, tears in her eyes, stinging her. She was too embarrassed to wipe at them. She did not look up. She could not.

The door led sideways from the building to a new street. The young man stood next to her and asked if she was all right. Grace was unable to answer. He stayed there, his hand on her arm, the rain falling on his blue shirt so that he crouched a little and hunched his shoulders and screwed up his face.

'Will I leave you here, then?' he asked. 'Will you be okay?'

She nodded and he let go of her and she felt a ring of cold where his hand had gripped her. She cried, but in the rain it was hard to see.

MARTIN

At some point the radio came on. He heard its muffled voice announce the news as if from under water. They would not let her go. The girl. The fourteen-year-old. They would not let her go.

Henry made coffee, but Martin could not drink it. The smell of it was like sweat. He sat in the kitchen, wearing two jumpers, sniffing, dazed. He found it impossible to talk. He refused to move to the living room or upstairs. In the end Henry gave up trying to communicate and went off somewhere and Martin could hear him moving about. He thought that he might be unpacking. When he reappeared he stood in the doorway and Martin could feel him looking down at him.

'I have to eat, Martin. I've had nothing since this morning.'

Martin nodded. He stared at his hands.

'Do you want something?'

He shook his head and formed two loose fists and pushed them together and saw how the knuckles interlocked like the cogs of soft wheels. He ran his chin over them and felt the smoothness and remembered that this was the same day as it had been that morning.

'Do you think I was wrong?' he asked.

Henry stayed where he was and sighed. He did not answer.

Martin laid his hands out in front of him and looked up. 'You didn't believe it, sure you didn't?'

'Believe what?'

'That she'd killed him.'

Henry sighed again.

'No, I suppose not. I'd hoped that Sean had got it wrong, or had made it up or something. He does that kind of thing.'

There was the rustle of tin foil, a chill from the open door of the fridge. A sound started like a roll. It was the kettle. Martin began to drum his fingers on the table top and slowly shook his head.

'She would have had to drive really fast. To be sure of killing him. She would have had to pick him out in the darkness and drive at him, go for him, and keep on going. She would have had to stop then and get out of the car and check that he was dead. Can you imagine that? Can you imagine lying on a road in the dark – dying – and this face looks down at you, pokes you with a foot to see if you're still breathing. Can you imagine knowing who it was that had killed you? Then she would have had to get back into the car and drive home. I can't understand that. How she could just leave him there and head off home and go to bed like nothing had happened. Then she would have rung me later on, and told me that my father was dead. "He's dead," she said, just like that. And she watched him buried. Actually, she didn't. She stood by his grave and she was bored. Bored silly. Then she comes up here and she laughs about it and forgets. She forgets the sight of him dying on the road. How do you forget doing something like that?'

'I'm sure you don't.'

Martin looked up at him. He was pulling rashers from a opened foil wrapper and holding them up to the light. Sniffing.

'She did. It's not like she broke down and confessed. She was caught. That's what it took. Someone to catch her out. If Sean hadn't seen that cop then we'd be none the wiser.'

'You don't know that.'

'You're taking her side.'

He was quiet for a moment, and then said, very calmly, 'I wasn't aware there were sides.'

'She murdered my father.'

'You didn't love him.'

'He was my father.'

'You hated him. You loved her. You knew stuff.'

'What stuff?'

He didn't answer. Martin looked at his hands. He bit on a nail. He wondered whether he had called out words, when they made love. Whether it had just been noise, or whether there had been words there too. He felt tired and disabled, heavy in his chair, breathing with a small pain somewhere in his chest.

'I'm going upstairs for a while, okay?'

'What's wrong?'

'I just want to sleep for a hour or so. Wake me up. Wake me up later. We'll talk then. I can't think straight now.'

Henry went upstairs with him and tidied the bed and closed the curtains and sat beside him as he settled. He kissed his forehead and stroked his hair and Martin was glad when he stopped and left. That kind of thing reminded him of his mother.

GRACE

Mrs Talbot opened the door and smiled immediately and said nothing. She stood aside and ushered Grace in and seemed to dance a little, a flurry of tiny steps without moving, and rubbed her hands together and smiled again like a child. Then she saw more, and her smile faded and she became businesslike and quick. She did not ask.

'The room you had is still empty. You'll want a shower and a change of clothes.'

She led the way up the stairs and fished in the pockets of her apron and produced the key that Grace had had the night before.

'I gave it the once-over this morning, but really you left it very tidy so I didn't have very much to do. I wish I could say the same about some of the other rooms. Do you ever wonder why trains and buses are so incredibly squalid? Well, never mind.'

She unlocked the door and pushed it open and sent Grace in ahead of her. Grace put her bags on the bed and took her money from her pocket. She had forgotten that it was all together in a bundle and was embarrassed at the sight of it. She peeled off fifteen pounds.

'Oh you're all right, dear,' said Mrs Talbot.

'No, I'd like to pay you now. That's your rule.'

Mrs Talbot smiled gently and stepped forward and took the money.

'Thank you, Mrs Wilson. I'm glad you came back.'

She folded the money deftly with the thick fingers of

one hand and looked at Grace kindly, her smile still hovering, more in her eyes than in her mouth.

'Can I do anything for you, dear? In the way of food, I mean. Are you hungry at all?'

Grace was hungry.

'No, thank you.'

'Are you sure, dear?'

'Yes, thanks. I'll be eating later.'

'All right then. But if you need anything, you just ask.'

She tucked the money into an apron pocket and moved backwards to the door.

'I'll be in the kitchen for the next while. So if you change your mind at all, it'll be no trouble.'

Grace smiled and nodded and Mrs Talbot paused for a moment and looked at her. Then she closed the door and was gone.

She had not asked, and Grace wondered at that. And she wondered too at the room, still warm, as if it had been kept for her. But Mrs Talbot could not have known. She could not. It could not have been dreamed of, except maybe in a sickness. A day begun here, unfolding in front of her like a Monaghan road – minutely, delicately ruined – a construction that had crumbled as it was built, that had come apart in front of her as she stepped along it. It would end here too. A circle of small fires. Her eyes in shock. She had lost her son. As quick as saying it, as sharp as that. And had found herself suddenly swaying, as if on the edge of a drop, the sudden threat of being caught like the ground cut away on all sides. She feared it. It was not the law. Not so much. It was the sound of her son, the anger – that. That was what she feared. The hate. As if she had murdered someone else. As if she had killed someone he loved. That. The idea that maybe she had got it wrong.

She could not have gone to the ferry. They would be ready for it. There would be men there watching out for her. They would have a photograph. They would get one

241

from the house, or from Martin. They would be at the airport as well. Why not? She was a murderer. She might kill again. It was what they would think. It was what Martin would say to them. As if there had been no reason. As if it had been a random thing.

She would not kill again. It had been very specific, her crime. Or, that was what she had thought. That it had been committed in a corner with her back to the world. That it had been a private thing, a personal moment plucked from the dark, like the striking of a single match. She had done it, and it was done. She had thought that it would be echoless.

Her clothes were wet and they smelled. She threw them in a heap in the corner and wondered about getting them washed. She emptied the contents of her suitcase on to the bed and retrieved her dressing-gown and her plastic bag of toiletries and crept quietly on to the landing, locking her door behind her. The television was on downstairs, and she heard voices from somewhere, she could not tell where.

In the bathroom she stood naked in front of the mirror and for a while she ran her hands over her body and smelled them. It was not unpleasant. It made her a little drowsy. Her hair was damaged and brittle and felt rough to the touch. In her armpits and beneath her breasts there was a slippery film of sweat that her fingers skated over quickly. On her shoulders and her thighs there seemed to be a layer of grime. Her legs were hard and her feet were swollen and her arms were soft and warm. She ran her palms over all of it and inhaled deeply. Wet wood. Fields in an autumn shower. Trees dripping leaves and water on the sodden grass. The earth down there.

She stepped into the shower and let the water hit her.

It was not echoless, what she had done. That had been her mistake. The echoes of it had reached Martin, and had reached a part of him that she had not known. And the echoes of it had reached Brady and the machine that he could not control, with its sense of measure and its eyes on the streets. And its eyes on the small roads where she had touched her husband quickly with the metal of his own crime and killed him there and then. Just the once. Pushed him away from her like bad food.

In his living she had been the only one to hear the echoes. In his death, though, everyone seemed woken.

MARTIN

The doorbell woke him. He heard the sound of it come from underneath as if he was on a platform, and he sat upright in the bed knowing that something was going on but forgetting for a moment exactly what it was. Then the doorbell went again and he heard Henry going to answer it and he remembered everything and looked at the clock and cursed and threw himself out of the bed and into a pair of jeans and a jumper and out the door. He met Henry on the stairs.

'Police,' said Henry, his face at an angle.

'Jesus. Have they got her?'

'No. They thought she was here.' He was slow, looking at Martin like he was just back, like it was all new.

'Why didn't you wake me?'

He said nothing, just got out of Martin's way, pressing back against the wall to let him pass. Then followed him.

Martin got to the door of the sitting room and paused. He straightened himself and coughed quietly and went in.

Too quick. He'd been too quick. Three minutes ago he'd been asleep. He could have let them wait, relaxed a little. Woken up a little. There were two of them. One was familiar – the man standing with his back to the television as if it was a fire. He had a bald head and a red face and still had his coat on. The other one sat in the armchair but stood as Martin came in. He also wore a coat. He was bearded and young. Martin nodded, felt that his eyes were not fully open. Henry was behind him.

'Mr Quinn,' said the red faced one. 'Pleased to meet you. I'm Detective Brady, Monaghan.'

Martin shook his outstretched hand, a damp fleshy thing without grip.

'Yes.'

'This is Detective Tom Crowley,' Brady went on. 'He's a Dublin man, Harcourt Street.'

The bearded one had a firmer clasp. He smiled. He'd grown the beard because of his baby face. Martin smiled back as best he could and glanced at Henry. He had closed the door. He stood there with his arms folded, like a bouncer.

'We were looking for your mother,' said baby face. Crowley. 'We believe she's no longer here.'

'That's right.'

'Where is she?'

'I don't know.'

He nodded. He looked at Brady. Brady looked at the floor, then at Martin. He smiled.

'When did you last see her?' asked Crowley.

'I don't know. A few hours ago. This afternoon. She came back for her things and left. She murdered my father.'

Crowley's eyebrows went up. A gap opened in his beard. Brady ran a hand over his head and sat down. Henry groaned. Almost. A noise like a groan. Martin glanced at him. His arms had unfolded.

'What makes you say that?' said Crowley.

The television was on. The sound turned down.

'Well, I imagine that's what you wanted to talk to her about. I mean.'

'We wanted to talk to her, yes,' said Brady, coughing a little. 'About that. Certain things have come to light . . .'

Crowley cut him off.

'What is it makes you think your mother killed your father?'

On the television now there was a man talking, like a shoulder-up ghost in the room, babbling, invisible.

'She said it. To a friend. You know him.' He gestured at Brady. 'He knows him. She said it to this friend and then went off. Disappeared. She turned up today again but now she's gone.'

Crowley shook his head.

'You're going to have to start from the beginning, Mr Quinn, if you don't mind. I'm not sure I follow you.'

Brady nodded, nodded at Martin, as if encouraging him, as if he knew him, as if Martin would think it mattered that he nodded, as if Martin was in need of that kind of thing. Crowley sat down. Henry had his hands in his pockets. For the first time, Martin noticed a half-eaten omelette on top of the television. There was a balled-up tissue beside it on the plate, a fork, face up. He sat down in the armchair. Brady had the other one, Crowley had the sofa to himself. Henry by the door.

'From where?'

'The beginning.'

'Where's that?'

He told them everything. Rolled it out like a little story, like a joke. It was words and sentences and he looked at the carpet as he said it, his hands on his knees, quickly. He wasn't sure how to finish. There was a silence. Then Brady asked again about Sean – about Sean's lie.

'That's a little journalistic prodding,' he said. 'That's what that is.'

Crowley looked at Brady, frowning, shaking his head minutely, very pissed off.

'Did your mother mention Detective Brady at all?' he said, not looking at Martin, looking at Brady.

'Yeah. That he was here.' Brady stared at him. A lesser red. 'She said you were keeping her informed.'

He nodded and sighed, twisting his lips.

'I told her it was all right for her to come and stay with you. Perhaps I should have kept a closer eye.'

He shook his head. Crowley looked at him as if he was mad. Henry coughed, shifted on his feet, one hand leaving a pocket, a red mark on the back of it, holding the opposite elbow.

'Did you not suspect her then?' he asked.

Brady sniffed.

'Ah well. Not really, no. Certain things though, now. Certain tests and so forth . . . We have a clearer picture.'

Martin smiled, shook his head. These guys.

'You're not very good at your job, are you? Sean thought of it. You'd think you might have. Christ, it's obvious.'

He sat back, folded his arms. Henry was looking at him. Very still. Nobody said anything.

They asked about Sean. Crowley carefully wrote down his address. Then they went, standing up at the same time as if synchronised. Crowley gave Martin a card with his name on it and two phone numbers, one at work, one at home. He told him to ring any time. He shook his hand. Brady did not.

On the street there was a Garda car with two uniformed men staring at Martin through the watery air. Brady and Crowley climbed into a plain black Ford and started talking to each other out of the corners of their mouths. Crowley drove. Martin watched them pull away, the squad car following, and it occurred to him that they had taken everything he'd told them at face value. They had believed him. They might have suspected him of collusion with his mother. They might even have suspected him of having done it himself. But no. They had listened and nodded and disputed nothing. As if he was easily known.

He closed the door, seeing in the crack of darkness that he shut out, the drunk, the woman, the wanker's claw woman, staring at him. He clicked the lock and turned in the hallway and saw Henry, returned, standing in the door of the kitchen, a plate of cold omelette in one hand, a fork in the other, his head up as if something had been said to him, his eyes a little wide, staring at him too.

GRACE

There was a mist in the morning, a fog that hung over the river. Grace peered out at it until her eyes hurt. She had caught a cold. Her throat was sore and her nose blocked and there was the ghost of a headache and an ache in her bones. She hoped it was not 'flu.

Mrs Talbot had not knocked on her door this time. Grace had not asked. She had stayed in her room, hungry, her mind turning, thinking about herself.

She dressed and went downstairs, late, just before half eight, expecting it to be quieter then. But there were three men chatting at one table, and a young couple at another, and Mrs Talbot seemed slightly flustered. She smiled, asked Grace had she slept well, and said nothing more. Grace could hear her talking to someone in the kitchen, another woman. There was laughter, and the sound of Mrs Talbot whispering, and more laughter.

The breakfast was big again, and this time Grace ate it all, hurriedly. Nobody had a newspaper. She left the room and went back upstairs while Mrs Talbot was in the kitchen, silent now.

The fog had lifted. She lay on the bed and wished that she had a radio. Perhaps she could buy one somewhere. A small one. Perhaps one that fitted in your pocket and had headphones that went inside your ears.

She had not slept much the night before, and dozed now, slipping away more easily for not trying. In her mind she saw Martin. Martin from years ago. She dreamed of summer, of the warmth of the grass, sitting with him by the small lake, the noise of her husband's tractor from over the hill. She would bring her husband sandwiches in the afternoon. Sandwiches and a bottle of milk and sometimes an apple. She dreamed that she was carrying a tray across the fields. On the tray there was a pot of tea and some cups and a cake. She dreamed that her husband saw her and stopped the tractor and it coughed itself quiet and he climbed down and wiped his brow and sat on a bale of hay and waited for her. When she reached him he held up his hands to take the tray, but she walked on past him and started to laugh. Then she was by the small lake and they were having a picnic – Martin and herself. There was no sound. It was like a television with the volume turned down.

It was cold. She shivered on the bed and felt her throat increasingly raw and sore. She swallowed and it hurt her, and she clenched her eyes and rolled over and felt the cold follow her and cling to her. She should get under the blankets.

She dreamed again. Her father at the top of the stairs, bouncing a football down the steps to her. She caught it and threw it up at him and he gently set it rolling again, bumping towards her, bouncing higher and higher the closer it came. She caught it and shrieked and her father put a finger to his lips and shushed her.

'Don't wake your mother.'

She sat in the garden with her sister, waiting. She could not think what they might be waiting for. They looked at each other nervously.

Grace started and sat up and listened. It came again, a light knock on the door. The room was dim, gloomy, and she felt the cold on her skin when she moved, and it hurt. Her throat was closed and stinging. She eased herself from the bed, her muscles aching, and switched on the bedside lamp. The knock came again, followed by the low voice of Mrs Talbot.

'Hello? Mrs Wilson?'

'Yes,' said Grace, sure that she could not be heard. 'Hold on.'

She looked at herself briefly in the mirror and drew the curtains. Then she looked at her watch and opened them again. It was only four o'clock. She paused by the door. Perhaps she had been caught. Or her picture had appeared in the evening papers. A description on the radio. Maybe Brady was there, at the door, at Mrs Talbot's shoulder, his big head frowning, getting ready to apologise. She swallowed hard to try and ease her throat and opened the door.

Mrs Talbot stood there alone, in the dark of the landing. She wore her apron and smiled for a moment and looked at Grace.

'I'm sorry, dear,' she said. 'Did I disturb you?'

'I was just having a snooze, actually.'

Mrs Talbot nodded her head slowly, her mouth in an oh shape, as if she did not quite believe it.

'I haven't seen you all day, dear. I thought you might be hungry. Perhaps you'd like to have dinner this evening?'

She spoke without seeming to think about what she was saying. She kept her eyes on Grace, watchful and curious. She had told Grace that she didn't do evening meals.

'No. No thank you.'

'Will you be going out, then?'

'No, well, I don't know, perhaps.'

Mrs Talbot laughed.

'I'm sorry, dear, I'm the nosiest old dragon you're ever likely to meet. You do what you like. It's none of my business. All I mean to say is that if you want anything, you just let me know.'

She balled her hands together and looked at them. She was trying to think of something to say. Grace thought she

251

looked like an upturned bowl, covering something. A cake. She sniffed.

'Do you have a cold, dear?'

'Well, yes, I think so.'

'Oh well, dear, now listen to me. You get back in there and close the door and snuggle up in bed and I'll bring you up some soup and a sandwich. I insist on it. It'll do you good. Does Anadin work for you at all?'

'I don't know, probably . . .'

'It works for me. I practically live on the stuff. I'll bring up some Anadin as well, and Lemsip later on for before you go to sleep. Now you get back in there and into bed. I won't be a minute.'

She closed the door. There was the noise of her on the stairs, careful, clumping. It was true that Grace was hungry. She did have a cold. She did not want to leave the room. But there, in that offer of hot soup, she had heard the promise of company. Talk. Grace did not want to talk. She could not afford it. She would blab and forget and reveal something. She would become confused.

She tried to remember the story she had told Mrs Talbot as she slowly undressed and put on her nightclothes and her dressing-gown and slipped into the bed. She had said that she was going to her son's house to get her things and then she was going away to Scotland. She had told her the truth then. No, she had said that there had been a misunderstanding and her son had gone away and that was why she had no clothes and was staying in a guesthouse.

Where was she from?

She shook the blankets and smoothed them down at her sides. She would have to invent a reason for not taking the ferry. Storms. There were no storms. Technical faults. A million things could go wrong with a rudder, she imagined. But those kinds of things were announced on the radio. Everybody heard them. And it would only mean that there would be a delay, that she would have to leave the next day, or the day after. There would have to be something else. She would say that she had changed her mind. Then why not stay with her son?

Where?

Mrs Talbot knocked and did not wait for an answer. She turned the handle and pushed the door open with her hip, holding out a large tray.

'Here we are,' she said, breathlessly. She closed the door with a small, delicate foot and made her way quickly, as if about to tip forwards, towards the dresser where she placed the tray and gave a loud sigh.

'Dear Lord, this house is getting smaller, I swear it is. Smaller and taller, if you know what I mean. It'll end up as one giant ladder, me stuck somewhere in the middle with my elbows squashed, too frightened to look down and too fat to keep going.'

Grace smiled at her and tried to see what was on the tray. She was very hungry.

'Do you know, if I die bringing someone their tea, I'll be livid. If I die cooking or washing or climbing stairs I'll arrive in heaven and cause such a scene that I'll be sent to hell on the spot.'

'You shouldn't have, really,' said Grace. 'I could have come downstairs.'

'Oh, I'm not complaining, Mrs Wilson. I really amn't. At least, not about you. I don't mind bringing you some soup and tea and a bit of bread. I don't mind at all, but there's some people here expect their breakfast in bed and then dinner and God knows what else, and me like the fool I am, I give in to them. I shouldn't. Shouldn't do it at all. Now, Anadin. Here you are, take those.'

She dropped two white tablets into Grace's palm and handed her a glass of water and stood with her hands on her hips. Grace swallowed. The cold water eased her throat a little.

'Good,' said Mrs Talbot. 'That'll make things better. I'm not sure if you should take them before or after food, but I don't suppose it matters.'

She took a large linen serviette and spread it out on Grace's lap and handed her a bowl of piping hot vegetable soup..

'I hope you like it. Home made. It'll warm you up, anyway. Warm you up.'

She gave Grace a spoon and placed a plate of buttered bread on the bedside table. Then she moved the chair from beside the wardrobe to nearer the bed and settled herself into it, shuffling, wedging.

'I'll sit with you for a while, Mrs Wilson, if you don't mind. There's no one around downstairs except Annie, and if you think I talk too much you should meet Annie Collins. Never shuts up. She comes in mornings and evenings during the week. Today now she's got a bee in her bonnet about this abortion business. I can't bear to listen to her.'

Grace smiled. She did not feel inclined to mind. She was too hungry, the soup was too good. Still on the tray was a pot of tea, and two mugs. At least she would not be expected to talk. Mouth full, working. Pieces of cake as well, she thought. Dark, chocolate-looking cake.

'And there's not much traffic through here on a Tuesday for some reason. It's the quietest day of the week. It's a bit of a nothing day really, Tuesday. Wednesday is midweek, Thursday is getting on for the weekend, Friday is the weekend, really, and so are Saturday and Sunday, and then Monday is the first day of the week and everyone gets through it by complaining about it, but Tuesday, well, Tuesday just sort of sits there and does nothing, doesn't it?'

Grace nodded and sipped soup from her spoon. Salty. Tongue curling.

'I once heard,' Mrs Talbot continued, 'that there are more burglaries on a Tuesday than there are on any other day.

Isn't that strange? Burglaries of all things. Statistics can be wonderful like that – throwing up the strangest notions.'

She made to fold her arms, but it seemed they were not long enough and they snapped back like elastic and left her hands there dangling over her lap. Grace slowed down.

'Did you know that red cars are involved in more accidents than any other colour? I read that just the other day. My husband drove a red car. Never had an accident. But the thing about statistics is that you're covered all kinds of ways. Men with wives called Ida are probably less likely to have an accident in a red car than men with wives called Eileen, or Bridget, or whatever. We fit into so many categories, you see, most of us, that it can't really be said what we might be likely to do or not do, or have done or not done, or are prone to or not prone to or what have you. Or what have you not.'

She gave a loud laugh and rocked a little back and forth, the chair not liking it. Grace thought of her naked. There would be wonderful warmth in the folds.

'Oh dear. You must tell me to shut up. I don't know what I'm talking about.'

Grace smiled and chewed bread and lifted the soup bowl towards her mouth so as not to spill any more. There were already two or three drops on the lapel of her dressing-gown. Mrs Talbot was silent for a moment, smiling to herself and looking at her fingers.

'So,' she said finally, in a tone that alerted Grace. Here it was. 'Did your son come back?'

'He did, yes,' said Grace, as brightly as she could. 'He came back.'

'Good for him. They're terribly unpredictable, sons. I have several. How many have you?'

'Just the one.'

'Really? What age is he?'

'He's twenty-four.'

'Is that all?'

How old did Grace look?

'Sure he's still a baby. But they get older younger now, if you know what I mean. All the pressure on them. School. Points. Then no work. Nothing. I feel so sorry for them. I have four sons. Two of them are still in Dublin, the older ones, both married and doing fine, although one was made redundant last year. He was very lucky to get another job. Very lucky. Then the other two are gone. Seamus is in London, and Mark in New York. Mark is the same age as your lad. Well, he's twenty-three actually, but it makes no difference as far as I'm concerned. Babies, all of them.'

'Yes,' said Grace. She was coming to the last of the soup and the start of the thirst. She eyed the glass of water by her side.

'And daughters?'

Grace shook her head.

'I've two. Paula is in Germany but doesn't like it and she's coming home. And Anne is in London, staying with her brother, with Seamus. He'll look after her. She's my youngest. Nineteen. She only left last summer. She used to help me here. She was back for Christmas, and to be honest I'm not sure that it was a good idea. Oh, I know that's awful to say, really. It was wonderful to have her back, but it was just that it took such a lot out of me. The sadness of it. When they come back for such a short time it only reminds you that they've gone, if you know what I mean. You should have seen me the day she left. New Year's Day it was. I never cried so much.'

She was silent, her voice going back into her and stopping, her head slipping down. Quietly, Grace put the empty soup bowl on the bedside table and lifted the water and drank it all without pausing, her eyes on the still shape of Mrs Talbot, the room spread out around her, a bird flashing by the window, the sky dying. She looked up. Frowned.

'Dear God, here's me rattling on and you sitting there,

gasping I'd say. Annie puts enough salt in her soups th.
you could walk across them.'

She shoved the chair away from her rising bulk, and
took away the empty bowl and the glass and stood at the
dresser, rearranging things on the tray.

'Tea, dear, do you take sugar?'

'No thanks, no sugar.'

'Fair play to you. I like it sweet. Sweet and hot.' She
turned with a mug in her hand and looked at Grace. A big
smile on her, a test in her eyes. 'Like a good man.' Grace
laughed. Reassured, Mrs Talbot gave a little shriek and
rocked back on her heels. She placed the mug of tea on the
table, chuckling, and turned to pour her own.

'Do you know, Mrs Wilson, since my husband died I've
been more inclined to be faithful to him. Isn't that a strange
thing?' She sat down at her chair once more and sipped
her tea. 'Not that I was ever unfaithful, you understand,
never once.'

She looked at Grace and gave another big smile. They
were loaded, these smiles. They came to Grace with paper-
work. Sign here. Receipt. Respond. Acknowledge.

'But I thought about it, dear. Dear Lord, did I think about
it. The Pope says that's just as bad, and I can see his point.
I really can. I don't agree with much he says, and I
wouldn't go as far as to call it sinning or any such nonsense, but I can see his point. It's not very loyal, is it? It
smacks a little of cowardice, I think. Being afraid to live
your own life, wanting all the time to live a different one.
But nevertheless, I can't deny it, it's what I did. I imagined
myself into all kinds of affairs with all kinds of men. You
wouldn't believe the half of it.'

She chuckled and sipped her tea busily and looked at
the backs of her hands.

'Never did a thing though. Thirty-six years we were
married, and I never so much as touched another man.
Just thought about it. And do you know, since my husband

257

died, I've not thought about it at all. Now that I'm well within my rights, now that I could quite easily make myself available for whoever wants me, not that there'd be many, but if there was you understand, then I could, and not a thing the Pope could say against it, and do you think I'm interested? Not a smidgen. And yes, I admit it, I flirt with the lads here, I'm sure you've seen me, but it's strictly business, my heart isn't in it. And if one of them suddenly whispered in my ear,' she hooted, her hand flailing towards the window, 'and wanted me to ride off on his train with him, ha, well, I can tell you honestly, it wouldn't matter if he was,' she shook her head, blew out her lips, flicking through a file of famous men, 'Richard Gere. I wouldn't budge because I couldn't be bothered.'

Grace laughed, explosively, with a burst of damp, warm, soupy breath. Mrs Talbot lifted her head, surprised, and laughed as well. Then she stopped.

'My God, dear, I've forgotten the cake.'

Grace laughed on. Mrs Talbot retrieved two plates from the tray and handed one of them to her. On it was a piece, not of chocolate cake, but of fruit cake.

'And it's nothing to do with the Church or anything,' Mrs Talbot continued, biting into the cake, largely, wiping something from her lip, lowering herself into her seat once more, holding her plate steady in mid air, as if she was impossibly suspended from it. 'I've never been much of a one for the Church,' she was down, 'and I haven't gone all religious in my old age. It's not that.'

She sipped her tea and had another bite, and another, placing her mug on the empty plate, balancing it on her knee.

'It's more . . ., excuse me, dear, but this cake is gorgeous.' Grace nodded. 'Annie's, you know. You wouldn't think it from looking at her, all dry and puckered as she is. Woody Woodpecker they call her. Skinny as a stick and yap yap yap all the time. You'd never think she could come up with something so rich and moist.' Her cheeks bulged, her face a machine. 'And just plain delicious.'

Grace was smiling, her nose wrinkled, her hands slippy. Mrs Talbot was like a show.

'What was I saying? It's not the Church or anything like that. It's more,' she wiped her mouth, dabbed it with a finger, 'personal. Dear. He was a sweet old thing, my husband. Very kind. Not the cleverest man in the world, but a good heart. And that's what matters, dear. And it's like what they say. That you don't know what you have till it's gone. Taken from you.' She held the mug gingerly, pressed her thumb to the plate, gathering crumbs. 'He was taken very suddenly, you see. It was a big shock, to lose someone who's been so close to you that you've forgotten they're there. And you only realise it when there's a space where there wasn't one before. There's a gap, a little chill, a draft. And you think – what's missing here? And then you realise.'

She was quiet for a moment. Grace frowned. The light from outside was no longer really working. Mrs Talbot was lost against the grey clouds, the rise of the landscape, the bare trees. Grace could see her, but she was not clear.

'So to me, you see, it's that space that has become special. The space beside me, the gap. The lack of him. If I filled it then I'd forget. And I don't want to forget. All I have left of him is the gap he left. It's very special to me.'

They were quiet for a moment, only distant road noise, and then the squawk of a bird, a scrape on the silence that pulled Mrs Talbot's head up.

'Oh, I'm sorry, dear. I'm talking nonsense.'

'No, no,' said Grace quickly. 'It's not nonsense.'

'I prattle on, though. It's my failing. I get started on something and I'm off, and before you know where you are you have my life story and my theory of the universe and my opinion on everything.'

'Really, it's good to have the company.'

259

More tea, dear?'

Grace nodded and Mrs Talbot rose and collected her ıg from her and poured fresh tea for them both. She sighed as she added milk and spooned sugar into her own.

'It's our children as well, Mrs Wilson. Your son up here in Dublin, away from you. My lot scattered all over the place. We remember them as they were the day they left us. And of course that's not the way they are. That's why it was so difficult for me to see my daughter at Christmas. Because she's changed and I don't know her. She's not a complete stranger, but you know it'd almost be better if she was. I kept on thinking I knew her, I kept on recognising her, and then thinking nothing had changed and saying something as if nothing had changed. But then she'd look at me. The same, but different.'

Mrs Talbot laughed.

'She's been taken over. Possessed. Invasion of The Body Snatchers. They've brainwashed our children, Mrs Wilson. They send them back to us at Christmas time to make us depressed.'

She shook her head and smiled broadly and looked at Grace.

'Is your son long away from you dear?'

Grace nodded. 'Five years.'

'Well, there you are, you see. You'll know exactly what I mean, then. And I bet you've spent more time thinking about him since he's gone than you ever did while he was with you. I know I do with mine. The very fact that they're not there makes them bigger, more important, makes them more there, if you follow me. It's like what I said about my husband. It's the gaps. We're all gaps. It's the gaps in our lives that take up the most space, Mrs Wilson.'

She stood by the bed, her mug in prayer hands, her eyes on Grace.

'I've noticed that.'

Grace nodded and sipped at her tea. She felt the hot

liquid scrape its way through her sore throat and she closed her eyes for a moment to let it pass. When she opened them Mrs Talbot sat across from her like a big doll, smiling, rolling her head a little as she looked at Grace. She had turned the light on. The bedside light. While Grace had had her eyes closed. In that time.

Gaps. Grace understood her, knew the sensation of spaces, of places cleared. They filled her mind.

'So, dear,' said the woman in the new light. 'Tell me about your husband.'

In the quiet of the room Grace could hear the distance between things. She could sense how far she was from the street, and it came to her as a sound, not the sound of the street or the sound of the room, but of the distance between them. And she could hear the distance between her and the river that moved all the time. There was a hum of distances, a small orchestra of other places. It sounded like the snapping tight of ropes, like the plucking sound that came when a climber fell and was stopped from falling further.

She told Mrs Talbot everything. And Mrs Talbot had become Ida, horrified and appalled and, in the end, saddened. She had shook her head slowly and cried a little, quietly. She had sat on the side of the bed and stroked Grace's hair and calmed her and held on to her when she came to the part about Martin, about the things he had said to her.

They were on first name terms by then, and their foreheads touched. From within her shaking and her sobbing Grace could see them clutched together on the bed and it made her shake all the more. She would be like this for ever now, reliant on strangers, at the mercy of people whom she did not know. Ida Talbot worked hard and spoke little and calmed her in the end and left her sleeping. She had awoken in the small hours and had slipped out to the bathroom and back again before remembering exactly what it was that had happened.

She had crouched by the river and tried to see the stars moving. She had only seen the spinning of the water, the way it continued.

Killed my husband, Mrs Talbot. Shot him dead with the bonnet of his car. Went then and had a bath. Tried not to sing.

'Oh, Mrs Wilson.'

She had stared deep into her eyes and Grace had stared back, focusing first on one eye and then the other, darting between the two, unable to decide.

'Oh, Grace.'

'I saw his legs snapped at the knees like match sticks. There was very little blood but I could see the white of his bones through the rips in his trousers. And I couldn't see his face, and I told myself that it was because of the way he was lying – that his face was hidden. But I think it was gone.'

They would have taken the car and looked underneath it and they would have sent pieces of skin and clothing to some laboratory and they would have waited. Measured the ground; waited. Skin and clothing.

'Oh.'

Ida Talbot had forgotten to bring a Lemsip and Grace's throat was nearly unbearable now. It had been worn ragged by the crying and the talking. Ragged. So much talking that she had worn her throat ragged. She remembered the river.

She went to the window and lifted the corner of the curtain and wiped away the condensation and cupped her hand to the glass and peered into the darkness, trying to see the river. It was too far.

She looked down, as if from a high hill – as if transported – the landscape of what she had done laid out before her. She stood there and felt the ripping of the trees by her side.

She stood and looked out over the wreck of the world. She saw herself in a red car. Red cars are involved in more accidents than any other colour. Ida had told her.

She stood at a great height over the land that had taken her and kept her and killed her child. She saw herself upon it, moving like the ink of a red pen. Writing herself across the world, telling her small, thin, story. Her sketch. But she knew that it was not what mattered. She knew that this is not the way the world is seen, from above. It is seen from the ground, from the pits and the ditches where people have fallen. She knew what would be seen of her. It would be just a single point, a small place, self-contained, no path leading to it, no path going away. Just a red dot.

For ever, she would be in a red car on a long narrow part of the road, killing her husband in the quiet of the night. That, now, was where she was fixed. It was what she was for the world. All. All she was.

She had described herself.

MRS TALBOT

Her keys tugged her downstairs. All that metal in her apron pockets, pulling at her, bringing her down. She jingled them with her fingers, made a sound like a slot machine paying out.

What was it? What? That made her the centre of this world. She had seen it so often, felt it. She had been the middle. As if she was cut out of a different air, made from something chemical, she didn't know, scientific, nuclear. Magnetic. Ida and her keys.

Arthur had known. He had noticed. Things happened near Ida Talbot, née Boyle. Good things, bad things. Things. Car crashes. Brain haemorrhages. Windfalls. Lightning. No, not lightning. A strange fire once. Love. Love happened near Ida Talbot. People met each other under her benevolent gaze. Found calm in the shelter of her shadow, space in her presence. Time. Something like that. Arthur had called it genius. Genius, he said, as in peculiar spirit, as if there was a ghost in her. She did not feel it like that. There was just a succession of events, and her watching, reviewing the parade. Arthur had thought sometimes that she'd been a cause, but she knew she was not. She watched, gawking, astonished.

They had been married by a priest who was now a cardinal. Yes. They had won the money for the guesthouse. Won it. When she heard the songs, the correct songs, three of them, in the right order, she picked up the telephone and dialled once and it was answered immediately and they teased her for a while and told her then that she was the tenth caller. Twenty thousand pounds. Just like that. Yes. The bank loved them. Arthur marvelled. 'River View', he wanted to call it. River View it was. He kept his job for a while, but there was no need for it. River View did well. Mostly because the guesthouse that CIE used for their Hueston Station train drivers had collapsed while being renovated, two weeks after River View opened. Yes.

Arthur noticed. He noticed.

While she was giving birth to Paula in the Rotunda, Nelson's Pillar had exploded a few hundred yards away. She had nodded during labour. There's the pillar gone, she muttered, while the nurse dabbed at her with a damp cloth. Once, on their only foreign holiday ever, she had walked across the beach towards the Mediterranean water and the water had crackled and a small boy flapped in the shallows like a fish, his arched back jumping. An electric cable in the sand, ruptured by storms, brought to his bare foot by the motion of the moon. He was quite dead. She stood and watched his mother behave as if she was the victim of a practical joke. On the plane back home they found themselves staring at a man who looked familiar. It was the cardinal. Incognito. The plane made an emergency landing in Birmingham.

Ida's mother was accidentally locked into a walk-in freezer in a warehouse in Cabinteely, and died there. Her father slipped in the shower at the age of seventy-three and bled to death from a gash to the groin. Her younger sister Hilda fell down two flights of stairs in a city centre theatre and received seventeen thousand pounds compensation, out of court, even though she had only suffered a sprained ankle and bruising. Ida had been in the lobby getting ice cream. Her sister landed at her feet. They had giggled.

Arthur had started keeping notes.

Ida introduced his spinster sister to a train driver called

PJ and they married each other at the ages of sixty-three and fifty-five. Arthur expected them to produce a child, so oddly did he regard his wife's influence. He used to buy sweep tickets and hide them under the cushion of Ida's armchair. Betting slips. Greedy paper. It didn't work.

He lost faith in her. He looked for control. Sought to direct things. That's men. Confused Ida's nature with luck. Thought her bafflement an idle thing, apathy. Tried to prod her into science. Interviewed her. Studied her story. Asked questions about her parentage, seeking perhaps an eastern European ancestor. A Romanian gypsy. A Balkan magician. A priest. A seer. Something. Anything. Ida shrugged and laughed. On her mother's side, whose people came from Donegal, there had been, way back, way back, the seventh son of a seventh son who cured animals and children and died strangely after a row with a Protestant minister rumoured to be in league with the devil. But she wasn't about to tell him that. He'd have made something of it.

Every time she went out she bumped into celebrities. Her opinion was regularly polled. Twice her photograph had appeared on the front page of newspapers. A summer scene, in colour, the Phoenix Park, sunbathers, children, Ida in the background chasing Seamus, barefoot, her hazel hair flying. Long time ago, that. And a winter scene, black and white, trudging down a deserted O'Connell Street in a blizzard, barely recognisable, on her way home from the cinema. Once, she went to see *Ryan's Daughter* with Hilda and saw the box office robbed as they queued for popcorn.

Arthur died the day before their anniversary. Disappointed, despite everything. Tired. Perplexed. A little resentful, maybe, that he had not known how to control it. The sense of an opportunity missed.

But there had never been anything quite like this. Never. It would have spooked him. He had not liked the dead boy in the blue water. He had not liked the odd fire in the bank manager's office, her mother in the freezer, her father in the shower. Not death. Death had spooked him. Murder would have shaken him badly. She saw his face, pale, thin-lipped, a flurry of his hands in a blessing, reaching for the telephone then. Murder, Ida. Murder.

She sat on the sofa in front of the blank television. There was a murderer in room four. She said it out loud.

'There is a murderer in room four.'

Wilma jumped up beside her, ran the bulb of her head along Ida's thigh.

'Wilma, Wilma, listen to me, pet. There is a murderer in room four.'

Wilma didn't seem to mind. She stretched her neck, groped with a loose paw for a finger upon which she could impale herself.

People found her. Events found her. Money found her. A steady stream of inconclusive oddities bubbled past her. Coincidences. Peculiarities. So what? It did not make her special. There was a woman in room four in trouble. More trouble than Ida could have imagined a person like Mrs Wilson, Grace, enduring in a whole lifetime. This was no time for thinking like Arthur. This was a time for a singular strength, a calm voice, a good ear. Space. Quiet. All that. Murder was a complicated thing.

Annie wanted to know what was wrong.

'You have a face on you. I know you. You'd never say it but you're asked. What's wrong with you?'

'Nothing's wrong with me.'

Annie scowled, cracking eggs on the lip of a bowl. Ida switched on the radio. Mrs Wilson, Grace, was staying in her room.

'How many is in?'

'Seven.'

'You'll go bust.'

'There'll be sixteen tomorrow and you'll tell me I don't need all that money.'

'You're in a right mood, Ida. Is it this X thing? It's fouled me up, it has. All that bloody nonsense for nothing. As if it was the end of the world.'

'May be. For some.'

'Oh, don't. Don't you start. That girl's more important. She's real.'

'That's not what I meant.'

'What then?'

'Mind those shells.'

'You've no business being in a mood, Ida Talbot. Your morning's got a day ahead of it.'

Annie whisked eggs like they might come at her. She threw in milk and salt and pepper as if casting a spell.

It was always the case that people arrived for breakfast as if they met in the hall and waited until there was enough of them. Then Annie would panic, and her mouth would start, and she seemed to feel that if she kept conversations going with enough of them then they wouldn't notice that she was lost. Now five of seven arrived at once. Five. And a sixth five minutes later.

'You all on the same train?' shouted Ida.

'They're lazy and late, the sleepy heads. Are you not going to shave, Michael?'

'I'm . . .'

'You're like a ghost. What time were you up till? Are you having scrambled or fried?'

'Scrambled.'

'Scrambled,' shouted Annie. 'And there's lovely bacon Mrs Talbot got in Buckley's. White pudding soaks up a hangover, Michael, I'll give you extra. Scrambled, Paul? Scrambled,' she shouted. 'This abortion case is a nightmare, isn't it?'

The radio was on about it. Ida turned it down a little.

'There's a lot of people feel this very bad.'

'Is there fried bread?'

Ida threw two slices in the pan.

'Fried bread,' shouted Annie. 'I wonder will the girl's family appeal. I hope to God they do. I hope to God they do.'

'The government are going to finance it,' someone said. 'The appeal. Going against their own judges.'

'They're not their judges,' said someone else.

'And to other news now,' said the radio.

Ida muttered. No hot plates. All stacked cold on the sideboard.

'Fried,' shouted Annie. 'They'll not overrule it, you know. How can they? It's what happened with the Birmingham Six.'

'An appalling vista,' said a gruff voice, in imitation.

'Mrs Grace Quinn,' said the radio. Ida held a ruptured egg shell in her fingers. The hiss was too loud. Annie nattered. Ida strained.

' . . . about the death of her husband. We think Mrs Quinn may be in Dublin.' It was a country voice, northern, a policeman.

'We know that she was in the South Circular Road area on Monday, eh, Monday afternoon. She may have left the city but we don't really think that likely. She may be in a hotel or guesthouse and we're very keen that she gets in touch with us. Or if anybody has seen her or knows where she might be, they should get in touch with the Gardai at Harcourt Street.'

'Can you describe her, Detective?' said David Hanley.

'Scrambled,' shouted Annie.

Ida dropped the shell into the bin.

'She's approximately five feet five in height, average build, greying hair. She was wearing a white blouse and blue jumper and, eh, a skirt, a blue skirt, and a beige raincoat. She would have had a suitcase as well. A grey suitcase.'

'Mrs Quinn's husband died in a hit-and-run.'

'That's right.'

'And I believe he was the same man who was involved in a hit-and-run some years ago in which a young woman died. Is that right?'

'Eh, yes. But in this instance we're just seeking the whereabouts of Mrs Quinn. We'd appreciate the public's, eh, help, in this, eh, matter.'

'Very well,' said David Hanley. 'Traffic news now, with . . .'

'Is there nothing ready?' squealed Annie, in the door and looking at her.

'You never put the plates in. They're cold.'

'They're still not in either. Where's the sausages?'

Ida concentrated, cut the sound of Annie out, did it, did the breakfasts, did them right. It was true, then. Well. She had known, she supposed. But still, she had half hoped, and her hopes were always halved, that Grace was wrong, forgetful, mistaken. That she was not what she thought she was. Not that. Not that. But she was. She was.

That.

GRACE

She had not left her room in thirty hours. Trips to the bathroom just. Rustling along the wallpaper, lights off, eyes on the stairs. Distrusting the silence. Jumping at the slightest sound. Then back. Examining the frame of the world open to her, counting the walls out there, the birds, the buildings, the trees, the branches.

Mrs Talbot brought her breakfast, and was quiet, and regarded her for a moment, and told her then that she had to give herself up.

'You can't live in a room,' she said, and then stopped, caught the look that Grace gave her, and frowned.

'I'm sorry, dear. That's a stupid thing to say.'

'You mean this room.'

'I do not. I do not mean this room. That's not what I mean at all.'

Grace said nothing. Why exchange one room for another? Why? She bit with a small mouth at burned fried bread.

'They have named you on the radio.'

She closed her eyes. A clog of food was in her mouth, where nothing should be. How could she eat? She opened her eyes, clutched the mug of tepid tea, cleared it, closed her eyes.

'Have they?'

'They have. Gave a useless little description. Hemmed and hawed. Want to talk to her about the death of her husband, sounded like a Monaghan man.'

'Brady.'

'Didn't say, dear. Or I didn't hear. How's your throat?'

'Fine.' She coughed. 'Fine.'

Mrs Talbot sat on the bed, her arms at her sides, as if supporting her weight, keeping her from sinking into the softness and disappearing. Big as she was. Her face was a mix. She was plainly perturbed, but it was in the way forward that her uncertainty seemed to lie. She wondered what Grace should do. But seemed not to wonder at what Grace had done. She had asked very little. Only, 'Was it a spur of the moment thing, dear?' and 'What colour car?', and she had held her. Held her.

'I'm sorry, Mrs Talbot. I can't stay here. It's not fair.'

'It's Ida, and it's absolutely fair, dear. This is your home for as long as you need it. You'll not hear me grumble. But it's you I'm worried about, not my room. You, dear. You have to decide. You have to decide what you're going to do.'

'I know.'

The day passed in a lack of words. And a torrent.

In the evening Grace allowed Mrs Talbot to sneak her downstairs to the private part of the house. 'For company.' Once the route had been checked and cleared, Grace was led there, on tiptoe, wearing a scarf tied tightly over her hair and a pair of men's reading glasses that Mrs Talbot said she had found in a drawer. She did not ask, but Grace assumed that they had belonged to her husband. They slid down her nose. She pushed at them.

As they passed the door of the television room Mrs Talbot turned and held a finger to her lips and made a hushing noise and a face. Grace giggled. Mrs Talbot turned on her with a frown and then smiled, and giggled herself. They scampered down the last flight of stairs, spluttering and stumbling, Grace, losing the glasses, squealing at the sight of Mrs Talbot quivering, her body like a bath, rippled, flowing, barely upright. They reached the basement and closed the door, and loud laughs roared out of them, two wide mouths, slowly closing, and they drew deep breaths and stood in silence for a moment. They looked at each other.

It was not funny.

Mrs Talbot's home consisted mostly of closed doors, behind which, Grace imagined, were the bedrooms of departed children. She was taken to a cluttered sitting room in which there was evidence of an attempt at a quick clean-up. A television flickered in the corner, the volume down, and the grey cat lay on a cushion on a threadbare armchair. She miaowed at Grace, and stretched, and followed things with her eyes.

'I'm sorry about the mess, dear. It's rare that I have midweek visitors and I tend to let things build up. Isn't that right, Wilma?'

She stroked the cat's small head.

'We used to have one called Fred, but she was a shifty thing and she upped and left us. Disappeared. Isn't that right, Wilma? She left you too, didn't she? Bold thing. Ran off to sea.'

They did not talk of the main thing. They drank coffee and watched television, and Mrs Talbot produced from the small kitchen a succession of biscuits and cakes. And when they had had their fill of them, she produced a bottle of whiskey. She spoke of her husband. She told Grace about her children, about their jobs, their homes. She commented on the politicians who filled the television screen – she seemed to have bumped into all of them. She broke off corners of biscuits and held them on the tip of her finger for the cat. She brushed crumbs from her lap. She fretted and laughed, sighed and filled their glasses.

'Oh, it's good to have company.'

The X case distracted them. The low sound of it spread about the room. A wringing of hands. Bewildered talk.

273

' . . . that a fourteen-year-old girl can be injuncted . . .'
said the presenter, as if fourteen was a magic number, an
extraordinary number, news just in. The girl is fourteen.
Still fourteen. ' . . . and now we learn that this girl has
talked of suicide with the psychologists . . .' What psychologists? Grace sipped her drink. Who organised
psychologists? Two politicians went at each other. A lawyer
read and re-read parts of the constitution, shook his head,
shrugged. Apparently. Yes. The presenter, with an unpro-
fessional quiver, went over the details, looking for a logic,
a sequence, a pattern: ' . . . rape . . .' she said, and was
interrupted by a red face, a blue suit, ' . . . tragic as it may
be, rape is not an issue here. It's irrelevant . . .' uproar now.
    'Well,' said Mrs Talbot.
    The presenter calmed it down, turned back to the lawyer:
' . . . yes, strictly speaking, under the law, the constitution,
yes, that's right . . .' The presenter became a little indignant.
' . . . Through no fault of their own then, their request to
the gardai for assistance on the collection of DNA evidence,
has led, it would seem, via the offices of the Attorney
General, to this injunction, and this impasse, and this situation that no one seems happy with . . .'
    'Your man seems delighted,' muttered Mrs Talbot.
    The constitution. It was the constitution. ' . . . So are you
pleased then that the amendment that you, you, supported,
has led to this mess . . .' Mess.
    'What if she went anyway?' Grace asked quietly. 'Would
she be arrested?'
    'Oh no, dear,' Mrs Talbot assured her. 'There'd be riots.'
    But Grace imagined it happening and it occurred to her,
gently, pleasantly, that she might end up meeting the girl
in prison. Murderers, the two of them. Grace would look
after her, become her friend. Together they would move
on from the places where they had been fixed. The girl
would cease to be fourteen. Grace would no longer be a
mad woman in a red car on a dark road. They would have

274

each other and the space of their cell, and they would move there, freely, in the tiny space of their cell. It would be enough.

'Besides,' Mrs Talbot was saying, 'there's nowhere to put her. She's too young for an adult prison, and they don't have one for girls. You hear judges always giving out about it.'

She poured another whiskey for Grace, but Grace knew she would not drink it. She did not like the way her head swam slightly. She did not trust her thinking.

Suddenly there was the sound of a loud buzzer. Grace jumped and stared. The cat yawned.

'It's all right, dear,' Mrs Talbot said, standing up. 'It's the front door. There's always two or three lads arrive in on a Wednesday night. I won't be five minutes. You just make yourself comfortable. And relax, dear. Don't worry.'

Grace watched her leave the room. Go up. She turned down the volume on the television and listened. She could hear nothing, except the vague and distant hum of voices, and she suspected that it might be nothing more than the leakage of sound from the muted TV.

One of two things. Stay. Wait. Spend little. Eat the food that's given. Hear the story of Mrs Talbot. Adopt it perhaps. Wait. Weeks. Months maybe. Then over the border, by train or bus, into Belfast. The ferry to Scotland. Hope that she would not be stopped, asked to produce something that said who she was. If she could wait long enough she might manage it. She had the money. The place. Weeks in the same room, Mrs Talbot below her, waiting.

One of two things. Give herself up. Call a police station and tell them where to find her. Go through it. Let it happen. Slump.

She sat in the silence of Ida Talbot's living room, watching the quiet mouths of politicians and lawyers working to explain the nation to the nation and she swirled whiskey in a glass and was confused. She did not want to

275

go to prison. She knew nothing of it. It was a different life. She would have to be born into it in some way, installed. She could not go there as she was. She would not fit. Something would have to reshape her, great hands, something. So that she could be contained in the enclosure, the measured space. Able to touch all the walls at once. She tried to think of it, and thought of being buried alive, but knew that that was not quite right. It was more complicated than that, more involving. She would be allowed to refuse visitors.

There was no dispute. She had murdered. She had done that, hung that word around her neck, and it led inexorably down. To specifics. Height by length by breadth. The clock. Either one thing or the other, it would be the same. Waiting for the clump of feet on the stairs. Straining to hear the hints in the still air. Waiting.

She heard nothing.

The X girl had not murdered. She had not done anything. But still. Nevertheless. The machinery worked on her like it worked on Grace. Grinding. Twice. First, the man who had breathed on her face and ran his hard hands over her, over her tears, smudging her world. Second, the law that creaked itself into position and raised its dead arm and let it fall, crashing down on her small frame, pinning her, making of her a hollow thing, a shell to squeeze a life from.

Grace watched the faces on the screen. She guessed that they were arguing, angry, shouting at each other. But without the sound they looked helpless, rambling, shocked. She was not the same as the girl. There would be no debate about her. No doubts.

She held her hands up to her mouth and breathed on them, and smelled the smell of whiskey and did not like it. She should not be drinking. It affected her.

There was still no sound from above. There was perhaps the creak of floorboards, but she could not be sure. She wondered if there was a wind. Rain. She put the glass to her lips and rolled it back and forth, imagining weather. She could not decide.

Martin hated her now. That was clear. It was something solid, something that she no longer had to wonder about. Her child hated her. It was a small ball in her stomach, a marble in the folds, inside, a pip. Would he like her again if she gave herself up? Or would it take something more intricate, the spinning out of some lie, some theory of explanation, some expression of regret? Some wailing? She could not do that. She did not feel it.

There were footsteps suddenly, very clear and quick, moving somewhere overhead, and then silence again. One person walking, and stopping.

She wondered where the girl was. With her mother somewhere. They would keep her away from the television and the newspapers, Grace hoped. It was enough to be falling headlong without knowing that the whole country was behind you, stumbling. She would be cold, and she would be awake.

Grace spun the whiskey around the glass, watching the coating it left behind, trapping the reflected room in a smooth storm. There was silence again. No footsteps, no voices, no noise of the wind or the rain. She closed her eyes and leaned her head back and wished that she could take the place of the girl. She wished that she could appear in her room like a ghost and slip beneath her skin, warming her, covering her heart with the shield of her hands. She could go through it for her. Let them take her and tie her and lock her away. They wanted someone. Somebody. It could be Grace. They would not notice the difference.

'Grace, dear?'

She jumped and sat up. Mrs Talbot was at her shoulder, her hands clasped together at her waist. She was alone.

'Oh, I'm sorry. I thought you'd fallen asleep.'

'No, I just had my eyes closed.'

'I'm sorry I took so long.' She sat beside Grace, picking

277

up her whiskey. 'I knew you'd be worried. It was three lads from the buses. I had to make a pot of tea for them. They're settled in now though. Awful men. Are you all right, dear?'

'I'm fine, yes. The whiskey makes me sleepy.'

'I know. I like a glass or two before bed. It's my little vice. My little indulgence. It's a sweet taste, tickles my throat. It'll be good for your cold.'

She found the remote control and restored the sound from the television. They sat together, slumped slightly, their arms touching, and listened to the debate that continued. Mrs Talbot made a comment now and then, but Grace drifted away and could not follow it. Her mind was filled with a mess of dim pictures that followed on one from the other. Her leaving home, Manchester, Martin leaving home, the X girl alone in a dark room, Martin's face when he told her to go, her husband, her father, her husband dead on the road, the X girl dead on the road. That was not right, that one. It made no sense.

She wondered what her mind was made of. It seemed to her that it was made of pictures, and pictures only. She did not see herself there. She did not know quite where she was placed, whether she was in the pictures or just observing them. She did not know how she could control it all, what order to put on it, what pattern to look for. She wondered whether other people were the same, whether Ida Talbot was caught in a swirl of scenes, unable to find a steady place, a centre. She doubted it. Perhaps that was the difference between them. Perhaps that was the difference between killers and other people. And she was a killer. She could see that.

Eventually there was no more that the television could think of to say, and Grace allowed herself to be led once more through the house in her ridiculous disguise. Mrs Talbot stayed with her for a while, watching her. They simmered about the X case, finding common dismay, and

278

it was sufficient to distract them, to haul them away from the other thing. They shrugged.

'It troubles me, dear. Deeply. I know of strange things, of things happening that are, well, strange. As if they're invented and built and left lying around, little toys that you stumble over and you pick them up and you can't figure them out at all.'

She tilted her head and seemed to recall.

'One of my boys had a robot, or a spaceship or something, the shape of a coffin. A tiny coffin like a coffin for a doll. Closed up it'd give you the creeps, seeing it there lying on his bed. But he'd open it up and there'd be buttons and bleeps and switches and dials.'

She rubbed at her arm.

'But this, dear. This is a different thing.'

Grace did not understand her. She nodded.

'This,' said Mrs Talbot, 'is about right and wrong. About that. It's not just something happening. It's a question. A decision. It's that. That's what it is.'

She did not look up. She kept on at her arm, her blank eyes towards the floor. Grace wondered whether they had avoided it at all.

Ida Talbot left her. Wished her good night and kissed her cheek. Grace heard her on the stairs clear her throat, and the sound of her seeped away.

She fell asleep quickly. Whiskey. In her mind her pictures slowed and stopped, leaving her facing the X girl, a child constructed like a collage of colours, a blend of other children. A child who looked to Grace like her dead son, like her son who had held her hand on the way to the lake. The girl stood beneath the tall spire of a narrow church nestled in the hills. At her feet was a dream of the world held in a shallow pool. From her hands fell drops of water, breaking on the ground with a splash of red and a flower of white bone. Grace saw her face again, and recognised it now. That mix of Sean and Martin. The source

279

of them. All motherhood and loss. The plain, concentrated look. The shadow in the eyes. The strength in the arms.

Woman slicing onions.

Grace.

MARTIN

He wanted his friends around him.

A fall of rain midweek woke him to the sight of Henry standing at the window, his forehead to the glass, making small gunshot noises in the dark. Martin asked him was he all right. Henry was still for a moment and then shot something else, and walked out of the room. Martin closed his eyes and slept. His sleep was dense with ricochets and pebbles and cuts on his knees.

Sean called him, wanted to know what had happened, why he was being interviewed by the police. He was not angry. He was misshapen, twisted in his voice so that Martin thought that he felt guilty, and tried to tell him that it was not his fault that she had told him, that it was not his fault she had disappeared, not his fault that she had murdered. Sean listened without saying a word, and then hung up.

Philip didn't understand anything. He didn't understand why Henry answered the phone, why Henry was home, why there was no good news in it. Martin could hear his voice. It rose and fell, and went quiet. He wanted to come over but Henry wouldn't let him.

Martin wanted his friends around him. Henry kept them away.

He wanted to go to work. He became tired of sitting in the house with the silence emanating out of Henry, waiting for something to happen. But he did not know how to say anything. How to say what he wanted. How to move. Henry was clamped. Tightened down. With anger, or maybe disgust. He shook his head a lot, rang Paris, ate little. He treated Martin with care, but it was the wrong kind of care. It was like distrust.

And Martin filled with need, watched Henry moving, watched the line of his body move through the rooms, watched his skin emerge and disappear, waited for a moment when he could touch him. He stood near to him. Henry breathed and tensed, hung in the air like a sound. Moved away.

Martin locked the bathroom door and uttered odd words convulsed with fear. He thrashed about in a small space, felt all the sky and all the world draw in a breath and hiss at him.

All week it was the same. He talked daily to the policeman, Crowley. He would call at the door, come in and look around.

'Any word?' he'd say.

'No.'

'You'd get in touch if there was?'

'Yes.'

And he would go away again.

But all the time an unmarked car with two detectives was parked across the street. And Henry said once he thought the phone was bugged. There was an echo on the line.

On Friday the car disappeared and Crowley did not call. Martin assumed they had found her. He put his arms around Henry, hung from him. Henry patted his back, said nothing. Broke away and hid his eyes. No word came.

Eventually Martin called the number on the card Crowley had given him.

'We've not seen her, no.'

'The car is gone from outside.'

Crowley was silent. Then he told Martin that there had been no sighting, no sign, and that they thought she might have left the country.

It was Martin who stayed awake that night, while Henry slept. He thought of his mother on a boat. Moving over water.

Henry slept and Martin watched him. Propped up on an elbow, he looked at him, at his face, his chest rising and falling, his shoulders and his arms. He reached out and gently placed a hand on Henry's. Rested it there, feeling the fingers beneath his palm. He did not move, afraid of disturbing him. He tried not to stare, tried to be as still as the air, as light, weightless. His hand on Henry's. He could feel his pulse. He was amazed that he could be so close, that he could feel the blood beneath his skin, the life that filled him.

The effort of being still became an ache in his arm, a burning in the dark, a hum in his ears, a pressure in his mouth as his teeth pressed together. He did not move. Nothing in him moved. For a long stretched moment, he had his hand on Henry's hand and did not move.

Then he suddenly flinched, twitched grotesquely, his hand flailing sideways, hitting Henry's hip with a patter of fingers. Henry snorted, half sat up, throwing Martin's hand backwards, away from him. He turned noisily and lay down again, seeming to mutter.

Martin closed his eyes.

There. So easy to lose it all. A muscle and a flicked wrist. The stepping off the edge. People did it all the time. They were afraid of heights and they jumped.

MRS TALBOT

'The last taxi I was in was kicked by a horse.'

'Jaysus.'

'Up in Smithfield, horse fair, a few Sundays ago. Yes. Big white thing, a flurry. Did for the headlights on one side and a fierce dent in that corner. That corner there.'

'The front left wing.'

'Yes.'

'Jaysus.'

The taxi driver shook his head slowly. Ida wanted to keep him talking. Keep his eyes off Grace, who, despite the scarf and the sunglasses, looked alarmingly like herself.

'That's a fine moustache,' she said.

'Thank you.'

'My husband had one once but electrocuted himself trying to trim it.'

He laughed.

'How?'

Ida glanced at Grace. Her mouth was open. Her eyes on the river wall, the south side over there, flags on flagpoles, grey grey sky. If the sun stayed away she'd have to take off the glasses. They'd only attract attention in the dull day. Jacqueline Kennedy Onassis.

'He bought an electric razor with a beard trim attachment and plugged it in forcibly, in the kitchen, using a biro as the third prong. It blew up in his hand. There was a big bang.'

He shook his head, checked his mirror, changed lanes, moving towards the leaning north, Bachelors' Walk.

'I was away at the time,' said Ida.

Something clinked beside her. Grace had let her head get tangled in the wind on the river, her sunglasses touching the glass, gravity.

'We're going marching,' said Ida, and her mouth made a noise. 'Marching in the street. Protesting.'

'Is that so? That explains this then. They're diverting. I'll let you off at the corner if you don't mind. I don't want to turn into it.'

'Yes.'

'What's it about, then?'

'The girl in the X case.'

'The girl in the suitcase,' said the taxi driver, and laughed loudly. The car was stopped, immobile. Grace's head shifted.

'X case,' she said, clearly. Her glasses were smudged. Great big fingerprints scrawled across them.

The driver stared into his mirror, squinting at her, peering. She coughed.

'Is this the girl wants an abortion?'

'Yes.'

'Oh well, now. I don't hold with that. It's a set-up. It's a cod, that. There's a boyfriend and a pair of Dublin Four parents in there somewhere and it's a big cod. Get us to change the law. Abortion on demand'll be in before you know what's happened. Mightn't even be pregnant at all. It's a set-up, that.'

'No,' said Grace. They hadn't moved. 'No.'

He flicked a switch on the meter.

'That's four twenty.'

'Are we going no further?' Ida quietly asked.

He did not answer. He plunged his hand into a leather pouch of jangling coins. Ida opened her purse, pulled out a fiver.

'There you are. I hope you're stuck in traffic for hours. We'll wave as we walk by.'

'Right, missus. You do that.'

She climbed out and Grace followed her.

'Stupid man.' She slammed the door. 'Stupid man.'

Grace shrugged and loosened her scarf, took off her sunglasses, squinted at the sky.

'They pinch. Besides . . .'

'I know, dear, leave them. Just stay close to me. We'll be all right. We will.'

She took her by the arm and led her to the corner of O'Connell Street, past the wide windows, peeling paint, the light, the smell of the water, past the glut of youngsters that clogged every pavement Ida walked on. Since, well, since years.

'They've stopped the traffic this side. Oh look, dear. Look.'

There were thousands. Thousands. What did a thousand look like? Ida didn't know. She hurried, held Grace tightly.

'All these people, dear. All these people. And we're not the oldest either, thank God. How many is there, do you think? And still coming. Still arriving. We're early yet. Look at the signs, dear. The police.'

They stood along the kerbs, little glints of gold on their dark blue tunics, their hands slapping together, their legs shifting, their heads laughing, joking, not minding, nodding, goodhumoured. Grace fiddled with her scarf. Ida led her right, then left, then straight up the middle, coming into the edge of things now, the youngsters, a banner, a man with a megaphone, women not unlike themselves.

'Where will we go, dear? Where's the front, do you think?'

Grace shook her head. Did not answer. How her face was set. She had not eaten. Not at breakfast. Not the night before. Before that there had been only morsels, small things, hopeless mouthfuls. She had gritted her teeth. Made a barely audible promise. This will be the day. Today. No further. Ida had stroked her cold arm, rested her forehead on her shoulder, helped her with her hair.

'I think we should stay at this side of things. It's the front, I presume, if we're going towards the Dail. Unless you want to be at the back, dear.'

She didn't answer for a moment. She scanned the faces, flinched a little at the policemen gathered by the first pillar of the GPO. She nodded at a placard that said: 'Internment for 14 year olds?'

'Yes,' she said. 'The front.'

She was not pale. That was not it. There was colour, for example, in her lips and her eyes. Ida Talbot saw her like a flame, pictured her as a flame, then decided that that was not it either. But there was something about colour, some contrast, some blend. Oh what was it? She was different. Not just that she was older than most, as was Ida of course, and the odd married couple unsure of the protocol, and groups of women who stood around waiting for the start like walkers in the foothills, clubs. But also that she was closer. Closer. Nearer. Everybody else was smiling, laughing, excited at the crowd, the atmosphere, the street closed just for them, so that they could walk and shout and be photographed. All that attention. All that belonging. But Grace was not smiling. She was not excited. She was terribly quiet.

They stood shoulder to shoulder with others. The air waited. All that belonging. As if there was only one thing to be said, and not many things. Ida Talbot clutched her new friend's arm. She prayed, with concentration. Prayed that, for once, beside her, in her space, nothing would happen.

MARTIN

He saw the trees flick in the lifeless wind. Not flick. Flick. He saw shoppers stream through the marchers, staring, nodding, shaking. He saw the marchers not march, the stewards trying to shape them, trying to make a column out of a crowd, a form from nothing. He guessed two thousand. Henry nodded. Philip pointed out the time. Early yet.

They had met by the river, Philip delighted to see them, curious, peering at Martin, trying tentative questions. But Henry had steered the talk away from all that. Sick of it. Martin wished that Henry wasn't there – so that he could talk to Philip. Or that Philip wasn't there, so that he could talk to Henry. As if he could now, when he hadn't been able before. As if the open air and other people's disasters might force a gap in his mind. He wished for a fracture in time – a small one or a large one – one that would put them where they had been, together, with nothing of his mother or his father to press down on them. With nothing but themselves. As if they could be nothing but themselves.

He saw a grey sky hang low, a small space in which this would take place, this thing. He didn't like it. Didn't see the point. Couldn't see how something so amateur as a march could alter anything. Henry had told him that that was not the motivation, particularly. Martin did not enquire as to what the motivation might be. Dangerous ground. He imagined something like a symbol. But life and death confused him, and he was defeated by the logic, by the hierarchy, one over the other, depending, as if value changed, altered. Depending. Everything depended. Right and wrong.

He saw the heads of many.

He saw the corridor ahead of them, cleared.

He saw more than he would admit. He understood why it was wrong for the girl to be forced into childbirth. Forced. But he did not understand the rest of it. Couldn't bring himself to take the next step. A confusion crept in. Or was it just that he was reeling?

He understood that his mother had done wrong and that he had done wrong in calling her wrong to have done it. Could see the twist. Could see the double back, the rico-chet, the odd logic. But he couldn't accept it. Perhaps it was just the tone he had used. The completeness of it. The biblical terms. Be gone. That had been wrong. Tactically wrong at least. From the point of view of putting an end to it. He should have kept her where she was. Let them come and get her. Not this mess. This undignified groping. Her name on the radio and the television, his search for a photograph, trying to describe her, forgetting the colour of her eyes. All the time Henry and his silence. Noisy silence. Screaming quiet. He could have avoided it all with an embrace and a tearful hanging on. Stay here mother. We'll work it out.

He saw the stewards make straight lines of the edges. He caught a glance of Philip picking his nose. He saw a tightening towards the front. He saw . . .

'Oh look, look.' Philip stood on tip toes. 'Sinead.'

'Sinead who?'

'O'Connor. Sinead. There. She's beautiful.'

They peered.

'Did you hear what she did?'

They nodded. Philip told them anyway.

'She stormed into the Dail demanding to see Albert Reynolds.'

'And the fucking eegit saw her too,' said Martin. Sinead O'Connor smiled and huddled. She swung her shoulders. Photographers. Martin saw her eyes. Big clear eyes. Smiling. Everyone seemed to stare at her. Everyone.

He saw a placard that said: 'Get your laws off my body'.

He saw a child in a pram.

He saw a balloon let loose, rising into the grey, a red dot on the sky.

He saw the city, out ahead of them. Ready.

He saw.

He saw his mother. Of course. A face like his own in the midst of strangers.

He coughed. Glanced at Henry and Philip, expecting them to have seen her too, to be staring at him, waiting for him to react. But they hadn't seen her. Henry was whispering something to Philip who had his head dipped, eyes to the ground. They didn't look at him. He checked again.

It was her. Wearing a scarf. Still. Linked to a fat woman in a blue coat. They were looking around. They turned away, their backs to him. He lost them in the shuffle.

Martin thought. He would ignore her. Pretend he hadn't seen her. Push it out of his mind. An unpleasantness. If one of the others saw her, well then, so be it. But he didn't want to do anything. What could he say? Oh look, there's my mother. Quick, call the police. Talk to her. Go and talk to her. No. He knew her, recognised her. Knew her face and her shape. There she was again now. That coat. Her shoulders without width. Her body. Fifty yards. Through a hundred people. His mother.

Whistles blew. The air cut his cheeks.

'Are we moving?'

'Philip?'

'Yes?'

'Am I . . .'

'What?'

He stared hard, tried to make her turn. See him. Then it'd be her decision. Why his? Always his. Always his responsibility. His fault. Her descending on him out of nothing, floating over his head.

'What, Martin?'

She would keep on doing this. Flitting across his line of sight like a ghost. Daring him to tell.

The buses roared on the left of him. The high windows glinted the grey light, doubled it. The stone. The crowds of people like a sprinkling. A fall of berries. The trees with their bulbs.

'There's TV cameras.'

'What else?'

'Will we get on the news? Us, I mean. Make a show.'

'I see my mother.'

'They'll focus on Sinead.'

'She'll hit someone.'

'I love her coat. Very *Heaven's Gate*.'

'I see my mother.'

'Martin?'

'What?'

'I see my mother.'

Silence. Then Philip whispered 'Fuck,' and was on his toes again. Henry was like a black hole in O'Connell Street. A star come down to spin things. He stood at Martin's side suddenly, almost touching. Touching. He stood there. His arm against Martin's.

'Leave her.'

Martin felt his arm taken, Henry's hand holding his wrist.

'No.'

'Leave her, I said.'

'No.'

He felt in his pocket.

291

'Why not?'

'Because. She's like a ghost.'

He pulled out the card.

'Martin, don't.'

'What?'

Henry grabbed it. Let go of him and grabbed it out of his hand. The card.

'Give it.'

'Martin, it's a big mistake. Really. Just leave it. They're going to get her anyway. God. Don't make her hate you.'

Martin feigned a glance to his left, a smile, a small sigh, left his hands loose. Then he swung as suddenly as he could, snatched the card from Henry, who looked at him as if there was something murderous in plucking a card from a man's hand. Martin couldn't stop smiling. He laughed even.

'Martin,' said Philip.

'What? Fucking what?'

'Henry's right.'

'No he's not. He's not right.'

He turned and walked and did not want to look behind him. That night in the sauna. He had turned in the small space of a room. He had let himself down. He had broken it already. She was like the observer, the eye in the lens. He was being consistent, that was all. Consistent. Honest. What was so wrong with that? You'd think that Henry . . . There were public telephones in the GPO. Henry was behind him.

'Why are you doing this? Why? Martin. Stop.'

It was a tugging, not that way but this, as if there was gravity. As if it might put an end to things. Most things.

'Leave me,' he said, and it was inaudible. He went past Sinead O'Connor. Past cameras. Into the indoors, the lack of gunfire, the place.

Henry held his arm. Hurt it.

'If you do this I won't be around for it. I swear. I'm gone.'

'Okay,' he nodded briskly, his brow furrowed, all the seriousness he could muster, his smile fighting out of his mouth like an animal in his skin.

'Jesus, Martin. You're so fucking stupid. Your father's son.'

It must have got a response, that. Because Henry was in front of him suddenly, as if Martin had stopped. He said it again.

'Your father's son.'

And gone. He walked out of the GPO and did not look back. Martin followed him with his eyes. Felt the space between them grow, and slowly fill with distance. And distance is the measurement. How you know where you are.

Gone.

He found an empty box, stood in it. Dialled. Coined. Was put through somehow, to a scratchy space, crackling, as if connected to a temporary life.

'Yes.'

'Crowley.'

'Yes.'

'This is Martin Quinn. My mother's marching on the march. She's a marcher. X . . .'

'Where are you?'

'GPO.'

'Stay.'

Martin stood under the high ceiling. The space above him filled with light. His smile went out. He looked up, took a breath, idled in his foot space, his allocation, felt the past go out of him. All the past. Go. Out of him. And up. Up. Fly up, weightless, and leave him where he was, solid, rooted to the spot.

Rooted to the spot.

He tried to laugh. Tried to giggle in the high air, be a child.

Hollow noises flooded him.

GRACE

Ida Talbot smelled thickly of perfume and talc. An old woman scent. Light as the air. Grace averted her face, tried to catch something of the moment. But that, that odour. It made the whole scene, the whole sky, the crowd, the bustle, the cleared light, the waiting, the issue, the issue, made it all seem crudely quaint. A visit to an elderly aunt. A chat over tea with a neighbour. Custard creams. My husband knows your husband.

She disconnected her arm, loosened the scarf knot at her chin, slipped the whole thing down on to her shoulders. Remained unlinked. Mrs Talbot smiled at her, then bit a lip.

'Do you not think . . .'

'No. It's all right.'

She could not determine Mrs Talbot's age. It was lost in the bulk, the generosity. Anything from fifty to seventy. And her bewildered world. As if Grace was a natural force come into it, come into her life as a kind of test, an obligation. You reap when the weather's right. She had followed Grace with her eyes and her voice and her feet. Yes, dear. Nodding. Agreeing. Protecting. Grace wondered what she might have done without her.

Concentrate. Listen.

There was a babble. Drummers tried out their drums. Whistlers their whistles. A platform, a trailer, was parked in front of the GPO. Men worked on it with cables. Tying down. The squeak of megaphones tilted her head, altered voices startling her. 'Please make sure you stick together. Don't gallop off at the front. Be loud.'

'Are we going to shout, do you think?' Mrs Talbot asked her, sending out a little powder wave, a plume.

Before Grace could answer, a finger tapped her shoulder. For a moment there was a silence, as the sound of the crowd fell away from her and she pictured Brady at her side. Just the march. Please. Just that. She turned slowly. It was not Brady. It was Philip.

'Mrs Quinn. Are you all right?'

'Philip. Oh.'

Ida Talbot stepped between them roughly, shielding Grace.

'Who are you?' she snapped.

'It's all right, Ida. This is Philip. I know him. He's a friend of my son's. Martin's friend.'

Ida stayed where she was and glared at him.

'What do you want?' she demanded. She made herself huge. Philip disappeared behind her, his flip of hair the only part of him visible.

'I just wanted to say hello. I don't know. I don't want anything.'

'Is Martin here?' Grace asked him, nudging Ida sideways. He squinted, looked behind him, shrugged.

'Yeah. I think he's ... well ... he's back there somewhere.'

'Did he see me?'

Philip nodded. Mrs Talbot looked at her, her lips apart, her chalky face rippling slightly, the air around her shifting.

'Philip, this is Ida Talbot, my friend.'

Philip offered his hand and Ida clutched it rather than shook it.

'Will he tell the police – is that what you mean?'

He shrugged.

'I don't know, really. I think though that he'll probably,

well, he probably will. I think he had it in mind to make a phone call.'

He blushed and Ida put a hand to her mouth and looked at Grace. Grace had to smile at her. It was the face she made.

There was suddenly a long loud blast of a whistle, answered by more whistles from behind, and a kind of rumbling cheer moved through the long line of people as those at the front began to walk forward. Grace hesitated for a moment. Begin it. End it. Walk. She raised her weak head. She set off. Briskly.

Ida was quickly at her side.

'We could slip off, dear, back home. They wouldn't know.'

Grace shook her head.

'It'll be all right, Ida. We'll be all right.'

She was afraid that they would swoop on her. Afraid that they might. All that blue, a panic of blue, swirling through the marchers and leading her away. But she could think of nothing else now. Just the march. The weakness of walking, the tread of her feet, the self-propulsion. The moving forward. Volition. They would trace a circle. So. She would go and come back. It was not wrong. Stamp a pattern in the ground. A shape. A sign. Like the saying of certain words. A prayer. It goes up. Finds an echo in the sky. Some mechanism takes it and makes it meaningful.

At her side she noticed that Philip was still there, glum looking, his head down. She looked at him and smiled, but he was lost in his own thoughts.

They walked on quietly, reaching O'Connell Bridge and feeling the cold of the wind that blew from the east, chopping the water. They crossed slowly, the marshals concerned that they were strung out too much, signalling a pause while the others caught up. Grace turned and looked behind her. She could not see the end of it. People and banners and placards filled the roadway. There were drums and whistles. Chants had started further back. Grace could not quite make them out. They moved into D'Olier Street and up towards College Green. Somebody in front of them shouted suddenly, 'Not the church, not the state, Women must control their fate,' and others took it up. She looked at Ida and Philip, but they both walked as if alone. She chanted once, almost inaudibly, and then once more, a little louder, and then again, louder still. She heard Philip join her and she glanced at him, but he did not look at her, he looked ahead. Ida stayed silent.

Grace's voice sounded good to her. She felt it in her chest as well as in her throat. It rolled through her and left her breathless. As they passed the gates of Trinity she took a rest, and Philip did the same.

'Mrs Quinn,' he said quietly. 'Did you kill your husband?'

Grace looked at him and saw only curiosity in his eyes. She was silent for a moment.

'Did Martin not talk to you?'

He shook his head.

'He talked to me, but he didn't say much. He's in a bit of a daze I think, a bit confused. I think maybe that he doesn't realise . . .'

He coughed. He was very handsome; with his strange hair turned up, making a surprise of his face, a rising. She did not answer his question. She stayed quiet. She took his arm as Mrs Talbot had taken hers. Ida walked nervously, glancing behind them, ahead of them. They followed the wall of the university, the drummers drumming, the chanting loud, angry. Pedestrians watched, stared. Some stood and applauded. They passed the stopped clocks, the buildings. She held Philip, pressed against him.

'Myself and Martin used to walk,' she said. 'We used to go out from the farm and walk around the hills and the lakes for miles and miles. He would talk all the time, and tell me about the world. He knew everything then, when he was little. He used to tell me about America and Africa and all the travelling he would do.'

She paused as the march paused once more, and the marshals allowed it to tighten up, condense, be stronger. The chants. Like handclaps in an old code.

'I would walk a steady pace on the way out, and he would circle me, running a little bit ahead, and a little to either side, exploring. Then on the way home he would hold my hand and stay with me.'

Philip smiled at her.

'I can't imagine Martin as a little boy.'

Grace nodded. She could understand that.

They turned into Kildare Street and towards the Green. Ida had relaxed a little. She tentatively joined in one of the chants. It was the abortion information telephone number. It was illegal to publish it or broadcast it. It echoed in the street against the walls of government departments.

'We would arrive back,' continued Grace, 'and it would be like remembering a dream suddenly. We would stop, and look at each other and we'd be startled at the strangeness of our home.'

She looked at Philip to see if he understood.

'At the threat of it,' she said, and he turned to her and nodded slowly.

They passed the Dail without stopping. Grace assumed that there would be nobody in there in any case. Ida seemed disappointed, sighing, shaking her head. Chanting now, full-throated, stern-eyed. Philip kept his head on one side, listening.

'I waited for him one night. I waited in his car, in the darkness, and saw him come towards me. I shouldn't have done it, but it was a certain night. It was its own time, its own moment. It all came as one, and I couldn't take one bit and leave the rest. I had to take it all.'

She glanced at Philip but was afraid to look at him too

long. Ida was a little way away from them now, her voice coming big out of her big frame.

'He stopped at the side of the road and I lost him for a moment. Then I saw him again. He was kneeling. Kneeling at the place where he had killed the girl, praying there at the spot where the flowers rested, kneeling and praying. I don't know what there is in that. When I was a child I might have guessed, but I don't know now. I shouldn't have done it. I wanted to be free of him, and so I did it, but I'm tied to him now like I never was. In signs and symbols and in ways I don't understand. I wanted to spit him out and I swallowed him instead. I shouldn't have done it.'

Philip looked at her for a moment and straightened then and looked ahead. He seemed constricted, his brow furrowed, as if he felt an obligation to answer. Say something. Grace knew she should tell him not to. It did not matter. But she was curious. This young man. Her son's friend. A part of all this. After a few steps he turned to her again.

'I think you were right to do it.'

She stared at him, and saw that he was unsure. She shook her head.

'Don't say that.'

There were photographers and camera crews gathered in front of them, walking backwards and scampering around the edges of the crowd. Grace wondered whether they would catch her face, whether any of them would recognise her, say something to a policeman.

They reached St Stephen's Green and turned left, past the Shelbourne Hotel where Grace had been the week before. They turned right then, staying on the square. They would come around on the other side she guessed, and go down Dawson Street. The chanting had died away a little and they moved at a quicker pace. There were not many people on this side of the Green. It was quiet here and the march did not seem that impressive against the wide road and the high buildings.

'Are you all right, dear?' asked Ida, taking her arm once more.

'Yes, I'm fine.'

'Will we keep going?'

'Yes, we will. Back to where we started.'

'You don't want to make a dash for it, dear?'

Grace smiled. Shook her head.

They wheeled around to the top of the Green and felt the wind behind them, not as cold as it had been. Grace took the scarf from around her neck and put it into her pocket. The walking had warmed her.

She gently took her arm from Philip's and moved as slowly as she could away from him. She walked a little faster so that by the time they approached the next corner and turned to face back towards the river, she was a yard or two in front of the others. She looked back at them and smiled. Ida returned her smile, and Philip looked worried. They made no move to catch up.

The chants started low and reached a peak and died away again, one taking the place of another. Whistles and drums wove through the words, and everywhere placards were poked at the sky like stubby little fingers. They approached the crowds at the top of Grafton Street and the chants came faster and louder and people stopped what they were doing and watched. Grace was surprised when, instead of continuing around the Green to Dawson Street, the police led them straight ahead, directly into the pedestrianised and packed street. She worried that there would be a crush, but the shoppers parted in front of them, standing to one side and waiting patiently for them to pass. It occurred to her that they would be a formidable sight and a shuddering sound. They would brook no argument. She raised her voice and chanted the number.

In her dreams she had seen the child, seen her waiting.

She had been a strange, lost thing, out beneath the stars, Grace with her back to her. On the road the child had knelt and the silence of the night had flowed from her hands clasped together to make a church. Against the web of the roads and the pattern of the lakes she had been set like a light in a shallow grave, only seen from the air.

Grace had killed her husband and it was the wrong thing to do. She had her son to tell her that. You have killed my father.

She turned her face to the sky and saw the grey hood that covered Dublin, enclosing the sound of the march, the shape it made on the earth, the spell it cast. He had been kneeling, praying. That had been his sign. This was hers.

Suddenly Ida was beside her, and Philip as well, and Ida tugged at her coat and nodded towards the side of the road. On each side of the marchers three or four policemen moved quickly, scanning the faces of the crowd.

'Where's your scarf?'

'It's all right, Ida. It doesn't matter.'

A hand was pointed at her from the right. She saw a mouth close to a radio and saw the men stop their search and stare at her. Others noticed them. Some of the marchers jeered at them. They made no move. They followed and stared.

'Jesus,' whispered Philip.

They passed again into College Green and Westmoreland Street and in the distance Grace could see the statue and the angels, their wings unfolding, always unfolding, never anything other than unfolding, and the trees behind them, sick in the shade of the city. It was cold. Her hands felt it most.

The crowd sang. 'Let her go. Let her go. Let her go.'

She had killed her husband and it was the wrong thing to do.

On the bridge whistles blew, and the marshals shouted,

302

and everybody sat down. Ida looked at her and asked her was she all right and sat next to her, Philip at her shoulder.

'I'm fine Ida, fine.'

The policemen did not sit. They stood and she saw again the mouth at the radio, and their eyes.

The sitting down confused her and she did not like it. Her body pressed to a road, her bones hurting. In her mind she tried to keep the picture of the girl. The X girl. She was small, smaller than Martin, smaller than Philip. She poked a stick at the ice of the lake and made it crack, and saw where the night was kept. Grace's husband's name was Michael. He had picked the girl up and put her in the back of his car and had driven home. Her hand pressed up against the window.

They stood up. How wrong was it?

It was wrong enough.

Into O'Connell Street and under the statue. Ida held her elbow and she could sense that it was Philip at her other side, and that he was nervous, and she put her arm through his.

The chanting died away as they returned to the place where they had started. Grace heard in the silence the sound of her own breathing and it amazed her to think that she had marched the full march and had not been halted. She had carved a promise out of concrete and the cold air. She had made her prayer.

She smiled and looked for her son.

He stood beside the first pillar of the GPO with Brady and another man. He was his father's shape, a cut of deep colour against the grey of the stone. His face was set blank, but she could tell that he was barely breathing, that he was lost from the place where he understood the world, and was flung now like she was, into a place where the world understood him.

As the crowd lost its momentum the policemen came closer, in a loop, pointing her towards her son, herding them together like a thing that was forced. Philip groaned and Ida stopped and would go no further.

'Grace,' she said. 'Is that your son?'

'Yes.'

Ida nodded. She looked at Martin for a moment, stuck out her head and examined him, as if he were below her and tiny. Then her neck gave way, relaxed, and her face lost its anger and she glanced at Grace and smiled.

'He's very handsome. Has your look.'

Grace let go of her, and of Philip, and felt the detachment very clearly, and recorded it, remembered it, put it away, safe. Then quickly, so that it would not seem important, she embraced Ida and whispered to her, and embraced Philip also so that he would not feel so strange in the world.

Then she turned and walked on alone and kept her eyes on Martin. He looked at the ground.

'Hello, Mrs Quinn.'

'Detective.'

'Are you ready to come in with us, then?'

'I am. You'll let the girl go.'

She had not meant it as a question, but Brady asked her:

'What girl?'

'The X girl.'

The man she did not know moved behind her and a woman garda took her firmly by the arm.

'We will, of course,' said Brady. 'Of course we will.'

Grace was moved away from Martin, towards a car that was parked on the footpath. She tried to look behind, to find him.

'Is my son there, Detective?'

They all stopped, and Grace was allowed to turn around. He had not moved. He stood with his back to the pillar, watching her. He was too far away for her to say anything. She looked at his face against the grey uneven surface, the pits of the pillar at his shoulders. She saw the difference between skin and stone, between light and the earth, between the heights where you begin and the jolt of arriving at the place where you begin again.

He nodded, maybe. She was not sure. Then he moved from the stone and disappeared in the colours of the crowd.

While *The Long Falling* is fiction, the details of the X case which it contains are accurate. The reader may wish to know that:

In February 1992 the then Attorney General, Mr Harry Whelehan, sought an injunction to stop X, a fourteen-year-old girl, from leaving the country to obtain an abortion in England. The injunction was granted on Monday, 17 February 1992 by Mr Justice Costello in the High Court. The judgement restrained X from procuring or arranging a termination of her pregnancy either within the state or abroad. Mr Justice Costello also restrained X, and her parents, from leaving the jurisdiction for nine months.

The parents of X took the case to appeal at the Supreme Court some days later, in a constitutional action funded by the government.

The march described at the end of this book took place on Saturday, 22 February 1992, and was one of many, both in Ireland and abroad.

The injunction was lifted four days later, on Wednesday, 26 February.

In a judgement delivered on 5 March, the Supreme Court ruled that abortion was lawful in certain limited circumstances. The judges felt that X's threat of suicide constituted a 'real and substantial risk to the life' of X, which could 'only be avoided by the termination of her pregnancy'.

It later emerged that two days before the ruling was delivered, X and her parents had travelled to St Mary's Hospital, Manchester, where X suffered a natural and spontaneous miscarriage.

On Thursday, 2 June, 1994, a forty-three-year-old man was sentenced to fourteen years' imprisonment at the Dublin Circuit Criminal Court after pleading guilty to three charges of sexual offences against a girl under fifteen. The girl was X. It was reported that DNA evidence in the case was conclusive.

The sentence was later reduced on appeal.